prais

Summer AT TILLINGFORD HALL

"Wow! I will be reading more from this author. What a fabulous, funny and romantic story. I loved every bit of it and now I am a bit sad the book's finished. Well worth a read!"
Lucy Mitchell, author of *The Car Share*

"I adored the setting – I could easily picture the house and its inhabitants – and Alice and Hatty were so likeable and authentic that I was rooting for them the whole way.
Summer at Tillingford Hall kept me guessing till the end."
Hannah Langdon, author of *Christmas with the Lords*

"A delightful romantic read that combines heart, humour, and a touch of nostalgia. A perfect choice for fans of romance and those looking for a feel-good book. Whether you're a long-time romance reader or new to the genre, there is something for everyone."
Reader, Cheam

"Immensely enjoyable, engaging and entertaining."
Reader, Wimbledon

"Summer at Tillingford Hall is an enchanting read that artistically leads you on an adventurous journey. It is filled with mystery, secrets, and deep truths shadowed by lies, ultimately ending in the greatest discovery of all – love."
Jacqueline Malcolm, author of *Slave*

"I still think about your lovely story!
The characters stayed with me.
I loved it; the setting, the characters who just fit,
the family intrigue. All in all, a wonderful book."
Ruth Kramer, writer

"The engaging characters kept me
turning the pages until the very end."
Rose, teacher, Surrey

"The characters are easy to relate to,
the plot sufficiently mysterious to keep the reader engaged,
and the outcome so emotionally satisfying and optimistic
that one leaves the book eager for more."
David, reader, Cambridge

"This is an engaging love story with an array of characters, many of whom have secrets to hide. Flora Dunn has created a delightful, authentic world, and I'm very much looking forward to the next book and to more tales from Tillingford."
Katharine Light, author of *Like Me*

"A gorgeous 5* read!"
Helen Hawkins, author of *A Concert for Christmas*

"If you're after a well-written romance with humour and a quintessential English countryside setting, then Summer at Tillingford Hall will not disappoint. I look forward to reading more of this author's work, she has a great comedic turn of phrase"
Angela Pearse, author of *Amusing Miss Austen*

Summer at Tillingford Hall

by

Flora Dunn

First published in Great Britain
by Lumina Publications 2024

Paperback – ISBN 978-1-0687494-0-7

Edition 1.1

Cover design:
Primavera Moretti and Sajeela Kiran
Instagram: @sajee_artandpatterns

To my husband, Martin, my knight in shining armour.

Dear Reader,

I'm so glad you've decided to visit Tillingford Hall. I hope you'll enjoy it as much as many other readers have done.

You will have noticed from the cover that £1 from the sale of every copy of this book goes to support The Daniel Spargo-Mabbs Foundation. This is part of an ongoing commitment by Lumina Publications to support charities through publishing.

We have a vision: to bring light to the world by creating educating and entertaining books and donating £1 from every book sold to our partner charities. You can learn more about our vision, mission and values, and how to apply to be our next charity partner at www.floradunn.com.

The Daniel Spargo-Mabbs Foundation was set up in 2014 by Fiona and Tim Spargo-Mabbs in response to the death of their sixteen-year-old son, Dan, who had taken an accidental overdose of ecstasy.

The aim of the drug education charity is to enable young people to make informed, empowered and safer decisions when in situations involving drugs and alcohol. The charity does this through workshops for young people and the adults in their lives, theatre performances, materials that school and college staff can deliver to students, and working with commissioners and policy makers to raise awareness of the importance of drug education. There's more information at www.dsmfoundation.org.uk.

If you would like to know more about the world of Tillingford Hall, including more about the history of the Hall, events, give-aways, and Mrs Powell's gluten free recipes, please sign up for my newsletter by filling in the form on my website www.floradunn.com – and please use the contact form there to get in touch and tell me what you think of this book.

Flora

Chapter One

I look at the two portraits in my hands, certain the one on the right is a fake.

For the past couple of hours, I've been sitting in the stifling, dusty Collections Room at Tillingford Hall poring over a tiny part of the huge collection of miniatures I'm here to catalogue. The blinds over the tall sash windows cut out a beautiful sun-soaked view of the hall's extensive grounds. The only ventilation is a wobbly desk-top fan, and the old-fashioned mercury thermometer reads nearly ninety degrees. Not only will this not do these delicate artefacts any good, it's also way over my own optimum operating temperature.

Luckily only the less important ones are in the Collections Room. Most of the collection is displayed around Tillingford Hall; on the walls, in cabinets and, incredibly, some just lying around.

But before going down to collect Hatty, my seven-year-old daughter from the housekeeper, Mrs Powell, who has been minding her, I thought I would just peek inside one last drawer. Inside, an oval portrait of an old lady with a narrow, cat-like gaze, caught my eye. There was a pale ring on the paper on which the miniature was resting, as though the picture had been moved, and although the frame was identical in shape to the others, it had a slightly different sheen. I noticed that the aged look on the picture seemed to have been created with paint or maybe some kind of dirt. Putting on my white cotton conservator's gloves, I carefully turned over the miniature. The paper tacked to the back of the frame was brand new.

Next to the picture of the lady was a portrait of an owlish gentleman in an identical frame, so I picked it up for comparison.

I'm now staring at them both; one in each hand. They are obviously a pair. The lady, turned to her left, and the gentleman, to his right, gaze lovingly at each other like *The Owl and The Pussycat.*

Against my principles as a curator, but very much in the name of scientific discovery, I take off my gloves and shut my eyes. I shuffle the two miniatures around so I can't be sure which is which. Then I weigh them in my hands, rub them gently and smell them again.

One smells like an old library. It has a rough, dusty feel, the vibes of antiquity emanating off it.

The other smells odd; it's got a chemically, plastic scent.

I open my eyes. There's definitely something not quite right about the lady's portrait; it's just not that good. The brushwork on the gentleman is so delicate; the artist has managed to get the effect of lace with the merest strokes of white. The paint on the other portrait is daubed on, and there's a wash of brown over it, but it's shiny, like acrylic ink, not the grime of antiquity.

There's no doubt this portrait of a lady is a modern fake.

Or a forgery.

I sit down, staring at the two pictures in my hands and wondering what to do.

I look around the dusty, disordered room. I've already got my work cut out here and only six weeks in which to do it.

I don't need the distraction of this mysterious lady. I think I'd better settle in, get my feet under the table and wait and see what else comes up. I carefully replace the pictures and lock the cabinets. Then I check the blinds are fully closed and leave the room, locking the door behind me and pocketing the large iron key.

As I enter the vast semi-basement crypt that is Mrs Powell's domain, Hatty rushes over and hugs me tight. One corner of the huge Kitchen has been fitted with a modern range cooker and a Nespresso machine, but the acres of marble worktop and the enormous scrubbed oak table hark back to the days when this space would have been a frenetic catering hub feeding a hundred people a day.

"How's your day been?" I ask my only child.

"OK," she says, burying her face in my tummy.

"We're a bit shy, aren't we?" says Mrs Powell, pursing her lips. "But we've done some cooking, and we watched a film."

"Which one?" I asked.

"*Frozen*," says Hatty gazing up at me with a cheeky smile.

"Again?"

Hatty nods.

"How about we go for a swim?" I suggest. "Lord Tillingford told me there's a lovely swimming pool here."

Hatty shakes her head.

"Oh, come on, it'll be fun – and so nice to cool off," I puff, ineffectually fanning myself with my hand.

Hatty's twisting her hair around her finger, so I promise that if she doesn't fancy getting in the water, she can just watch me. I thank Mrs Powell, praying silently that Hatty will warm to her and settle in. Otherwise, it's going to be a very long summer.

"Can we bring Beebee?" asks Hatty as we climb up the servants' staircase to our bedroom under the eaves to get changed. She snatches up her blue beany bunny from her suitcase and clings to him. She's been gradually detaching herself from him, but my heart tightens knowing that she's feeling a bit insecure again today.

"I don't think Beebee knows how to swim!" I laugh. "And anyway, his beans would get all soggy."

"I *know* he can't swim, Mummy! But I think he'd like to watch," she says in a small, firm voice. "I think he'll be a bit scared if we leave him on his own up here."

"I think Beebee will be more scared if he falls in the pool or gets lost in the gardens, don't you? And anyway, he'll have Mousy to keep him company if he stays up here, won't he?"

Hatty agrees this is true, but I can see she doesn't really want to let go of him. We make Beebee comfy with Mousy on the bed and leave them some mini raisin packs and a book to look at, so they don't get bored or hungry, and head off for the garden.

I'm wearing a new navy one-piece – I never was a bikini girl – and a beautiful cream linen kaftan embroidered with crewel-work flowers. It's blown my clothes budget for three months. Part of me wants to keep it safe, wrapped in its aqua-coloured tissue paper and teal-and-gold paper bag, but I just can't bear to see beautiful things, like Lord Tillingford's miniatures, shut away.

A few minutes later, we're walking through the Shrubbery, following the path past the Knot Garden while Hatty tells me about how she helped Mrs Powell make bread, chopped some onions that made her cry, and heard about Sir Aubrey Tillingford who married an Indian Princess *thousands* of years ago.

It sounds like she got on well with Mrs P and actually had some fun, which is a huge relief.

Passing through a shaggy arch in an ancient yew hedge, we enter a shady grove filled with classical statues. There's Apollo, the sun-god, looking handsome in a mossy kind of way, and that must be Diana the huntress, goddess of the moon, with her bow and arrow. She stands, highlighted in a shaft of sunlight that breaks through the overhanging plane trees. A dribble of greenish water trickles from a conch shell held aloft by a bearded Poseidon, the fierce sea-god, into a large marble pool.

"Are you *sure* this is the pool, Mummy?" asks Hatty, tightening her grip on my hand.

"Mrs Powell definitely said to follow the path around the Knot Garden," I reassure her.

We giggle at the idea of swimming with the stone water nymphs and crusty dolphins, but this is Tillingford Hall, and we must embrace its quirks. The water does look rather murky, but there are steps on the opposite side leading down into the water and I can just imagine Lord Tillingford coming down here for his morning dip.

I carefully lay my kaftan and towel on a stone seat, encrusted with ancient grey-green lichen. Normally, I'd ease myself into the water by walking down the steps. But New Alice, the Alice who said 'yes' to this secondment at Tillingford Hall, who is pretending to be ready for anything and wants to be a good role-model for her daughter, takes the plunge.

I gasp at the shock of the cold. The sunlight hardly reaches the water here. What's worse, there's at least a foot of slimy goop enveloping my ankles at the bottom of the pool. I purse my lips to stop myself crying out in disgust, relieved that Hatty is still hesitating on the side.

As I tread water, trying to clean the sludge off my feet before swimming back to the edge, a shadow falls across the pool.

Someone's there.

I look up, but a single beam of sunlight is shining between the leaves into my eyes. I have no choice but to swim to the steps in full view of the unknown watcher. I get out and turn around, teeth chattering, the silky slime coating my body from the knees down. There, laughing, is Apollo himself, lit by the sun so that his golden hair and beard forms an aura around his unfeasibly handsome face. He is naked from his broad shoulders down to his waist.

His swimming trunks break the illusion and I realise the statues haven't come alive – this is actually a modern-day human being addressing me.

"Are you alright?" he asks in a voice that conveys both concern and bewilderment, as you'd expect from someone who's just found a house guest floundering in the garden pond. "You must be The Miniature Girl," he says, squinting at me and holding out his hand.

I'm not *that* small, nor since I'm a thirty-seven-year-old divorcee with a seven-year-old daughter, really a *girl*. My hand stays firmly by my side as I try to take in what's happening.

"Sorry," he says, "I should know your name, but Mrs Powell couldn't remember, and Dad just calls you 'The Miniature Girl'."

Oh crap! This demi-god is the heir to Tillingford Hall, *The Honourable Guy Tillingford*, no less and here am I, supposedly a professional art curator, emerging green and slimy like some creature of the swamp from his garden pond.

"Hello," I say, unsure how to address him and shivering as I attempt something like a curtsey. "I'm Alice," I manage to say. "Alice Merrow, from the London Portrait Gallery, and this is my daughter Hatty."

"I'm Guy," he says enveloping my damp, chilly hand in a warm, strong grip that sends a momentary thrill up my arm and into my stomach. "Welcome to Tillingford Hall, Alice. And hello, Hatty," he says cheerfully shaking her hand too. "I'm sure you'll have lots of fun here."

Hatty looks up at me and whispers "Is he a prince?".

I explained to her before we came that Tillingford Hall is *not* a palace, just a large country house, and it's *not* inhabited by a prince and princess, just a baron. But she thought a baron must be *wicked,* so that didn't really help.

Fairy stories have a lot to answer for.

"Hatty, it's not polite to whisper. You'll have to ask Guy yours-s-self," I insist, stammering with cold.

"Are you a prince?" she asks in the tiniest voice, looking at the ground.

Guy laughs. "No. My father is a baron," he says, "but that doesn't make me anything special. I'm just Guy, although my title is 'The Honourable' but really… just don't worry about it," he sighs. "So, Alice, do you make a habit of jumping into people's garden ponds?" he asks as he shifts his attention to me and I can feel his eyes on my legs.

"Silly Mummy," giggles Hatty tugging my hand and swinging it from side to side as she throws her head back and looks up at me cheekily, "I *told* you this didn't look right!"

"S-s-so, I'm guessing this isn't the s-s-swimming pool?"

I ask pointlessly. My thighs are pasty white and covered in goosebumps, my shins are green and coated in stuff I don't even want to think about, and my face must be as pink as Barbie's knickers.

"Does it look like one to you?" says Guy with a chuckle.

"M-m-maybe not," I admit, my teeth chattering, "but it might've been one once – there *are* steps leading down into the water," I point out, trying to look fractionally less stupid.

"Oh yeah, I'd never thought of that," he says as he hands me my towel.

I try to rub the green goo off my legs with it. It doesn't make much difference and just ruins the towel.

As I wrap the stained towel round my middle to cover my wobbly bits and stop myself shivering, he picks up my kaftan and, examining the crewel-work details, says, "This is exquisite."

"Thank you. Are you into textiles?" I ask.

"Not especially," he says, "but I always admire beauty where I find it." And he looks directly at me.

I find myself blushing again. My heart starts to thump, but I'm under no illusions; I'm nothing special to look at, and I'm sure he can't be making a pass at me. Someone as heart-stoppingly gorgeous and eligible as The Honourable Guy Tillingford won't be single, nor consider a nearly middle-aged divorcee with a daughter in tow as a potential match for a nanosecond. I tell myself to stop even considering the possibility, but as I do, I feel a kick of disappointment that New Alice is nowhere to be found.

She would definitely take a compliment and run with it.

"I'll show you the real pool," says Guy. "There's a shower there you can use to… deslime," he adds, looking at my legs again, “and loads of clean towels. Come on, Hatty,” he says, holding out his hand to her.

Amazingly, she takes it.

Chapter Two

I leave squishy footprints behind as Guy leads us the other way round the Knot Garden. We soon come upon a twenty-metre infinity pool, lined with blue mosaic tiles. It has Indian sandstone borders on three sides, the fourth merging into the landscape beyond. A well-built man, about Guy's age, with a full beard is fishing leaves and other debris out of the pool with a large net. He's wearing one of those loose cut-away vests, which shows off his chunky shoulders, his mass of fair curls tied up with garden twine.

"Hi, Seb," calls Guy.

"Yo, Dude," the man replies with a nonchalant wave.

"Still here?"

"Yeah, Max just came back and there was more to do than usual, so I thought I'd stick around," Seb drawls in a surprisingly plummy accent.

"Alice, Hatty, this is Seb," says Guy, "Seb this is Alice and Hatty. Alice is here to catalogue the collections."

"Hey, guys," Seb says, glancing at my pasty legs, still stained with tell-tale streaks of green. He goes to put his net in the cedar-clad pool house. It contains a couple of elegant sofas and a few potted palms. A set of teak sun loungers is scattered around the pool. There's also an outside shower which Guy turns on and laughingly orders me to use before I get in. He pulls a giant inflatable ring with a fluorescent flamingo's head out of the water and throws it contemptuously behind the loungers.

Guy puts his arm round Seb's shoulder and exchanges a few words, before Seb lopes away across the grass in bare feet. I had assumed Seb was the pool boy, but his accent and the warmth between the two men makes me wonder if they're friends or maybe even brothers.

As I shower off the slime, I try to wash away my anxiety. It was difficult taking Hatty away from her friends for the summer holidays so that I could work. She wasn't overly happy about being away from our little flat in Southwest London for the first time since we moved there after The Divorce.

But I've been in a rut, and I know I need to get back out there and be braver. So, when my boss, Desmond Kingston-Campbell – you've probably seen him on Antiques Roadshow: the flamboyant Trinidadian who always wears amazing waistcoats and cravats – gave me the chance to come here on secondment, it seemed like the perfect opportunity. Especially when Lord Tillingford was so sympathetic about Hatty and offered me free childcare.

But right now, I'm overwhelmed by the enormity of the task ahead, and I've made myself look completely stupid in front of my employer's son, who also happens to be the most gorgeous man I've ever seen, not that his looks or how I feel about them really matter as he's clearly way out of my league.

I thought The Divorce had cauterised my emotions but apparently there's still a flicker of life there.

A second later, Guy's in the pool doing butterfly stroke. I've only ever seen Olympians do that, but clearly Guy is no mere mortal. I'm not a strong swimmer and suddenly feel incredibly tired, so lying on a sun lounger feels more tempting just now.

But Hatty, her legs dangling over the side, is watching Guy. She's a real water baby, one of the few things I can actually thank Philip, her dad, for. She walks to the less splashy side of the pool and jumps in, calling me into the water.

My heart is pounding with fear and embarrassment and maybe just a hint of excitement. I don't want to show myself up yet again in front of Guy, but Brave New Alice won't let me chicken out like that. Before I have time to regret it, I'm grabbing the fluorescent pink flamingo and jumping in the water with an un-Alice-like whoop that makes Hatty shake with laughter. I want to show her that Mummy *can* be fun – occasionally.

"I say," bellows a deep voice, "what are you doing with my miniature girls?"

"Just cooling off after a hard day doing *your* accounts, Dad," says Guy wearily.

I'm now fully stuck, helplessly bobbing round and round with my bottom in the flamingo ring. I spin to face Lord Tillingford, but the inflatable keeps going in lazy circles, my cheeks matching its fluorescent pink as everything I do to stop it seems to make it – and my head – spin even faster.

"Room for another one?" says Lord Tillingford, easing himself down the ladder and into the pool. "I see you found Maxine's tasteful pool toys," he laughs eyeing up my flamingo. I'm practically doubled-up with self-consciousness, floating in an overcrowded pool with a half-dressed peer of the realm and his handsome son and heir. Only the flamingo is stopping me from drowning with sheer embarrassment.

Suddenly, the most enormous Great Dane I've ever seen

bounds across the grass. It belly flops into the pool and Hatty screams.

"Algie! What the…" shouts Guy. "Dad, get him out of here!"

"He's just joining in the fun," laughs Lord T, but Hatty shrieks and scrabbles desperately to reach the side of the pool, which only excites Algie even more, and waves from the canine commotion break over Hatty's head. I flail about in my flamingo trying to get to her, but I'm properly stuck. I should never have got into it bottom first!

With one underwater stroke, Guy's underneath Hatty. He has her in his arms and plonks her onto the side of the pool. "You'll be fine!" he insists, then jumps out of the pool, calls off the dog and shuts it up in the pool house.

"Sorry about that!" he says to me and Hatty. "Algie's a gentle giant; he wouldn't hurt a fly, but he takes some getting used to." He comes to sit next to my daughter, putting his arm around her. "Are you OK, Hatty?" he says. She looks up at him and nods solemnly.

I'm still trying to propel myself to where she's sitting. But as I unsuccessfully attempt to direct the plastic flamingo to Hatty's side of the pool, it makes awkward farting noises and Hatty starts laughing, pointing at me. She then jumps back in the water and spins me around, even though I beg her not to because it'll make me dizzy. But then I discover it's actually kind of relaxing if you just go with it.

Luckily, she gets bored after a moment and starts to swim about in that non-directional way children do. Lord Tillingford continues his slow breaststroke as though nothing happened, methodically working his way up the pool. Guy matches his pace to keep him company and I decide to lie back, ignore them all, and look at the sky.

The air is so much cleaner here than in London and there are loads of house martins and swallows zooming about above our heads and, much higher up, a hawk of some kind.

After a couple more lengths in companionable silence, Lord T says "Right. That's enough for me!"

"You've only done four lengths!" Guy chides.

"I'm not a strapping young thing like you," retorts his father, climbing slowly up the ladder. "And I did forty-six this morning, I'll have you know."

"Oh Dad, that's great," says Guy. "I'm glad you're exercising."

"Stop nannying me, silly boy. These last four lengths are just so I can say I've done my full fifty, like the Adonis I am," Lord Tillingford explains, flexing his wiry biceps and his son laughs.

"Are we doing drinks tonight?" asks Guy as Lord Tillingford picks up a robe from one of the loungers.

"Yes, we'll have them on the Terrace as it's such a balmy evening and your mother's home," he says, putting on the robe.

"OK, I'll go down and help Mrs Powell in a few minutes," calls Guy. "See you in a bit."

I can hear Lord T pushing on some sandals. "Six-thirty sharp as usual!" he calls, as he lets Algie out of the pool house. Holding onto the dog's collar, he drags Algie past the pool and then lets The Beast romp on ahead of him towards the house.

Guy powers up again into butterfly stroke, which makes me bob up and down, as he passes, and I realise I'm enjoying just lying here, gazing at the sky. *You are allowed to relax,* I remind myself and my shoulders loosen a little. I might even be dozing off a bit. A distant bell strikes six, and the splashing dies down.

I'm aware of Guy approaching. "Alice," he says softly. "We'll be doing what Dad calls 'drinkies' on the Terrace in half an hour, so you might want some time to get changed. We don't dress formally for dinner, but Mum's a bit of a snob, so I'd put on something nice if you want to make a good first impression."

"Thanks for the tip!" I say, struggling to get out of the flamingo.

Guy laughs again and tilts the inflatable up.

"I didn't mean that kind of tip!" I shriek as I slide out.

He grabs me and something like a spark of electricity passes between us as we touch. I gasp.

"It's cold!" I lie to justify my sudden exhalation. I couldn't bear to have Guy think I have a crush on him. For all I know he's a womanising axe murderer. Or gay. Or married.

But whatever his status in the potential romance department, I can't deny he sets my heart racing like a giddy schoolgirl's.

"I'll do a few more lengths," Guy says, his muscular arms resting on the edge of the pool, as he watches me. I get out, towel myself off, and try to drop my kaftan over my head as naturally as possible, even though I'm achingly conscious of his gaze.

"Come on, Hatty," I call, desperate for a quiet moment away from all this. "Time to get out."

"Can't I stay a bit longer?" Hatty asks. "Guy could look after me."

Trying to hide my astonishment that she's keener to spend time with a stranger than with me, I say, "Guy wants to do some serious swimming, Hatty. Anyway, we need to make ourselves look pretty for dinner with Lord and Lady Tillingford."

"I'll see you on the Terrace," says Guy, helping Hatty get out. "That's the bit outside the Ballroom, right? Just go through the Entrance Hall, into the Ballroom and out of the open French doors at the other side. Don't get lost," he says with a cheeky smile.

"Got it," I say with a withering look. Taking Hatty's hand, I walk off worrying about what I'm going to wear.

Chapter Three

Our little bedroom under the eaves is a bomb site. I've only brought one suitcase of clothes, but they are all, without exception, scattered across the bed, the chair, the desk and floor. I'm panicky, like a teenager who's got *nothing to wear* for an impromptu date.

My cotton print dresses and smocks are too informal, and so are T-shirts or shorts, and my linen slacks emerge too crushed from my case to be wearable. I've got a couple of blouse-skirt combos that are a bit too worky, while my maxi dress is too daytime and, if I'm honest, a bit too *maxi* for my petite frame; I really must try and shorten it a bit.

But I've not got long, so I settle on the one formal thing I have that fits properly and actually somewhat flatters me: my black linen sheath dress. I dress it up with my smartest necklace – a string of river pearls my English granny gave me. I've treasured it as my only piece of serious jewellery and only wear it on special occasions, unlike the silver oak-leaf bracelet my other grandmother made for me, which I wear every day.

And then, looking at my limited shoe options, I dress it down a little with black ballet pumps.

Hatty's in a pretty sundress and cardy, which she chose herself and will easily do. She was ready fifteen minutes ago and is quietly reading a book, Beebee wedged under her elbow so she can still turn the pages.

It's 6.25pm. I dare not be late, and it's going to take a few minutes to get all the way downstairs and find the right place, so I don't have time to do a full face of make-up. I'm not very good at doing it quickly because I hardly ever wear any. Instead, I add a slick of lip gloss, quickly towel-dry my frizzy hair, twist it and pin it up with a comb, hoping no one will notice it's still wet.

"I'm ready," I say to Hatty, even though I'm anything but. As I usher her out, I take a few drops of Rescue Remedy and shut the door behind us.

We hesitate at the door of the Ballroom. Hatty's eyes widen as she pushes open the door to the marble-floored room filled with ceiling height gold mirrors. I can imagine the scenes from many a Disney movie playing on the cinema screen of her mind as she practises a few ballet steps in the cavernous space.

There are three figures on the Terrace, and I catch my breath, wiping my sweaty palms on my dress. Then I realise the female figure is just Mrs Powell, not Lady Tillingford, and relax slightly. We cross the Ballroom, the clack of Hatty's sandals echoing horribly on the marble floor. Through the open French doors, we're greeted by the smell of sun-warmed lavender and thyme from ornamental pots lined up along the balustrade. A conservator would have a fit about letting all this fresh, damp air into the room, but this isn't a museum, I remind myself. It's the Tillingfords' home, and it can't be preserved in aspic.

Guy is looking intellectual in steel-rimmed specs. A sky-blue Oxford shirt, worn over stone-coloured chinos, perfectly suits his complexion. It's open at the neck, showing a little golden chest hair, and his well-muscled arms are tight inside the rolled-up sleeves. I catch a hint of his fresh, citrussy cologne as he hands me a G&T. I thank him and take a swig.

"I'm scared, Mummy," says Hatty, clutching my skirt. She's nervously watching Algie romp about on the lawn with two lively beagles.

"Don't be silly," I say, more confidently than I feel.

"Dogs can be quite scary if you're not used to them," says Guy, crouching down to look Hatty in the eye. "Their great-great-great-great-great-great-great grandads were wolves, so it's totally fine to be a bit scared of them. But Algie's a gentle giant, and Bertie and Bailey are decent chaps when they've had plenty of exercise. They might want to play with you because you're small and they think you must be one of them. But if they get a bit lively for you, just stand still like a tree and totally ignore them. They'll soon get bored and go away."

Hatty looks at him with huge eyes as she takes in this life-saving piece of wisdom.

"I'll introduce you to them properly later so you can stroke them. They've got such lovely velvety fur. If you give them some treats, I'm sure you'll be best friends. Now then, Miss Hatty," he says, straightening up, "would you like orange juice or apple juice?"

"Apple juice, please," she says, relaxing her grip on my skirt and craning her neck to look up at Guy.

Once he's served Hatty, Guy takes a sip of his G&T. "How much gin did you put in this, Dad?"

"There's no point in a G&T if you can't taste the G," Lord T replies cheerfully. I would think he'd be boiling in burgundy moleskin slacks and a checked twill shirt with a cravat and a navy blazer, but he looks completely comfortable.

Guy's phone rings, and he swears under his breath as he switches it off. "These bloody kids in the office never go home! There's one called Gus who I swear sleeps under his desk. I mean, seriously, it's Saturday evening. Don't they have parties to go to?"

I take another small sip of my super-strength G&T then nurse my glass wistfully, resolving not to drink any more until there's some food to steady it. Although, goodness knows, I could certainly do with the Dutch courage. I turn at the sound of footsteps crossing the Ballroom.

"Ah, Maxine!" says Lord Tillingford, warmly.

Billowing through the French windows and milking her entrance for all it's worth as she allows Guy to kiss her on each cheek, is an elegant lady with soft, shoulder-length blond hair. She's carrying a ridiculously fluffy Bichon Frisée, and she has that high-maintenance look that makes it hard to tell if she's an expensively preserved fifty-five or a slightly tired forty-five. Maths dictates the former. Like me, she's wearing a black linen sheath dress, but hers is dressed up with a diamond pendant the size of a quail's egg and black patent killer heels. As she balances to peck her husband on the cheek, I catch a flash of red Christian Louboutin sole.

I can't decide if I'm relieved that I've picked the right kind of thing to wear, or dismayed that I've accidentally stolen her look, albeit a thousand times cheaper. I also can't help but wonder what seeing me and his mum identically dressed must be doing to Guy's head.

I take a very large swig of G&T. Dutch courage is going to be essential.

"How was your flight, my dear?" asks Lord Tillingford,

handing Maxine a glass.

"No worse than usual, Honey!" his wife replies with a faint accent that might be American East Coast tempered by a few decades in England.

"Well, you look fresh as a daisy!" says Lord T, adding more gin to his glass.

"Thank you, Sweetie. It was kind of you to send Sebastian to collect me," she says, an enigmatic smile flickering on her lips.

"Well, I didn't want you being rushed over by some ghastly rickshaw-driver in a Prius," he says through the opening hiss of another bottle of tonic.

"I'd have thought Neville would be far worse than a Prius!" laughs Guy.

"Don't be daft, Boy! You know your mother wouldn't be seen dead in a camper van; I let him take the Rangie. Anyway, this is my cataloguing girl, Alice," says Lord T, waving his glass in my general direction. "And her daughter, Hatty."

"So sweet of you to invite them to dinner, Giles," says Maxine. Her eyebrows struggle to raise themselves in a Botox-frozen forehead as she puts down her drink. "Coco says, *You are sooo welcome*!" Maxine says in a doggy sort of voice while making the Bichon wave its tiny white paw.

Hatty giggles. It would be impossible to be scared of that little ball of fluff.

"She's so pleased you've come to help out!" Maxine looks at me properly for the first time. "And look at us in our little matching outfits!" She peals with laughter. "*We love the way you've paired pearls with pumps*," she says in the doggy voice again, as though Coco herself were delivering this observation.

"*So charming and casual!* And what a pretty dress," she says to Hatty, patting her on the cheek. "This *is* slimline tonic, isn't it, Honey?" she asks Giles. She sets Coco down with Algie and the two beagles and makes a fuss over all of them, interrupting the important ritual between the four dogs. They quickly ignore her and carry on sniffing each other's bottoms, which is clearly much more fun than being petted, even if there's no way Coco can reach anywhere near the relevant part of Algie's anatomy.

I keep my smile fixed while Maxine's whirlwind of brittle niceness flurries past me. But inside, I feel like a child whose poorly stacked ice cream has just dropped off the cone and landed on the floor.

I'm aware of Guy on my left, with a bowl in his hand. "Have some of Mrs Powell's Spicy Bar Nuts," he murmurs, gently cupping my elbow, "for fortification." He winks as I gratefully take a handful before he passes the bowl to Hatty.

"So, *Amelia*," Maxine – or is it Coco? – says, turning to me with a tight grin just as I've popped about twenty nuts in my mouth, "how are the miniatures?"

I'm frantically chewing, trying to wash the nuts down with what's left in my glass, which is already surprisingly empty.

"The miniatures are great!" I reply, trying not to choke. "There's a lot to do, but I'm really excited! I was looking at the Belgians this afternoon," I add.

"The Belgians! Those are some of our most valuable ones," she says brightly. "One very similar to the Lady Vroeningen snuffbox sold in Boston yesterday for $165,000."

"Really? The estimate was 180-200," I say, thoughtfully. "So they sold it with no reserve? Someone must have been keen to get rid of it. I thought there'd be more interest."

Lady Tillingford looks at me intently, her eyes fractionally narrowing.

"Shall we go in for dinner, Giles?" she says, glancing at my already empty glass.

"Mrs Powell will call us in when it's ready, I'm sure."

"She's probably waiting for us," insists Lady Tillingford. "Let's go in."

She puts her arm into her husband's and all but drags him towards the Dining Room, which is just off the Ballroom. Guy takes my arm in the same way but holds back a bit.

"We normally just eat in the Kitchen," he whispers, his breath warm on my ear, tantalising with a waft of lemons and juniper, "but Mum likes a more formal dinner when she gets home, just to assert her rights as Lady of the Manor. You mustn't mind her – she's always a bit tetchy when she's been travelling." He squeezes my hand reassuringly, then rests it on his arm, just below his elbow. He holds out his other hand for Hatty, who shyly obliges, and we process into the Dining Room, walking on either side of him like two maiden aunts in a period drama.

As we enter the magnificent room, Hatty gazes around, eyes wide. I dimly take in the sombre oil paintings on the dark red walls until my eyes settle on the exquisitely carved mantlepiece.

"The mantelpiece," says Lady T with evident pride as she catches my admiring gaze.

"Grinling Gibbons, isn't it?"

"We're not completely sure," Lord T admits. "It could be *school of*. We're not quite happy with the turn of that putto's bottom; it's slightly less pert than you'd expect from a classic

Gibbons, and there are pineapples too, which are either unique, or fraudulent – who's to say? There are precious few Grinling Gibbons experts around these days."

"True, but I can certainly get Alexander Sopwith to come and have a look if you like," I say.

"*The* Alexander Sopwith?" asks Lady T, with an attempt to raise her frozen brow.

"Well, of course!" I say. "Is there more than one?" And we laugh, as Alexander is one of the most distinctive eccentrics in the world of decorative arts. He's the expert on Stuart and Early Georgian decorative arts on *The Arty Farty Show* on Channel Four who always wears a bow tie.

"Well, that's wonderful," says Lady Tillingford, crisply. "*We'd love to host Alexander Sopwith, wouldn't we, Daddy*?" 'says' Coco. "You really must invite him to come down," Maxine continues in her own voice. "Tell him to bring that Kirsten too. The more experts we can get looking around, the better," she adds with a bright little laugh that doesn't reach her eyes.

As Lord Tillingford said, dinner isn't quite ready, so he shows Hatty and me around for few more minutes, pointing out a freaky little monkey in one picture and asking Hatty to spot the rabbit in another, while Lady Tillingford chats with Guy. They seem to be catching up about some family friends in America, presumably the people Maxine's just been visiting, but I'm not paying attention; I'm rapt by the astonishing richness of art in this one room. My mind boggles at the thought of how much there is to learn about the treasures of Tillingford Hall.

When I spot two miniatures hanging by the fireplace, I make a beeline for them. "Are these ancestors of yours?" I ask, unnecessarily. Even seven or eight generations on, I can see the family likeness.

"Yes, indeed," confirms Lord Tillingford. "But can you tell me who they're by?" he asks, fixing me with his gaze as he leans against the mantelpiece, and I know this is a test.

"I think this one's a Thomas Lawrence, probably from the 1790s," I say hesitantly, pointing to the larger of the two.

"Spot on!" he says, clearly impressed. "But I bet you won't know the second one!" he teases, wagging a finger at me. I'm under pressure now, and there's a flush rising in my cheeks, as I seem to have drawn Guy and Maxine's attention too.

I look at it closely, but to me, it's unmistakable. "Richard Cosway, middle period, about 1800."

"Are you sure?" asks Lord Tillingford. "We had a man from Christie's a few years back, and he didn't know."

"Yes, I'm quite sure; I'm doing my PhD on him."

And as I've been working on said PhD for ten years, I don't think anyone alive knows more about Richard Cosway than I do. I'm finally feeling in my element.

Before the stunned silence becomes oppressive, Mrs Powell plonks a tureen of soup on the sideboard. I'm relieved the soup has taken the spotlight off me, but for a moment, as Guy shows me to my seat, I'm aware of him looking at me intently. As he pushes my chair in so I can sit down, I can smell his cologne and feel the warmth of him.

Mrs Powell ladles out the soup and Guy takes the bowls to the table. "French Onion, my favourite," says Lord T, rubbing his hands together.

I give Hatty the secret look we agreed on the way down here

which means 'I know you won't like it, so just pretend to eat it and leave it quietly'. "Mmm, look at this lovely homemade bread," I say, looking at her significantly, willing her to munch on that.

Lord Tillingford wishes us *Bon Appetit,* and we all set to while he questions his wife about her trip.

"Chelsea sends you her love, Honey," Maxine says to Guy. "She can't wait to see you – so she's coming over soon."

"Oh, when?" asks Guy.

"In a month's time," replies Maxine.

"That's nice," he replies. "I haven't seen her since the funeral – when was that? This time last year, wasn't it?"

"Yes, it's the first break she's had since her mother died, poor thing."

But even while I'm wondering who Chelsea is and why she can't wait to see Guy, I'm aware of the warmth from his leg under the table, a few inches closer to mine than it needs to be, and suddenly I lose my appetite.

Chapter Four

It's Sunday, and Guy insisted I wouldn't do any work today, which I'm glad of as I had a restless night. I couldn't help thinking about him and wondering whether he'd deliberately sat so close to me at the table last night. And whether Chelsea is anyone important in his life.

As he and I walk with Hatty across the fields to the pub in the village of Tillingham, Guy explains that all the farmland round the village belongs to the Tillingford estate. The half of the estate to the east of the house is managed – not very successfully, I get the impression – by the Tillingfords' own estate manager, while the half to the west is on a long lease to Susan, the widow of the late Formula One driver Sir Jason Irving-McAuley. The land is farmed on organic principles by her son and daughter, James and Allegra. They run a farm shop and have their own brand of organic produce while 'Lady Susan' (as she styles herself, even though she's since remarried) swans around being a Society hostess, a role which Lady Tillingford seems to be only too happy to pass over to her.

There certainly seem to be a huge number of birds and bugs around, generating the occasional squeak from Hatty, who's not very good with creepy crawlies. But she is very excited to use steppingstones to cross a ford; she's never seen one before, and she crouches down to run her fingers through the water, asking if we can come back another day to paddle. Of course I agree, thinking that splashing around in freezing cold water is just the kind of thing New Alice would do.

Guy takes us on a slightly longer route through Tillingham village so we can see some of the pretty cottages and the old Village Stores, which are being turned into a community shop, and the church which, it being a Sunday, is open. Inside, Guy shows us the tombs of some of his ancestors, including his great-grandfather, Brigadier General Lord Algernon Tillingford, who was killed in the Second World War.

We arrive at the Tillingford Arms, a charming coaching inn on the village green, with a cobbled courtyard and a pretty beer garden with summer herbs and flowers overflowing from mismatched barrels. The car park is full, as you'd expect at Sunday lunchtime, and the restaurant is busy with families and couples, the bar propped up by a gaggle of locals quaffing pints.

Guy goes to order our food and drinks while Hatty and I wait in the garden. I try to persuade her to go into the playground.

"But there are *other people* there," Hatty whispers.

Two girls her age are on the swings. One has glasses, but they look so similar I'm sure they must be twins.

"I'm sure they'll share," I reason.

Hatty looks uncertain.

"Why don't we go and see? They might be Nice Little Girls. Maybe they could be new friends while you're here."

Hatty looks doubtful, but she allows me to take her by the hand and 'go and have a look'.

"Hello!" says the little girl with glasses. She stops swinging her legs.

"We're Lily and Poppy," says the other as the swings lose momentum.

Both girls jump off the swings at exactly the same moment and end up sprawling on the patchy grass, giggling as their Boden sundresses get covered in grass clippings.

"What's your name?" the one with glasses asks Hatty from the dust, without even getting up.

"Hatty," says my daughter, a bemused smile to match mine playing on her lips.

"That's a nice name! Come and play with us," says the other girl – though we still don't know which is Lily and which is Poppy.

Hatty looks to me for encouragement, which of course I give, and goes to join them.

Pleasantly surprised, I return to our table just as Guy appears with a couple of packets of fancy-looking crisps, two glasses, and a bottle in a cooler. It's Chablis – my favourite. Guy pours the beautiful, pale yellow liquid delicately into my glass and then his, then chinks glasses with me.

"This is really nice," I say, taking an appreciative sip.

"Surprised we have decent wine in Hillbilly Hell?" says Guy with a smirk, but before I can make some lame protest, he explains that The Tillingford Arms is an award-winning gastropub and offers a top wine selection.

"Where's Hatty?" he asks, looking about while he opens the Mature Cheddar Cheese and Hampshire Spring Onion crisps from Tillingford Manor Farm Organics.

"In the playground with Lily and Poppy, the precocious twins," I say, craning my neck to take a look.

"She's in safe hands then! You can honestly relax and leave

them to it," he says, pushing the crisps towards me.

"You know them?" I ask, taking a huge, thick crisp from the top of the pile.

"Sure. Their parents moved into the Old Vicarage a year ago. Mike's at Megacorp, and Elizabeth's a yummy mummy with an engineering degree from Cambridge who's expending her enormous energy and talents reorganising the village," he laughs. "She's one of the ones setting up the new community shop and a bit of a Queen Bee, by all accounts. But they're lovely," he adds when he sees the face I must've just pulled. "You'll like them. We're very lucky to have some excellent people in the village."

His phone buzzes, and he glances at it. "I thought it was Gus from the office, but it's actually Sinitta; I'd better take this one," he excuses himself.

He turns away for a few moments, exchanges a few words with the caller, then turns his phone right off. "Sinitta's the coordinator for a mentoring programme for boys at risk of getting into gangs I volunteer for. One of my mentees has a hearing at Southwark Magistrates tomorrow, and she was just checking I could get out of work to go with him."

"Will you be able to?"

"Hogghedge will have to do without me – his dad's in prison and his mum's having chemo tomorrow, so there's literally no one else to go with him. This is definitely more important."

I'm really not getting an impression of an axe murderer from Guy.

I smile at him while we sit in companionable silence, looking about at the people enjoying their leisure time, stuffing their faces with Sunday Roast in this lovely garden.

"Thank you for coming out with me," he says, taking a handful of crisps.

"It's my pleasure," I say and take another sip of wine.

"I like a Sunday lunch out," he says, "I feel like it extends the weekend before I have to get back to the Smoke."

"So, you don't really think of London as home, then?"

"No – it's just where I work. Don't get me wrong, I've got a very nice flat overlooking London Bridge, but it's just a one-bed bachelor pad. I'm often in the office by six and sometimes don't get home till midnight, so I barely notice the place. I think the cleaner spends more waking hours there than I do. Hogghedge let me take time out once or twice a week to do my mentoring because it looks good for their CSR, but I'm always back in the office afterwards, making up the time.

"No, Tillingford Hall will always be my home and where the future Lady Tillingford and I will bring up our children – if I ever find her, that is."

For a second, I feel a frisson of desire in my solar plexus – until I remind myself that someone like me, boring little Alice Merrow, a divorcee living in a rented flat at the rear end of South-west London, a frumpy nobody from the basement of a dusty museum, will never be a catch for someone like The Honourable Guy Tillingford. He's obviously only brought Hatty and me here to be hospitable, or because he wanted to 'extend the weekend'.

As I glance at him, I reckon he's in his mid-thirties like me, and I'm wondering what his story is – how it is that he hasn't found his Lady Tillingford yet. Goodness knows, the candidates must be queuing round the block.

"Hi James," Guy calls to a well-built man in cricket whites

who has his arm around the waist of an ethereal, willowy blonde. She looks somehow familiar.

"Guy!" says James, coming over to give his friend a great bear hug. "How's tricks?" His accent is plummy as a fruitcake.

The beautiful woman with sad eyes silently kisses Guy on both cheeks, and he leans his forehead on hers as he holds her tenderly. Then he turns to me.

"Alice, this is my tenant, neighbour and old school friend, James Irving-McAuley. And of course, I don't need to introduce Sahara," he says.

Oh my God! It *is* actually Sahara Seaton-Smyth, the supermodel, but she doesn't look anything like she used to on the cover of Vogue. She's frail, with sallow skin and bags under her eyes. I hold out my hand to her and mumble something, feeling incredibly awkward amid these luminaries. But Sahara takes my hand in both hers, gives it a gentle squeeze, and looks so genuinely and kindly into my eyes as she says a few welcoming words that I immediately start to relax.

"And this is Alice," says Guy with a smile. "She's come on secondment from the London Portrait Gallery to catalogue our miniatures."

"Ha! Good luck trying to sort out that dusty old junk," laughs James with a twinkle in his eye, kissing me on both cheeks. "I'm taking Sahara back to the Manor now," he tells Guy.

"Won't you stay for lunch?" asks Guy. "The cricket can't be starting for another hour at least."

"Exactly," laughs Sahara, "just enough time for me to get home for my siesta. I saw my brother at the bar though – I'm sure he'll come and keep you company!"

"If it's company you want..." James adds with a somewhat lecherous look in my direction.

I can feel my cheeks burning under his gaze.

And is that Sahara rolling her eyes?

"He'll no doubt find us in a minute," says Guy, sitting back down.

And with a few parting words, James and Sahara take their leave. Guy splits open the second bag of crisps, and I reach out to take one. I don't want to spoil my appetite, but who doesn't want a crisp with a chilled glass of white? "Nice people," I comment, looking at the receding forms of James and Sahara.

"Yeah. Seb – who you met by the pool – is Sahara's brother. He and James were at Winchester with me."

"Are James and Sahara a couple?" I ask, taking a sip of my wine.

"Sometimes!" says Guy. "It's complicated."

I cock my head on one side, willing him to explain.

"He's got commitment issues and she's not exactly marriage material either," he says with a sigh.

"What do you mean?"

Guy takes a sharp in-breath, scrutinising the table, then looks at me over the rim of his glasses. "I *mean* James is a sex addict who thinks he has *droit du seigneur*, although technically I'm the *seigneur* around here, I suppose. But because I'm away a lot and Mum and Dad don't get much involved in the village, people see him more as the Lord of the Manor, and anyway, I'm very much a one-woman man.

"And Sahara..." here he looks with great interest and a furrowed brow at the signet ring on his left little finger.

"Sahara's addicted to whatever the thing is at the moment – sometimes cocaine, sometimes vodka. She even went through a heroin phase, though thank God we managed to get her into rehab," he bites his lower lip. "Luckily it's raw food and Reiki at the moment." He attempts a smile.

"Do lots of your friends do drugs?" I can't help asking.

"Not these days. I'll admit I tried the odd spliff or line of coke when I was a teenager. And there's quite a bit goes on at work." He looks almost angry. "But I never touch anything illegal these days. If people could see how drugs ruin lives – not just the people who take them, but the people who supply them, like the kid I'm helping tomorrow, who basically didn't stand a chance once he got in the sights of his local gang – they'd never start. Anyway, life's rich and full enough without all that crap, don't you think?"

"Totally! I've never done drugs. I've always been too scared, too skint, and to be honest, I never really came across them, even at Uni."

He looks surprised. I don't explain, because I don't want to look too dull, that my friends were quiet people, heads down in the library with the occasional warm chardonnay in the students' union or tea at Fortnum's as a special treat.

"Although my best friend Charlotte got a bit alternative in her last year, and I think she made a few pots of mushroom tea when she went to live out of halls. And now she definitely likes the odd smoke – *odd* being the operative word – and hangs round with some quite unconventional people."

"Sounds like Seb," Guy muses. "Anyway, I'm the only heir to Tillingford Hall. It would be stupid for me to waste money on drugs that I could use on the upkeep of the Hall, or to end up killing myself with an overdose for some obscure relative to inherit it."

"You take your role as heir to Tillingford Hall very seriously, then?"

"Totally," he replies, raking his hand through his hair.

"Don't you see it as a burden?" I ask, taking a sip of Chablis.

"Sometimes – particularly the money side. The estate always seems to be making a loss, and I'm constantly bailing Mum and Dad out. I've spent millions of quid – my own money, honestly most of what I've earned in the last ten years – on the roof, the guttering, the damp-proofing, putting in a new boiler! But mostly I see it as an honour to be born an Honourable. Who has the right to say they don't want that or that it's a load of crap? I can't bear whingers like Prince Harry," he says, turning away and taking a deep draught of wine.

"Have you ever met him?" I ask, feeling even more inadequate.

"Yeah, a couple of times…" he mumbles into his glass. "Some guys I rowed with at uni knew him at Eton."

"I don't think I've ever met any aristocrats before," I admit.

"*Aristocrats!* How did we get onto this?" He puts his hands behind his head and flexes his arms. "At the end of the day, I'm just this guy," he smiles. "Let's talk about you, Alice Merrow, fascinating, clever art curator, a great mum with the sweetest little daughter in tow – so much more interesting than some boring old hedge fund manager trying to rub two pennies together to keep a roof over his dad's head!"

"I don't think I'm fascinating or clever," I say, looking into my drink, "and as for being a great mother…"

"Modest too!" he says, putting his hand over mine for a moment. It feels nice – warm and comforting like a big paw – and I'm sorry when he takes it away a second later.

So, I tell him about my very ordinary middle-class upbringing in Hemel Hempstead, my successful older brothers: Tim, an army officer, and Nick, a barrister, and how no one else in my family has an artistic bone in their body and how they can't understand why I'd want to spend all day making lists of old stuff. It was my lovely French granny, Sylvie, who gave me my love of the arts.

"What did she do?"

"She was a ballet dancer and, when she retired, she became a jewellery designer. She would stay with us for weeks every summer and show me how to draw and make jewellery, and we'd spend hours and hours in the museums. She loved the V&A especially."

"Is that what gave you the bug for 'dusty old junk'?" asks Guy.

"A bit, but I think it was more to do with Bagpuss, really," I giggle.

"Sounds like you've been smoking one of your friend Charlotte's special cigarettes!"

Now I'm giggling so much I can hardly get the words out. "Bagpuss was a big baggy old pink-and-white plush cat that lived in a shop with a rag doll and some felt mice and other characters. Emily, the little girl he lived with, used to bring him lost objects."

"And what would he do with them?" asks Guy with a twinkle in his eye.

I try not to laugh as I explain my serious point. "He and his chums would mend the stuff and tell the story behind it. I loved him because he was squashy and cute and reunited people with their lost things. But Granny Sylvie loved him because he showed how everything, from an old coin to a shoe, has a story to tell.

"Ah! I get it," says Guy. "That's why you decided to become a curator – because you wanted to tell the stories that old things have locked inside them."

"That's just it," I say, staring at him. No one has ever understood this about me before, except my beloved granny.

She made this for me," I say, showing Guy the delicate silver bracelet, decorated with tiny oak leaves I always wear. He holds my wrist as he looks at it, and I can feel my pulse pounding. His firm but gentle fingers grip my arm, brushing my skin as he lifts the metal to examine it closer.

"That's really lovely," he says, slowly returning my wrist to the table. "What's the significance of the oak leaves?"

"For England and our heritage," I explain. "She always used to call me *Aleece* with the French pronunciation and *ma petite Anglaise* and tried to get me to be more French, but it never worked! I just don't feel at home in France… although I do love a good Chablis!" I laugh.

He pours me another glass. "I shouldn't," I say, feeling pretty woozy by now.

"Oh, go on… you don't have to work this afternoon."

"But I do have a daughter to look after," I say, "and I want to get going on the catalogue this evening."

"It's Sunday!" he says, chinking glasses with me.

"I know, but there's so much to do, I thought I'd do a couple of hours when Hatty's in bed."

"I admire your work ethic, but we don't expect you to work

at the weekends!" he exclaims. "And I'd like to get to know you both. Next weekend, I want to take you out somewhere, show you our glorious Hampshire countryside. We could take Hatty to feed the penguins at Bird World or go to the coast. I could borrow a friend's yacht for the day."

My heart is thumping in my throat. I've never felt so attracted to someone, and here he is saying he wants to spend more time with me, with us both. This feels dangerous and silly. I don't trust it. My priority is my daughter, and I know there isn't space for pointless flirting in my life.

"I don't know what to say," I admit.

"Just say 'that would be nice'," he suggests, sounding slightly peeved. I seem to have this effect on people.

"It would be nice, of course, but I'm here to work. Don't feel you have to entertain us… you've been so welcoming already and… well, Hatty will be with her dad next weekend," I manage before my mouth goes dry.

"Then I get you all to myself," he says huskily, and my stomach is attacked by a flurry of butterflies. I dare not look at him.

"I should check up on her," I say, looking towards the playground.

"She's having fun, just relax and let her chill," he says, putting his hand on mine to stop me getting up.

And it's true – she and the twins are crouching in a corner, giggling and poking something with a stick. I'm not sure I want to know what it is.

Suddenly a girl who can't be more than sixteen appears with two laden plates in her hands and one balancing on an arm. I do need to go over and interrupt Hatty, who's clearly having the best fun. She doesn't really want her lunch, but I insist, adding that Lily and Poppy are welcome to come and help her with her chips, which they do, until their parents come over to collect them.

"We can't stay," says Elizabeth. "Father Matthew and some of the shop committee are coming over to ours for a meeting."

Elizabeth and I exchange numbers so we can arrange for the girls to meet up during the week while Guy talks to Mike about getting some decent IT set up for me. They agree it would be good to ask Father Matthew for help as apparently he used to be some IT whiz in his previous life.

When they've gone, Guy says that Lily and Poppy are more than welcome to come to the Hall at any time, and while we're living there, Hatty and I should treat his home as ours. I don't know if it's the wine or the food or the lovely summer day, but I breathe a sigh and feel that, for the first time in about four years, I'm really starting to relax.

I eat as much of the roast as I can manage, but the pub portions defeat me. Hatty struggles to finish her fish fingers and chips too, even though it's a child's portion and Lily and Poppy have been helping. I finish my glass of wine and excuse myself to go to the loo while Guy promises he'll keep an eye on Hatty. As I look back, he's magicking a coin out of her ear, which utterly delights her and sends a smile shooting across my face.

When I get back, Seb's sitting at our table with Guy and Hatty, swigging from a bottle of $J_2 0$.

As I approach, he's on his feet and giving me a loose hug, his beard tickling my neck. "Hi Alice," he drawls, "you saw me by the pool?" he says with an upward inflection as though he's looking for reassurance that I recognise him.

I warm to him instantly; he's laid back and has a sweet, goofy smile. He's good-looking, too, though not in a way that sets *my* heart racing. With his thick beard, long, curly hair, and un-ironed t-shirt and shorts, he's a bit scruffy and less refined than Guy. He's how I imagine a typical surfer dude looks, not that I've ever met a surfer dude in real life.

Hatty whinges that she's tired, but I suspect she's just bored now The Twins have gone.

"Do you think we should go?" I ask Guy, aware that this enchanted afternoon is slipping away from us.

"Yes, probably," Guy sighs, looking at me. Our eyes lock and my stomach fizzes. I look away and pretend to be fascinated by a beer mat.

"I'll take you guys home," offers Seb, waving his J_2O bottle to reassure us that he's OK to drive.

"Thanks," I sigh. The walk across the fields was lovely, but I'm so full – and slightly muzzy from the wine – so I'd happily not bother this time.

We follow Seb to the car park.

"Meet Neville," sighs Guy, rolling his eyes.

"Who's Neville?" I ask, the name vaguely coming back to me from the conversation last night.

Seb affectionately pats the bonnet of a refurbished 1960s VW Campervan, then slides open the side door so Hatty and I can climb inside. He evidently lives in Neville full time, and it doesn't smell too fresh. As we set off over the bumps and curves of the country road, I try hard not to throw up.

Thankfully it's only a five-minute drive to Tillingford Hall. Even so, Hatty has already fallen asleep on the sofa bed by the time we arrive. Guy carefully unclips her seat belt and lifts her out of the van. She stirs, but nestles into him like she belongs against his chest.

"Which room's yours?" he asks.

"The one on the top floor at the end near the servant's stairs," I say. It's the furthest away we could possibly be from the front door, but Hatty, who's now too heavy for me to lift, seems like a little doll in Guy's arms, and he has no trouble carrying her all the way.

When we get to our room, I go ahead to open the door. Guy places Hatty on her bed as carefully as a gilder would dab a sheet of gold leaf on a picture frame.

"Thank you, Guy," I whisper as he turns to face me. "It was lovely to go out for lunch."

"Yes, it was," he says, looking right into my eyes. He tells me how much he's looking forward to next weekend and says he'll talk to me about the catalogue just before he leaves this evening. Then he silently disappears out of the room, leaving me with that *what just happened?* feeling as I flop onto the bed.

Am I so deprived of affection that I've fallen for the first handsome man to cross my path? I'm not exaggerating when I say I've never felt like this about anyone. He's so good-looking and so kind. He's a million miles above anyone I've met before. Most of the men I meet through work are old, married, or gay, and the few single straight ones tend to be a bit odd.

And then there was my ex-husband, Philip, a manipulative, grey, corporate man with no real hobbies or interests. We fell into a relationship when we were students and married as the obvious next step. I was glad when we agreed to separate, especially once

I discovered it was an open secret that he'd had affairs with more than one colleague, which left me feeling utterly humiliated and totally devoid of self-confidence.

But I was fine on my own. Just fine. Before today, my life was a tight ship. My daughter was safe, learning, and loved. My career was slowly progressing. We had an adequate home and enough to eat. I was an independent woman, coping perfectly well on my own.

Now I realise how much I long for a strong man to love me, to help bring up my daughter, to make me laugh and to take care of me. And all that pent-up sadness, fear, and anger at my failed marriage and lonely future bubble up inside me until I'm shaking with self-pity and pent-up rage.

Why am I such an *idiot*? Why do I have to fall for someone like Guy? Even if he does like me, he's probably just toying with me. I'm so obviously not right for someone like him, or for his posh friends and family. I should have just eaten in the Kitchen with the other servants and kept my distance, like the other employees. I bet Mrs Powell doesn't have fantasies about getting off with Lord Tillingford.

I took this secondment at Tillingford Hall because I knew I needed to get out of my shell. I've been doing the same job in the bowels of the London Portrait Gallery since I graduated fifteen years ago, and I realised I wouldn't go anywhere in my career – or my life – unless I got out of that basement and did something new. So, when my boss, Desmond, offered this job around the team, I became Brave New Alice and put my hand up. And, without wanting to sound big-headed, Desmond knew I was the best person for the job. I do know more about miniatures than anyone else at the Gallery, except maybe Desmond himself, so it was right up my street.

And now I've messed everything up by falling for someone way out of my league on my first weekend here. I'm heading for a summer of misery worse than if I'd just stayed in my lonely little hole in London. The tears keep coming, and I curl up in a ball.

I get up and rummage through my suitcase for my battered copy of Jane Austen's *Northanger Abbey*. I feel like Catherine Morland catapulted straight to the Abbey with none of the fun in Bath beforehand. But eventually dear Jane's familiar lines soothe me and, with my book in my hand, I fall into a doze.

Chapter Five

I wake up from my catnap to find Hatty bending over me. "Mummy?" she says.

A blackbird trills its evening song not far from our window, and I'm confused about the time, so I look at my watch.

"Oh crap! It's five o'clock already!" I gasp, sitting up suddenly and giving myself a head-rush. "I promised Guy we'd have a look at the catalogue before he goes back to London."

I get up and splash water on my face to try and wake myself up before we hurry down the servants' stairs near our room, bumping into Guy as he's coming up from the Kitchen.

"Sorry I'm late," I say. "I must've dozed off."

"Hey! Don't worry – it's Sunday. I should be apologising for asking you to talk work on your day off. Anyway, I don't have to leave for a while, and we only need an hour or so. What would you like to do while your mum and I are working, Hatty?"

"Can I watch something?" she asks quietly.

"Of course!" says Guy, taking her into the Snug, a cosy little room next to the Kitchen that I guess was once a storeroom or a scullery. Now it's warmly carpeted and furnished with squishy sofas, beanbags and a big-screen TV. I head to the Kitchen to make us some good, strong builder's tea.

After a few minutes, I hear Guy's firm tread coming back into the Kitchen, and a little smile creeps over my face. I know

I shouldn't be excited about spending an hour in a confined space with Guy, but I can't help myself.

"All set," he says with a grin. "She's watching *Encanto.* It's about an eccentric family that live in a huge, magical house, but they've all got personality issues, and it takes a normal girl to sort them out," he says with a chuckle. "Sound familiar?"

"No way!" I laugh. "You all seem pretty normal to me!"

"We like to give that impression," he says, raising his eyebrows, "but it's all a front! Come on, let's go and look at Art Stuff."

"I'm not sure we should be bringing tea into the Collections Room," I say. It probably sounds rather prim, but I need to uphold my professional standards.

"You're right… we'll drink it here." He dives for the biscuit barrel and pulls out some gorgeous, homemade choc chip shortbread. I know I shouldn't after that huge lunch, but I can't resist tea-time treats.

So, as we sit there munching our shortbread and sipping tea, he gives me some background to the collection: how it grew organically at first before his great grandfather, The Brigadier General, got a bit obsessed with it and started the catalogue. And then Guy's father kept adding to it, and Maxine created a computer catalogue in the noughties on a giant old Gateway laptop but then she let it slip. There are lots of new acquisitions, all with proper provenance and authentication certificates, which haven't been added, and a bunch of stuff which is on there but might be a bit sketchy or incorrectly attributed. And then he thinks some things might be missing from the catalogue altogether while other things that are in the catalogue aren't where they should be and might need to be found and rehung or stored in archive boxes.

"My dad's dream is to get the whole collection fit for display to the public and allow visitors. We must be one of the few great houses that still never opens to the public – and we're missing a trick there, not just because we're depriving people of an opportunity to see something wonderful, but also because we could be making some money out of it, and that would help us with the upkeep of the place."

"So why haven't you done it yet?" I ask, eyeing up a second biscuit.

"Mum's really not keen – she doesn't want Joe Public snooping around. And I'm too busy trying to earn a living, and Dad's, well… not that organised. Have you finished?" he asks eagerly. When I nod, he grabs my mug and shoves it in the dishwasher. "Come on, let's go!"

We climb the stairs to the upper ground floor. "Have you got the key?" he asks.

I put it in the lock and the door swings open.

"I don't think anyone's been in here for at least two years," he says, standing behind me and looking over my shoulder into the room.

"I spent a couple of hours here when I arrived yesterday," I explain as I walk in, "so don't be surprised by the fingerprints!"

But they're not all mine. Even yesterday, I could tell that someone had been in the Collections Room in the last few weeks. Maybe Mrs Powell tidying up?

The late afternoon sun pierces the edges of the UV-blocking blinds, catching the dust motes and making them wink and shimmer as they dance on the eddies of our movements and breath. For a moment, we're silent, and I feel the weight of Guy's expectation and the responsibility of the task before me. That's when I realise that Guy's looking at me.

"What?"

"I don't know…" he says. "I…" he hesitates, listening. "I feel… history calling."

I break into a smile. Like I said, I've never met anyone quite like Guy.

"You think I'm being whimsical?" he asks.

"No… not at all. I know exactly what you mean – this PC is on Windows 3.1!"

He playfully punches my arm. "I don't think you're taking me seriously," he says.

"No, I am – I really, totally get what you mean," and I admit to him how nervous I am about getting the project right.

"But there's no one better qualified than you," he reassures me, and taking a step towards me, he reaches out, as if to touch me. Then, as if recalling himself, he drops his hand. "We know how lucky we are to have you here."

He's so close. His fresh cologne, bright with citrus and juniper, gently teases my nose, and the tiny hairs on my arms are standing on end – with nerves or static or something else, I'm not quite sure. But the air is alive with expectation.

"Alice…" he says, delicately reaching the back of his index finger towards my cheek.

"Oh! You're both in here!" says Maxine barging in. Guy takes a step back, suddenly fascinated by some dust on the table.

"We saw the door was ajar," she says, scrutinising me, "and Coco thought it might have blown open."

"We're just checking out what new equipment Alice needs," Guy explains, looking like a five-year-old caught with his hand in the biscuit barrel. "Can you believe this laptop's actually still got Windows 3.1 on it?" he says.

"But it should still work," says Maxine frostily. She obviously doesn't understand much about operating systems.

"Will you need a printer, do you think, Alice?" Guy asks, sitting down in the office chair and swinging it from side to side.

"Probably not," I answer, not wanting to add unnecessary expense. "I should be able to do everything digitally."

"Dad has one in his Study you could Bluetooth to if you need…" suggests Guy.

"We don't think anyone should be going into Giles's office, do we, Coco?" says Maxine looking into the Bichon's indifferent eyes.

"OK, we'll get Alice her own printer if she finds she needs one," says Guy, spinning round. "Just let me know. And we'll obviously get you a new laptop and a booster for the Wi-Fi."

"That would all be great, thanks, but what I do need is some proper ventilation that's going to make it bearable to work in here but won't ruin the collection," I say, tapping the thermometer to check it really is reading eighty-five degrees, which must be approaching thirty Celsius. I get out my organiser and start making note of things I need, including a hygrometer and some specialist cleaning tools, as well as some less specialist ones – a Hoover and a feather duster would be a good start.

"*But that's a job for the servants*!" Maxine says in the doggy voice, as though Coco herself had expressed this opinion.

"Don't worry – I'm happy to do it," I reassure her. "I'm

sure you know historical artefacts require specialist techniques. Has Mrs Powell been trained?"

Guy and Maxine look at each other.

"No... should she be?" asks Guy.

I purse my lips as I think what untold damage Mrs Powell could be doing spraying Pledge on a priceless Grinling Gibbons fireplace surround and decide to change the subject:

"I'm worried about how I'm going to transfer the data from that laptop – I doubt it's even got a modem."

"There's an external one down here," Guy says. "Maybe it used to connect to that. Can you remember, Mum?"

"*You know we don't have a head for that kind of thing!*" 'says' Coco with a bored voice that belies the sharpness in Maxine's eyes, which seem to be darting around the room, taking everything in. "We'll leave you to it, won't we, Coco?" she says, sailing out of the room with a farewell flicker of her fingers.

"What about flash drives?" Guy says.

"But there won't be a USB port..." I reply.

"And if you could burn a CD, how would you read it back?" he puzzles.

"I might have to try the dial-up, although where one dials to these days is a mystery to me," I say.

We spend the next hour trying to fathom which of these ancient pieces of kit work and how I'm going to convert those twenty-year-old files into a readable format. Digging out the original paper catalogue Guy's great-grandfather made, that magical moment that passed between us is soon forgotten. At least, I suppose Guy's forgotten it. I don't think I'll ever forget how I felt in that moment, and how much I longed for him to touch me.

And then it's time for Guy to go, and Hatty's film finishes, and the prospect of the working week ahead looms like a lonely voyage on stormy winter seas.

"I've really enjoyed spending time with you both this weekend," says Guy, as I stand by his Aston Martin to see him off. Hatty's in the driver's seat, making brumming noises and pressing a button that Guy told her was the rocket launcher, him having reassured me there was no way she could accidentally start the engine and drive off.

"Hatty's adorable," he says. "You're a very lucky woman – and she's a lucky girl to have you for a mother". I feel my heart warming and my cheeks colouring at his kind words. "I'm sorry I have to go," he goes on. "When I'm in London, I'll have to be totally focused on my work – everyone at Hogghedge is a workaholic lab rat, but someone round here's got to earn some money, and this is the only way I know to earn a decent living.

"But I promise I'll be on the end of the phone if you need me, so give me your number. Let me know if you find anything interesting going on, anything odd at all. Just message me and I'll call you back when I can."

Other than the fake I found the other day, I wonder what sort of *odd thing* could be *going on* with a catalogue of miniature portraits, but I tell him my number, and he punches it into his phone, sending me a smiley face emoji so I can save his number too.

"Please don't think I've forgotten about you if I'm not texting every five minutes," he says.

"Of course not!" I say. *Why would I expect to hear from him at all?* But I do want to hear from him, and my phone is burning my hand now that I know I could be in touch with him at any time.

I don't want him to go. I don't want to say anything that will sound too needy, but I feel a little seed growing in my heart, and I don't want to see it shrivel and die before it's had a chance to turn its face to the sun.

"I hope I can be as focused as you," I say, before realising that's exactly the kind of thing that could make it totally obvious I've got a massive crush on him.

"I hope so too; what you're doing here could be much more important than you think," he says, confidentially. "We really do need your help, Alice, so please do your best. I want to see a full appraisal of the collection because there's something not quite right – I just can't put my finger on it."

With more conviction in my voice than in my heart, which is now going at about 290 bps, I tell him I will.

Then he takes my hand and, playing with the oak leaves on my bracelet, says, "I'm really looking forward to spending time with you next weekend, Alice." And with a quick goodbye, he kisses me on the forehead, which sends a jolt of electricity down my entire body.

"Come on, out you get!" he says cheerily to Hatty, who obliges. He gives her a hug, and then he's in the car and off with a crunch of gravel and a small cloud of dust, while I stand gazing after him, my face still tingling with the lingering memory of his touch.

Chapter Six

A couple of hours later, Hatty's tucked up in bed, but it's too early to go to sleep, so I've popped down to the Kitchen to make myself a cup of herbal tea to help me wind down. Mrs Powell is sitting at the far end of the oversized kitchen table with Herbert, the Tillingfords' ancient Jamaican gardener.

"Oh, sorry," I say, ducking back into the doorway.

"Come on in, gurl," calls Herbert in his lilting accent, gesturing towards me with his *I am the Stig* mug. "Come have a nice cuppa tea and tell us how you bewitched the man."

"What are you talking about?" I say, trying to pull a serious, innocent face as I cross the tiled floor towards them. But I can tell the corners of my mouth are betraying me.

Herbert leans across to me, winks conspiratorially, and says, "You know what I mean, gurl. Normally weekends he comes here and spends the whole time checking up on us, climbing up on the roof, fixing things, talking to the surveyor. He never stops – maybe a bit of cricket or a bit of riding, but with you here, he's just chilling the whole day."

I can feel a blush spreading right up my face as I fill the kettle. "I'm sure he was just trying to help me and Hatty settle in."

Mrs Powell and Herbert look at each other.

"Looks like you bin fallen for him big time, gurl," chortles Herbert.

"Well, who wouldn't?" Mrs Powell says, taking a sip out of an old, chipped mug bearing the faded legend: *A balanced diet is a cookie in each hand.*

"Beautiful, clever gurl like you," says Herbert, "Lucky boy."

As I search for a herbal teabag, I feel it's suddenly rather hot in here. I don't think I've been described as beautiful for at least a decade, and even though it's an elderly Jamaican gardener saying it as a bit of flattery, it still sounds nice. And I wonder, just wonder, if perhaps I'm not so bad-looking after all and mightn't scrub up alright if I actually ever got a haircut, used some kind of serum, or wore any makeup.

"A girl couldn't do much better than our Honourable," says Mrs Powell picking up her mug. "Such a gent! Mind you, I haven't seen him serious about a girl for years," she says, looking thoughtful as she takes a sip.

"Not since Sahara," says Herbert.

I almost drop my camomile. Sahara Seaton-Smyth, the ethereally beautiful super model, is *Guy's ex*?

"Man, was she trouble, that gurl. Let that Irving-McAuley, have her, I say. They deserve each other… they're one of a kind."

"Were Guy and Sahara together?" I ask, trying to sound casual and turning to hunt for a mug so Herbert and Mrs P can't see my face.

"*Were they*? Didn't you ever read *HELLO! Magazine*?" laughs Mrs Powell.

"Celebrity gossip isn't really my kind of thing," I explain as I select a bone china mug featuring a silhouette of Jane Austen on one side and the quote *…but indeed I would rather have nothing but tea…* on the other.

"Well, each to his own," says Mrs Powell, "But if you had of, you'd know as how they was engaged a while back."

Engaged! So, it was a really major thing. I remember how he held her when we met in the pub, and I shiver, wondering if he's ever really got over her and who broke it off.

"But she had such bad habits, if you know what I mean," says Mrs Powell with a disapproving tut.

"You mean… drugs?" I ask, remembering what Guy said.

"Oh, it was terrible, poor girl. She almost died. Guy tried to help her – he cared so much for her – but her habit just took over her life. She was in trouble all the time, and it tore them apart. She's hardly over thirty, but she looks nearer forty if you meet her in the flesh. Such a shame. She was beautiful in her heyday – you must have seen her on posters a while back."

I can't help but agree that, in person, she doesn't look like the photos. For a moment, I wonder if Sahara's lighting and makeup artists could make me look as good as she used to, and then I feel bad for thinking that. I'd far rather have my life, my indifferent bone structure and rubbish haircut, if all they're saying about her is true.

"The Hon did his best," agrees Herbert, "but you couldn't hold that gurl more than you could catch a moonbeam." He holds out his fingers as if a handful of sand is pouring away between them. "That Irving-McAuley's the only one who can keep her close," he adds.

"That's because he doesn't keep her at all," Mrs P says, and Herbert nods. "They're each off doing their own thing, no commitment. Our Hon's the kind of person who wants to be everything to someone – and that someone to be his everything in their turn.

He needs to be with a decent, hard-working woman who's worthy of being the next Lady Tillingford, God bless her."

"Someone like Maxine?" I ask, pouring boiling water into the Jane Austen mug.

A look passes between Herbert and Mrs Powell. "More like Beatrice, Lord Giles's mother," says Mrs Powell with a sniff.

"Maybe we said enough," Herbert says, nodding in my direction.

"I shall speak my mind below stairs," says Mrs Powell, "and even though they invited her upstairs on Friday, Alice is one of us, an employee, and I shall speak freely when she's down here. I'm sure she has enough common sense to know that what's said in the Kitchen is never spoken in the Dining Room."

I'm surprised to hear Mrs P talking referring to 'upstairs' and 'downstairs' in this day and age. I'm not sure whether I'm pleased to be welcomed as 'one of us' or slightly disappointed that I'm not considered 'upstairs', but country house politics is not something I want to get caught up in. If Guy did turn out to be interested in me, then I suppose I'd have to learn to navigate it, but while I'm accepted below stairs, I might as well make the most of it and try to get some answers.

"So, what about this Chelsea who's coming over in a month's time?" I ask, squeezing the teabag.

"Is she, Lord love us?" says Mrs Powell, dunking a Rich Tea in her mug. "I hadn't been told. Handy you passing that on!"

"But who is she?" I ask.

Another brief look passes between Herbert and Mrs Powell.

"Chelsea's father, Brad Masters, and his brother are the construction kings of Boston. They're family friends of

Lady T's," says Mrs Powell, taking a great interest in the biscuit she's dunking. "I think Lady T's dad was one of their suppliers – he was in air conditioning or something. Chelsea's mum, Barbara, passed away last year and Guy flew out for the funeral and spent a few days with them.

"They used to come over here most years when Brad was in London on business and would stay here a week or so at a time. Guy spent a chunk of time out there as well, when he was doing an internship at some fancy American bank. He's very close to them." She drains her mug. "Right," I'm done!" she says, getting up.

Herbert gets up too and shuffles towards the dishwasher with his mug, the sound of his footsteps on the tiled floor echoing round the huge room.

"Be careful, Alice," Mrs Powell says to me quietly as Herbert stacks his mug in the machine. "You're a lovely girl and obviously super clever and all that, but you're not really in his league, are you, dear? The Hon would never *mean* to hurt you, I'm sure, but apart from Sahara, he's always gone for sharp city lawyers or horsey boarding-school girls who fit in with the scene, if you know what I'd mean. Just look out for yourself, won't you?"

I nod while she shoots her barbed arrows into my heart.

Her well-meant advice might have come too late.

Just then, my phone rings. It's Charlotte, my best friend from university, Facetiming me.

"Do you mind if I get this?" I ask. "It's an old friend, and I haven't heard from her for ages."

"Don't mind us," says Mrs Powell as Herbert gives a nonchalant thumbs up. "I'm off to bed anyway. Goodnight!"

I mouth 'goodnight' and wave to them both as I answer the phone. "Hello, Charlie!"

"Alice! You picked up!" The light catches the silver stud in her nose, creating a flash on the screen. "I guess this is a good moment for once!"

She's surprised simply because over the past seven years, the ratio of missed calls and voicemails to actual conversations has probably been about five to one. I'm grateful to Charlotte for her loyalty, though. Like most mums, I've found my child-free friends have dropped off over the years, especially post-divorce. I expect they're bored of hearing me moan about my ex – or terrified of being called on for their babysitting services. And lots of the friends I knew as a couple with Philip have drifted away, at a loss for what to say, I suppose, or feeling that they have to choose between me and him.

"Hatty's asleep," I tell Charlie, "and I'm just having a camomile before I turn in."

"So, the nightlife at Downton Abbey's really exciting, then?" she says with a laugh, twirling the single strand of hair she's dyed purple, her 'rebellious streak' as she calls it.

Checking that Mrs P and Herbert are out of earshot, I start telling Charlie about my first weekend here. She thinks the pool story is hilarious and can't believe I've actually met Sahara Seaton-Smyth. She says she read in *HELLO!* this week that James and Sahara are engaged, which just goes to show that Mrs P doesn't know everything and also feels like something of a relief. Although, after what Mrs P and Herbert said, I'm not sure how binding that engagement is going to be.

"So, we started looking at the catalogue this afternoon,"

I say, taking a sip of the rapidly-cooling camomile from my Jane Austen mug.

"Who's *we*?" Charlie picks up on the pronoun immediately.

"Me and Guy," I say, trying to sound casual. "The Honourable Guy Tillingford to you, young lady."

"Ooh. The heir to the throne! So, it's *we* now, is it?" Charlie teases.

"Don't be silly!" I say, hoping she can't see my cheeks burning on her phone screen.

"*Aliiice….*" she says in that tone that means 'don't try to pull the wool over my eyes'.

"OK! OK! Guy is utterly adorable. He's mid-thirties and he's a hedge-fund manager, but he's just doing it for the money, and really, he just wants to restore the house and open it to the public."

"And what does he look like?" she demands.

I hesitate. "Does it matter?" I ask.

"Of course!" she insists.

"He's tall… and has floppy dark blond hair and a beard – but a short, smart beard, not a massive hipster beard – and glasses."

"Hmn… sexy but intellectual," she butts in with a cheeky grin.

I know my face is beetroot-red by now, but this is Charlie, and I have to tell her. "And he's a fantastic swimmer – I mean, he does butterfly stroke for fun. And he's got an Aston Martin – not that I care much about cars, but even I can see it's a very nice car – and he's so sweet and… according to the housekeeper, he's totally the committing type…." It all gushes out. To hide my blush, I take a sip of tepid tea, which tastes like pond water.

"Wow," says Charlie, stunned. "I mean… wow. Is that actually possible?"

"Apparently..." I say, only now objectively taking in everything that I've just said and realising I must be dreaming.

"Oh, come on, Alice. There's got to be *something*. Guys like that just don't..."

"...exist," I finish. "Yes, OK... and he's way out of my league." I attempt to take another sip of tea, but I'm down to the cold gritty bit at the bottom.

"That's not insurmountable, Alice. You're not exactly the woodcutter's daughter."

"No, but... I mean, his dad's a *baron* for goodness' sake. And he used to be engaged to Sahara Seaton-Smyth – before James Irving-McAuley, obviously... I think he's still got a soft spot for her, and there's this other girl called Chelsea, whose dad's an American billionaire or something."

"Oh my God," says Charlie, momentarily stunned. "Wow. He really *is* out of your league, isn't he?"

"You know how to pop a girl's balloon, don't you?" I say, taking my mug over to the dishwasher.

"Well, let's be realistic, Alice."

"I know. I'm a frumpy middle-aged divorcee with a young daughter. I understand."

"Well, you're not quite middle-aged yet," Charlie reassures me. "Though you act and dress like you are."

"Thanks for bolstering my self-confidence," I say, going to put my mug in the dishwasher and remembering it's on already.

"I just don't want to see you get hurt, not after Philip," says Charlie.

"I'd rather be on my own than with someone like Philip," I say, looking for a sponge and some washing up liquid, "but I'm tired of managing everything by myself all the time. I think I deserve another stab at happiness with someone, don't you?"

"Of course, you do," agrees Charlie as I prop my phone on the windowsill so I can put on some Marigolds. "Do you think he likes you too?"

"When he went back to London, he said he was really looking forward to seeing me next weekend. He knows Hatty's at her dad's, so I'll be here all on my own. It's really freaking me out. I mean, I really want to spend time with him, but I'm worried that…"

"What? Unchaperoned by your seven-year-old daughter, he's going to ravish you in the shrubbery?"

I take a deep breath, grab the sponge, and put washing up liquid on it.

"Oh my God!" says Charlie. "You *are*! Alice! That *so* isn't going to happen, not unless…"

"Yes?" I say, scrubbing at the mug.

"Not unless you both want it to."

I lean on the sink with the mug in my hand and take a deep breath. There's the rub! It's the *both* that's the operative word here. I'm too scared, and he's probably not actually interested. And what if he realises I fancy him and leads me on? My breath catches in my throat.

"Can I come to yours instead?" I ask, rinsing off the foam so Jane Austen's face peeps through. I'm sure Dear Jane would approve of a trip to see my best friend in Bath.

"Just to avoid him? No way!" retorts Charlie. "You told him you'd be there this weekend. Think how disappointed he'll be if you suddenly make plans to be somewhere else."

"It's not that I want to put him off, Charlie. I just want to get to know him a bit more first. Like maybe try in a fortnight…"

"That'll be a deliberate snub, Alice. If you really like him, you should face up to this and see where it takes you. Anyway, I'm busy this weekend. Pentangle are headlining at the Melksham Aquarius Festival, and my little pub gang are all going. You'd hate it."

"You are absolutely right," I say, picturing Charlotte and her crusty friends drinking mushroom tea in a too-small family tent as seventy-year-old stoned naturist hippies wander by. I shudder, wanting to wash my brain with the soap suds just to get that thought out of my head.

You might wonder why Charlie and I are friends when we're so different, but at university, we were very similar. We were both studying Art History, but she became a landscape historian, while my thing was portraits. We used to wear Alice Temperley (when we could afford it) and vintage Laura Ashley when we couldn't, and we both fancied Colin Firth in the BBC adaptation of *Pride and Prejudice*. Charlotte's father is an Anglican bishop, and her mother was the head teacher of a choir school, and they used to call her Tottie. She shook that off after her first day at secondary school went rather badly, but I kind of like it.

Charlotte drifted towards a more alternative lifestyle as the horticulture part of her job came to the fore. She swapped her ballet pumps for steel toe-capped boots (or colourful Doc Martens at the very least), while I stayed firmly in the striped wallpaper department (not that I can really indulge my tastes in my little post-divorce rental in Morden). But we must still be the same girls underneath. I actually love the way she's freer and more relaxed than me, and I think she envied me my settled married lifestyle – until it all fell apart, of course.

I sigh. "I guess I'd better throw myself at the mercy of the most gorgeous, eligible bachelor I ever clapped eyes on, then."

"Uh-huh. Hobson's choice, Alice."

And when she puts it that way, my heart starts doing a sparkly little dragonfly dance, and I swear Jane winks at me as I set the mug on the draining board.

"Why don't you come down the last weekend of August?" Charlie says brightly. "My flatmate's away then, and it'll give you a mini break before Hatty starts back at school. I'll make sure I keep it free – assuming you're not shacked up with Lord Farquhar by then."

"Don't be daft! Even if I was, I'd still want to come and see you," I say.

"I'm honoured," says Charlie, turning to scrawl the date on a WWF Endangered Species calendar in her kitchenette with what looks like a piece of charcoal. I type it into my personal Google Calendar and send an invite to the 'Hatty Calendar' that Philip and I share, just so he knows that I'm really, actually not around that weekend and can't be called at the last minute to pick up Hatty early, as seems to happen more often than it should.

"I can't wait for you to come to Bath," says Charlotte. "There's this hilarious stall I want you to see in the Green Street market. There's this old slapper who dresses up in Regency clothes and does silhouettes and Jane-Austen-style portraits for the tourists. It's so unbelievably tacky I just have to show you. And they're opening this Bridgerton Experience place in a warehouse on the edge of town."

"I can't wait," I say, somewhat sarcastically; to me history is about facts and I really struggle with stuff that messes around with it. "I really wish I could show you Tillingford Hall. There's nothing tacky here, apart from an inflatable flamingo in the pool. I think you'd find the gardens really interesting; they were designed by Capability Brown in the 1760s about fifty years after the house was first built. They need a complete restoration, which would be totally up your street. But I don't really think I can be inviting house guests."

"Don't worry – I totally get that. If you become the next Lady Tillingford, I'll take service as the under-gardener and keep below stairs, where I belong!" she jokes.

"Stop it!" I chide, grabbing my phone and hoping I look menacing in close-up.

"I can just see it!" Charlie crows. "The double-page spread in *HELLO! Magazine – Lord Farquhar and Dr Alice Merrow's engagement party took place last Thursday evening at The House of Lords. Present were The Prince and Princess of Wales and supermodel Sahara Seaton-Smyth...*"

"Shut up, Charlie!" I squeak. And I really wish she would, as she's making me realise how ridiculous I am, falling for Guy. But I did kind of enjoy her little fantasy... until she mentioned Sahara.

"I'll see you in August!" I say firmly. I can't decide if six weeks is a long time or no time at all. It doesn't feel like nearly long enough to tackle the project and far too long to spend feeling heartsick.

Chapter Seven

Monday's come round at last and I'm about to start my first proper day of work at Tillingford Hall and get on with what I came for. This is where I feel comfortable – in my hobbit hole full of 'dusty old junk', as James Irving-McAuley called these wonderful works of art.

Many of the miniatures in the collection are portraits of the Tillingford family going back generations. Now that I can't help having an interest in one particular member of that family, looking at their faces and preserving his heritage means more to me than I ever expected. I'm trying so hard to remind myself that to him, I'm just another employee, but I can't stop my heart racing as he steals into my mind for the thousandth time today.

I tell myself off, determined to concentrate. Regardless of how I might feel about Guy, I want to do something amazing here and get noticed. I don't want to be a worker ant anymore. I've been at the London Portrait Gallery for fifteen years, quietly cataloguing and researching down in the basement so that my succession of self-confident bosses can take the credit, even though by now, I probably know more about the subject than the rest of them put together.

But since The Divorce, I've been re-evaluating things. I've realised I could end up being the Gromit to their Wallace for the rest of my life if I don't blow my own trumpet a bit more. I also know I need to get out more and start rebuilding my confidence, but I could break my heart all over again if I fall for someone out of my league like The Honourable Guy Tillingford.

After breakfast below stairs and once Hatty is settled with some colouring books, Mrs Powell lends me a Hoover, a bucket, and some cloths. She offers to clean the Collections Room herself, but I tell her not to worry. I can reorganise while I clean (and I'm not sure I trust her old-fashioned elbow-grease-and-caustic-soda methods). And anyway, someone needs to keep an eye on Hatty. Even though she's inherited my patience and focus, she's only seven, so she's going to get bored of those colouring books in half an hour or so.

"I like a girl who mucks in," Mrs Powell says. "Ask if you need anything else. If you want a hand lifting things, Sebastian could come over, and I could get those curtains washed if you like."

I assure her I will ask if I need anything. I'm only here for six weeks, so I just need to make the room vaguely hygienic, not clinically safe. Washing the Edwardian curtains may be a step too far, not least because they may well fall into shreds if we try to take them down, or worse, release a shower of dormant typhoid bacillus and start a pandemic.

A while later, I'm about to check the bag on the Hoover as I think it might be full already when there's a knock on the door. Mrs Powell appears with a couple of parcels. "These are for you," she says.

I look around for a sharp object I can use to cut open the boxes. A letter opener I find on the desk sort of works. Inside are a Wi-Fi booster, a state-of-the-art laptop, and an external hard drive.

"Wow. This is amazing. Where did all this come from?"

"PC Warehouse by the looks of it," says Mrs Powell.

"But I didn't order it," I say. "And how did it come so quickly?" I had been planning to go into Winchester this afternoon to buy things like this on my credit card, and I was worrying how long it might take to claim it back, so this is a huge relief.

"That'll be The Hon," says Mrs P with a fond smile. "He must've pulled some strings when you told him what you needed so you wouldn't have to waste any time – it's just like him. He thinks of everything and never lets the grass grow under his feet."

She takes away the Hoover, saying she'll empty the bag and sort it all out, but first she'll be back with another box. I take the opportunity to unpack the equipment. Inside the first box is a delivery note addressed to Matthew Causton.

"Who's Matthew Causton?" I ask Mrs P when she returns, carrying a tall, thin box. She also has a black bin bag and a recycling bag tucked in the waistband of her apron.

"He's the new curate down in Tillingham. He was head of IT for a big company before he became a priest," she explains.

"Oh yes, Elizabeth and Mike mentioned him."

"So you've met them, then?" says Mrs Powell. "I suppose Hatty played with the terrible twins!"

"Yes, that's right. Hatty's going to theirs for a playdate on Thursday, so you can have a break."

Mrs Powell brightens up visibly and helps me open the last box. It contains a state-of-the-art pillar fan – much more efficient but less blowy than the old one, perfect for a room full of dust and paper. "He's so considerate, our Hon," Mrs Powell says quietly.

I feel almost teary that Guy's thought of all these things.

"He is a lovely person, Alice," says Mrs Powell, catching sight of the look on my face. "And I don't mean to be unkind, Ducks, but you're here to work. Like I said, don't forget who you are – and who he is."

"I won't," I assure her as she leaves the room, but I feel like Eeyore putting his popped birthday balloon into his empty honey pot.

Sitting on the now slightly less dusty Persian rug, surrounded by all these boxes, I allow myself a moment of frustration. I've only got a few weeks to sort out this catalogue, and it's going to take all day just to get this lot set up. I sigh as I take out the instructions for the Wi-Fi booster.

I hear footsteps in the hall and a knock on the door. "Hi, Babe," says Seb. "Want some help with your tech?"

"Oh, Seb! You're a saviour!" I say as I hug him. His long, golden hair is brushed into a neat bun that makes him look cute – kind of rustic, yet respectable, like I imagine the farmer Robert Martin in Jane Austen's *Emma* – and he's wearing jeans and a white shirt. I think he might even have trimmed his beard, and he has a faint, clean smell of cypress and driftwood.

I suddenly find myself acutely aware of his masculine presence. Have I been so deprived of male company that any old hunk will do? But there's no doubting… he *is* a hunk. I take a deep breath, laugh at myself, and try to focus.

Although I'm not too bad at tech, it's not my forte. Two heads will definitely be better than one, especially as I'm trying to set up several things. Once we get the Wi-Fi booster on and get a decent signal, everything else goes quite well. The old PC was a good spec twenty years ago, so it still kind of works.

Seb leaves me to set up the new laptop and burn CDs off the old PC: multitasking which requires my utmost concentration. As he walks out to get an external CD reader from some storage crate he keeps in one of the outbuildings, he leaves a faint trace of the ocean behind.

When he returns, Seb says, “Giles and Guy are total dudes for giving me a base here while I get myself sorted out.”

I delve a bit deeper, and he admits that Maxine isn’t too keen on having Neville parked by the Stables. “It’s not like it’s going to be for that long,” he says, pulling at his beard. “I know I need to get a proper job. I’m not stupid, I’ve just done some stupid stuff,” he explains. “Trouble is, I hate sitting behind a desk. I’m more of a doer than a sitter; that’s why I just couldn’t deal with A-levels and I dropped out. I did one Calvin Klein campaign with Sahara then came to my senses and went to college. I trained as a cabinet maker, but my dream is to set up a surf school.” He says, his face lighting up.

“Why don’t you?”

“Money. I asked my sister, but she’s spent all hers on rehab.”

He goes over to the window and looks a bit annoyed when I say he can’t open it because it will affect the moisture balance in the room. “But anyway, I’ve got a plan,” he says. “Shouldn’t be long now, and I’ll be out of here.”

But he doesn’t elaborate.

Seb helps me finish the laptop set-up, me working at the desk with him watching over my shoulder, so close that I can feel the heat of him. He leans across to tap a couple of keys, and his cypress cologne envelopes me as he whistles.

I have a feeling it’s by Pentangle, the seventies hippy band that Charlie likes but I'm too busy concentrating to give it much thought.

"I'm going to install some anti-virus software that's much more powerful than the one that came with the machine. Never use a laptop straight out of the box," he says, but I thought there was a full year's subscription to Norton Antivirus included with the laptop, so I'm not sure what he's changing it for.

My tummy rumbles, and I realise I could really do with a break. Seb says he'll get the software set up and join me in a minute, so I go down to the Kitchen, where I find Hatty and Mrs P making brownies together.

"Is Seb coming?" Mrs P asks.

"Yes."

"Then I expect he'll be wanting some detox tea."

"Botox tea?" squeaks Hatty.

"Not *botox*, Little One, *detox!*"

"O-o-o-h," she says. "*Deeee*tox. I don't know what that is, but I hope it's nice."

"I'll try the detox," I laugh. "I'm sure it'll be *very* nice."

I'm glad to see my daughter finding her tongue again – she can be quite funny when it's just her and me, so she must be settling in with Mrs P.

I wait for my tea to cool and munch on a biscuit from Mrs P's bottomless cookie jar until Seb comes down. He tells us about his travels around the world with his surfboard, and Hatty stops 'helping' Mrs Powell to listen, wide eyed. Seb offers to take me and Hatty to Sandbanks in Neville so he can teach us to surf but I know I would feel incredibly shy and wouldn't be strong enough.

Seb doesn't make my pulse race like Guy does, but there's

something about Seb – he's certainly an attractive man, and the thought of being in the sea with him watching me closely, maybe holding me, hoisting me up onto a surfboard is making me blush horribly. I make some excuse about the sea not being good for my eczema, and he starts talking about this amazing cream he found in South America.

At least that's got us off the subject of Seb in a wetsuit.

Our detox teas drunk, Seb and I head back to the Collections Room. The laptop is asking permission to restart, and as I click to allow it, an icon I don't recognise flashes in the corner of the desktop. But when the PC restarts, it's gone.

Now we need to copy the catalogue across. It looks like someone has recently updated the file, but Seb says it was probably an automatic update, which makes no sense to me. I'm sure Lord Tillingford and Guy both told me no one had done any work on it for years, and new acquisitions are on a spreadsheet which Lord T has already emailed to me. But Seb seems so confident and has been so helpful that I don't feel I should press him.

His phone rings. "Sorry, I've got to go," he says. "Just let that last piece of software finish installing itself, and it'll restart automatically."

I thank him, glad that we've managed in a morning what might have taken me a day or two on my own.

Chapter Eight

Just after lunch, I get a call from Guy. My heart pounds as I answer the phone.

"How are you getting on?" he asks.

"Oh, fine," I begin, thanking him profusely for all the stuff and asking how he got it all so quickly.

"Father Matthew pulled a few strings," he explains.

I particularly thank him for the fan and tell him how Sebastian helped me get set up.

"OK," Guy says, sounding doubtful. "Was he helpful, then?"

I'd better be diplomatic. I know he's very close to Seb and assume it was he who asked Seb to help. "It was useful to have two pairs of eyes on the set-up," I say, noncommittally.

"I guess. I've got to get back to work now, Alice, but keep me posted, OK?"

A couple of hours later, just as it's getting unbearably stuffy despite my state-of-the-art fan, there's a knock on the Collections Room door. When I reply, the lady of the house herself enters, wearing black linen palazzo pants, a crisp white shirt, and a chunky silver necklace with matching bangles, her little Bichon Frisée sniffing around at her feet.

"Coco wants to know if you're ready for your tour, Sweetie."

"Of course! I'm looking forward to it," I say, putting my laptop in sleep mode, genuinely grateful for the interruption.

As we climb the creaking Grand Staircase, Maxine grills me again on my credentials. So I tell her that I studied History of Art at University College London and then did an MA in Art Gallery and Museum Studies at Leeds and repeat what I said on Saturday about my work and my PhD. I don't want to sound arrogant, but although I'm a thirty-seven-year-old single mother and rather shy and really have no life other than my work, I *am* extremely knowledgeable about my subject. And I have everyone who matters in the miniatures world in my contacts book.

"Well, well, we really couldn't hope for a better qualified person to come and help us, could we, Coco darling? she says.

Maxine stops on the landing, picks up the Bichon, which is panting at the exertion of pulling its non-existent legs up the stairs, and buries her face in its fur.

I breathe a sigh of relief; I'm so desperate to make a good impression on Lady T that when she suggests I should write a book I tell her that I certainly hope to, when I get the chance. I don't need to explain that I'm too busy being a single mum to have a side hustle as an author right now.

"Oh look, Coco! how sweet!" she says, glancing out of the window.

I follow her gaze and see Lord Tillingford patting the trunk of a cedar tree and helping Hatty up onto the lower branches. My heart's in my mouth, but when Maxine catches my eye she says, "*Don't worry, Miss Alice,*" in Coco's doggy voice. "*The branches are perfectly spaced for climbing, and the lower ones are very close to the ground. Mr Guy used to climb it all the time when he was little, didn't he, Mummy?* Yes, he did!" she carries on in her own voice. "It's perfectly safe, and we know that Giles is the best daddy in the world. Hatty will be having such fun!" she says with a tinkly laugh.

"So, let's start here," she says leading me to the Portrait Gallery. "There's a dinky guidebook written in the 1920s which they sold to tourists for a penny when they used to open the house sometimes. It pretty much covers everything in here and the other state rooms – the Salon, the Library, the Ballroom, the Dining Room and Grand Staircase. There'll be a copy in the Collections Room. It's got a yellow cover. It doesn't include anything else up here, though. They used to sleep in the state bedrooms in those days, so they didn't open them to the public, and there aren't any important paintings in them anyway, or in the basement, obviously."

"Not even in the Billiards Room or the Smoking Room?" I ask.

"None worth looking at!" she replies breezily. "The good ones are in the Drawing Room. She should definitely concentrate on those, shouldn't she, Coco? *Yes, yes, she should! Only the Drawing Room ones – don't bother with the Billiards Room!*" the dog 'says'.

"We'll just show you the Portrait Gallery so you can understand the family history," Maxine explains. I wince as she yanks open the ancient blue damask curtains with a proprietorial flourish, sending a maelstrom of dust motes hurtling across the shaft of sunlight that bursts from the window. "We won't bore you with the other paintings – or the furniture – because you're here for the miniatures and you've only got a few weeks, although, of course, they're so fascinating! We could go on for hours, couldn't we, Coco?" She gives a high, brittle laugh while

Coco looks at me with a baleful eye.

"It's a pity;" I reply, shielding my eyes from the damaging UV light that's now pouring onto the historic images, "the collection is so big, and there's only so much I can do in such a short time."

"Oh, I *knooow*, Sweetie! We'd *love* to have her here all year, wouldn't we, Coco? But there really isn't the money, is there, Munchkin? How would Coco get her venison-ear chews if we gave all our money to clever ladies like Alice? *We're only opening to the public because we need the money*," adds Coco.

I remember the diamond jewellery and Christian Louboutin shoes she was wearing Saturday night for supper, and I wonder what 'we need the money' means for people like her.

She goes on to tell me that the Tillingfords aren't that artistic – they've always been more interested in hunting and farming, although farming being what it is at the moment, it's hard to make money from the estate and the house costs so much to keep up. It's usually been the Ladies Tillingford who have added to the art collection, when their husbands have allowed them a little 'pin money' (as she puts it) to do so.

"We keep telling Giles we need to get something more fashionable. We love Banksy, don't we Coco? And we think a Hirst spin painting would look just amazing in the Entrance Hall, as we obviously can't afford the Warhol of Queen Elizabeth that I wanted. But fussy old Daddy says it wouldn't be 'in keeping'. We disagree, though, don't we, Coco? Guy put up a Tracey Emin of Sahara Seaton-Smyth above the fireplace in the Salon a few years ago when he was dating her. Did you know they were an item back then?"

I nod.

"Giles said he could live with it as she was sort of family, and it was really only three little scribbles and could hardly clash with anything. But I couldn't stand seeing her bush every time I sat down to watch TV, especially once she turned crazy," she fiddles with her necklace and sighs. "So I sold it and bought a Porsche 911. I don't think Guy was too pleased. But Coco thinks we should have more contemporary art on the walls, move with the times."

"It would certainly be a good investment," I agree.

"*Oh boy, wouldn't it?*" 'says' Coco. "That's what we keep telling Daddy, don't we, Coco? And you'd think Guy would go for that, but he cares more about 'preserving the artistic integrity of the house' than his investments, which is a bit crazy considering he's a hedge fund manager."

The more I hear about Guy Tillingford, the more I warm to him and the more I want to know. So I'm really focused as Maxine launches into a potted history of the family from 1066 to the present. Luckily Coco doesn't seem to know much about the topic, and Maxine continues in a stream of relatively normal English.

I had already found out before I came that the De Lain family were baronets. When they were given the western part of the current estate by William the Conqueror, they took the name Tillingford after the Saxon village they'd ravaged on their arrival, building the villagers a lovely new church by way of apology. Commonly, the sons are given 'Delain' as a middle name in recognition of this ancient heritage, so I'm guessing that's Guy's middle name too. The Tillingfords were able to add to the estate during the Reformation, when Sir Christopher Tillingford, one of Henry VIII's most trusted cronies, was given the Tillingford

Abbey lands to the east, in recognition of services rendered.

During the Regency period, Admiral Sir William Tillingford (who started out as an unpromising second son) led a fleet to victory in the Mediterranean, while his older brother (the Baronet, General Sir Thomas Tillingford) was killed in the Peninsular War. As a result, William not only inherited the title and estate but was also ennobled. The Admiral, now Lord, continued the Tillingford line by marrying an older cousin of Queen Victoria's, and an anchor was added to the family crest. The current Baron, Giles, is the seventh Baron Tillingford.

"They're not the handsomest family," she admits, pointing out the third Baron, whose massive Victorian dad beard fails to hide his goofy overbite, "but luckily, some of the Ladies Tillingford have injected their good looks over the years."

Maxine fills me in on some gossip about past wives, including Poll Furnival, who was a mistress to Charles II before she won a Tillingford's heart. He had to give the King half his art collection to buy her release. And then there was Connie Bucket, a guttersnipe music hall girl who changed her name to Constance Beckwith, was a celebrated muse to the pre-Raphaelites, and eventually became the second Baroness in the late nineteenth century.

At the end of the gallery is a splodgy Renoir-like portrait of an Edwardian lady, the fourth Baroness, in satin leg-of-mutton sleeves dreamily sniffing a rose. Next to her is a severe seventies daub in prison-chic neutrals of a commanding lady with steel-grey hair, sitting in front of a well-stocked bookcase. "My late mother-in-law, Beatrice, the sixth Baroness," says Maxine, staring up at this last picture with her lips pursed. There is clearly little love lost there, but Beatrice's wise eyes shine, despite the austerity of the painting.

And finally, the *pièce de résistance* which I noticed the moment I walked into the gallery – who wouldn't? – is a life-size portrait of a young and somewhat vacant-looking Maxine, resplendent in an '80s off-the-shoulder puffy-sleeved wedding dress, complete with satin train, humongous diamond necklace, and a massive 'do, like an unholy hybrid of Brooke Shields and Princess Diana. Unfeasibly small in the background, as though Maxine's standing in a cow field at least a mile from the house, is Tillingford Hall, messily rendered, like an afterthought.

"Isn't Mummy gorgeous?" she asks, holding up Coco for a good look.

For the sake of my continuing employment, I will perjure myself. "It's lovely. You look so happy."

Her mouth twitches into something that isn't quite a smile.

Chapter Nine

It's finally Friday afternoon, and I just can't concentrate. The sky is hazy, and it's hard to tell where the sun is, but it's definitely blasting away out there somewhere – the temperature is in the high twenties. The Collections Room is so stuffy that I've had to prop the door open a couple of times. I'm still working hard because Guy will be arriving back from London this evening. I want to make sure I've got as much as possible to show for my week of work.

And, I admit, the thought that, at the end of my working day, he might be powering up and down the pool is alternately distracting me and keeping me going.

By around three o'clock, my head is throbbing, and I'm about to stop to make myself a cup of tea when there's a knock on the door just before it swings open.

"Hi Alice," says Guy.

My cheeks lift as I can't help mirroring the beaming smile on his face. Somehow, I've resisted Googling him all week, telling myself that my memories of his good looks are exaggerated and he's actually not that handsome, but in fact he's even more gorgeous than I remember. I jump up from my chair, ready to throw my arms around him, but I pull back, remembering that I need to be professional.

Sensing my hesitation, he rakes a hand through his floppy

golden hair, but then he draws close for an air kiss, lingering just a moment.

"How are things in Town?" I manage to ask, dry-mouthed.

"Pretty shit. I always miss home during the week, but this week's been a humdinger. That's why I took this afternoon off and came down early. I just couldn't wait to see y… erm…" he coughs, "see how you're getting on."

"I've made some good progress on the catalogue," I say, trying to look cool and ignore the storm of butterflies in my stomach. "Do you want me to show you?"

"I do, but tell me about your week first – I mean you and Hatty, how you're settling in."

So, I tell him about my tour with Maxine and Hatty's play date and how I enjoyed tea and a chat with Elizabeth when I picked Hatty up.

His phone rings. He glances at the screen, turns it off as he swears under his breath, and pretends to drop it in the bin. And then he wants to see what I've been working on. I draw up a chair so he can sit next to me and look at the screen. His lemon-and-juniper cologne wafts through a muskier man-on-a-hot-Friday-afternoon smell, and my neck and lips tingle with the closeness of him.

Trying to concentrate, I show him how I've created a new traffic light field on the database, which basically shows items that are present and correct (green); ones that I haven't yet checked (yellow), which is most of them – I've still got eight hundred of those, but I'm speeding up now I've got a system in place; and then the ones I've found but I'm not happy with and need more research or a second opinion on (amber). The final category is for ones which I can't find at all (red). There are meant to be one thousand and sixteen items in the collection, and I've got six in the amber and thirty-six in the red category already.

Guy laughs at me. "You really are an art geek, aren't you?" he says affectionately, putting his arm round me, which sets all my nerve endings on fire.

"Well, yes, I guess so," I reply. "That's why I'm here."

"And I'm glad," he says, squeezing my shoulder. "We really need this. So, what about the red ones?" he asks, pointing at the screen.

"I'm not worried about the reds because I expect there are places in the house I haven't looked. I know there are some miniatures in the Billiards Room, but I haven't got around to them yet. I've sorted the catalogue according to location so that I can start in one part of the house and work my way around, rather than age or some other criterion which could mean skipping all over the building. I think it'll be more efficient that way," I hesitate, wondering if this is boring, but he's clearly fascinated. "Only half the items have images, which isn't really helping as *Head of a Regency gentleman thought to be by Thomas Lawrence* could be several of the ones I've looked at. Although lots do have catalogue numbers written in pencil on the back.

"And there are a few entries that don't make sense to me at the moment, but I'll revisit them. It might be clearer once I've checked most of the catalogue."

"It must be doing your head in," he says, leaning back and running his hands through his floppy blond hair.

"Well, yes, but I love it. This is probably the best collection in the country, second only to the Royal Collection."

"Wow – really?" he asks.

"Yes, if we could get it fully catalogued and opened to the public, Tillingford Hall could become a major destination for art lovers. I'd be proud to be part of that."

"Mum's really not keen on opening the Hall to the public," he says, looking tired. "She says it's an invasion of our privacy and too much hassle. But Dad and I have been wanting to for such a long time. What's the point of preserving our heritage if no one gets to see it?"

"I completely agree, Guy. There are loads of beautiful things here that would bring joy to so many people. And this particular collection is so comprehensive, it will also be really important for scholars; I'm finding treasures every day. I just can't wait to get Desmond back down here. I know he had a quick look when he accepted the job for us, but I don't think he had a chance to study the collection in detail; he'll be bowled over."

"Well, you must invite him, then," says Guy with a smile. "Dad and Desmond got on like a house on fire when he first came to see us, and it was Dad who suggested the secondment. Desmond turned up in a lovely little ivory 1957 MGA Roadster with luscious oxblood leather seats. He made himself very much at home and we had to practically push the car down the drive to get him to leave. But we really enjoyed his company. He'd be more than welcome as our guest for the weekend."

"He'd love that," I agree. "His husband Federico died five years ago, and he's buried himself in his work as a way of coping. He hasn't taken a proper holiday for years. I'm sure that a couple of days' break in the countryside would do him a lot of good."

"Talking of breaks, are you going to be much longer?" he asks.

"Well, officially I should keep going until five…" I sigh.

"I give you permission to knock off early, seeing as it's Friday! I'll race you to the pool!" he says, jumping up with a cheeky grin.

"I wish! I've got to take Hatty to her dad's – well, technically, her Granny's. It's his weekend with her, but since Granny Janet's only in Basingstoke, we all agreed it made sense for me to drop her there."

"Can't he come here to pick her up?" asks Guy.

"I don't want him to," I say defensively.

"Whyever not?" he asks.

"I just… I want to keep things separate," I try to explain. "And if I can drop Hatty at Granny's soon, it means I don't have to see him and get a massive lecture about how hugely inconvenient it is that I'm taking a six-week holiday, forcing him to come out of London for three weekends, which will be a bonus, because it really winds me up that he thinks I'm on holiday!"

"OK! I get it," says Guy. "Listen, I'll give you both a lift – I know the shortcuts, and – " here he laughs, "my car's a little faster than yours," which is the understatement of the century. "So if you knock off now and get Hatty ready, we've got plenty of time for a dip beforehand."

It isn't even four yet, and the idea of a swim followed by a drive with Guy across the glorious sun-soaked Hampshire countryside is hard to turn down.

"I need to say 'hi' to Mum and Dad first," he says, "but I'll see you and Hatty at the pool in twenty minutes!"

"OK!" I say to his back as he disappears. It's sweet of him to think of Hatty, so why do I feel a bit disappointed that he mentioned her? I love my daughter like my own life, and I accept that I will be dedicating at least the next decade to her, but sometimes, just sometimes, I wish I wasn't *always* 'Hatty's mum' but just me, Alice, a woman with desires and needs of my own.

I save my work and make a few notes to myself for Monday. As I shut the laptop and lock up the Collections Room, it dawns on me that the moment Guy got home, before he'd even seen his parents, he came to see *me*. Maybe it's because the Collections Room is near the front door and he wasn't sure where Lord and Lady Tillingford were. Or maybe he really did want me to be the first person he saw when he got back. I think about that fumbled air kiss and how I wanted to melt into him, even though I know he's going to break my heart. I'm longing for it to be true that maybe, just maybe, he likes me the way I like him too. I tell myself not to be silly, although I'm still fizzing as I remember how the room filled with light as he walked in.

I go to collect Hatty and find her and Mrs Powell busy making pinwheel biscuits.

"Guy's here," I tell Hatty. "He thinks it would be fun for us to have a swim!"

"Well, that *would* be lovely," says Hatty earnestly, "but I'm helping Mrs Powell to make biscuits, and I don't want to let her down."

"I see," I say, smirking as I catch Mrs Powell's eye. I have no idea how I bred such a solemn little girl. I worry that The Divorce has made her feel she needs to grow up and be responsible, which would be a terrible burden for a such a young child. At least she doesn't have siblings. I've done my utmost not to place any unnecessary responsibilities on her, but I constantly beat myself up about it, of course. "Well, Mrs Powell, can you spare Hatty?"

"I can indeed, but I'm just as happy to have her help me finish these biscuits. So shall we let her decide?"

"Yes, I'm fine with that," I say.

"Mmm," Hatty ponders, with her head to one side. "If you don't mind, Mummy, I'd really love to stay here and help Mrs Powell finish making the biscuits."

I laugh, secretly thrilled I get Guy to myself for a few minutes. "Well, don't eat them all up!" I say, knowing that, like any child, she's as much after the baked results as taking part in the process of making them.

"Of course not, Mummy. That would be *greedy*. I might try one or two to make sure they're OK, though." She looks hopefully at Mrs Powell.

"Of course," agrees Mrs P. "We need to test them before we let anyone else try them, just in case they're not good enough." She gives me a knowing look.

"Absolutely – you can't go serving us dodgy biscuits. Well, if you're sure you're both fine, then I'll have a swim. I'll bring your swimming stuff to the pool so you can come by when you're done here, Hatty, and we can see if there's time for you to join us before we go to Granny Janet's."

"I don't want to go to Granny's."

"Why not?" I ask. She's normally more than happy to spend time with Janet.

"I want to see Guy and play with Lily and Poppy at the pub again," says Hatty.

"Daddy and Granny can't wait to see you – and Guy's going to give us a lift!" I cajole.

"Does that mean we get to go in the James Bond car?"

Hatty's dad is a Bond fan, and he tried to show her a couple of the milder films until I pointed out that none of them are really suitable for a seven-year-old, even the PGs. When he actually thought about it, he did see what I was getting at, but his obsession ensured that she does at least appreciate the significance of an Aston Martin.

"Yes," I say.

Hatty gives an excited smile. "OK!" she says.

"So I'll see you in a bit," I say with a little wave. And as she turns back to the biscuit making, I race upstairs to get into my swimming stuff. I grab Hatty's things – swimsuit, goggles, sun cream and two of the aqua-coloured towels from the pool house which have ended up in our room – and shove them into a supermarket bag. Not very elegant, I know, but I don't have anything else. And even though it's mad, before heading down, I turn back and brush on some slightly crusty waterproof mascara.

When I get downstairs, Guy is already powering up and down the pool. I allow myself a sneaky look at those muscular shoulders, and for a moment, I imagine running my hands over them. I shake my head. This just isn't me: academic, quiet Alice who studies pictures of long-dead people, generally from the shoulders up – not real, living, hot blokes with their shoulders (and practically everything else) naked. Honestly, I never used to be interested in muscle – until now. I lower myself onto the edge of the pool and dangle my legs in the water.

Guy swims up and pulls me in.

The shock makes me shriek, and then we both start laughing. I feel silly and giddy like an over-excited schoolgirl. And then the realisation that he's still holding me hits, and electricity courses through my limbs. He looks at me in a way that's anything but childish and I catch my breath.

"Alice," he says, flicking his hair out of his eyes. "I've really missed you this week."

I take all my courage in my hands.

"I've missed you too, Guy," I say clearly.

Our eyes lock and for a moment, the swifts stop wheeling overhead.

"May I kiss you?" he says.

I laugh. Even for me, this polite request is so quaint and charming that, without a moment's hesitation or analysis, I lean towards him and press my lips to his. We melt into each other, and my brain explodes with desire and happiness.

"Mummy! WHAT ARE YOU DOING?"

I look up to see a shocked little girl looking down at me. There's a flicker of guilt in the back of my brain, but I've nothing to be ashamed of; I'm a single woman kissing a single man. I didn't make a vow of chastity when Hatty's dad left me, and Guy is smiling, obviously amused.

"Guy!" she admonishes. "Mummy!" Hatty puts her hands on her hips like a cartoon housewife.

"Hatty. I apologise," says Guy, becoming more serious. "I think your mother is beautiful and lovely and I just couldn't help wanting to kiss her." I melt as he says this. "I hope you don't mind?"

"Well!" she says huffily, looking down at us both like a miniature headmistress. "She *is* beautiful *and* lovely, and it wasn't her fault Daddy went away, so… If you promise to be kind to her and not hurt her feelings like Daddy did, then I guess that's fine."

I'm not sure whether to laugh or cry at this little speech, but it's certainly put cold water on my desire.

"I'll try my best never to hurt either of you," says Guy quietly. He looks at his watch. "We'll need to go in twenty minutes, so you've got time for a super quick swim if you want, Hatty."

"I'm alright," she says, sitting primly on the nearest lounger with her knees pressed together.

"OK, Hatty," I say, "I'll just do a couple of lengths and then we'll get ready."

I dive underwater, breathing out very slowly while my mind whirrs overtime, guilt and frustration mixing with amusement and fear. What if Hatty's right? I've only known Guy for a week. How do I know he's not some Casanova, or still in love with Sahara? And what about this Chelsea person?

"Can you take me in *our* car, Mummy?" asks Hatty quietly as my head pops above the water a few moments later.

"I was looking forward to riding in Guy's James Bond car," I whisper as I get out and towel off.

"You've got *all weekend* without me," she points out, quite reasonably, even if she is pouting. "And I want to see *you*. You've been working *all day*."

"OK," I say, aware that she's not wrong, while my mind whirls through the billion possibilities of what Guy's going to think when we turn down his offer of a lift.

"Guy," I call, and he stops, propping his arms on the poolside. "Hatty would like *me* to take her to Granny's after all."

He's taken aback but says, "I understand, Hatty. You want time with your mum before you go away. I get that. Will I see you on Sunday evening when you get back?"

Hatty looks at me for confirmation, and I nod.

"Yes, you will," she tells him solemnly.

"Oh good, because I wondered if you'd like a TV supper with us in front of a Disney film when you get home?"

"Really?"

"Of course! You know we've got Disney+, so you'd better watch everything on there by the end of the summer!"

"Yes, please!" she's beaming. I know there are several Disney films she hasn't been able to watch yet, and although lots of her friends have shockingly already grown out of Disney and say it's for babies, she still adores *Frozen*, *Cinderella*, and all the greats.

I flash Guy a grateful smile. "Why don't you chat to Guy about which one you'd like to watch while I change? I'll be down in ten minutes."

"Do you want to take my car?" offers Guy.

"God, no! I can't believe you'd trust me with it… I wouldn't trust me with it!"

"It's got Isofix…" says Guy with a wry smile, referring to the child car seat locking system I more readily associate with family estate cars.

"That was the least of my concerns," I say with a laugh.

When I get back down, Hatty is talking nineteen to the dozen about her favourite Disney films to Guy, who's sitting on a bench in a polo shirt and shorts. He's clearly pulled them on over his wet trunks, and I'm grateful to him for his sense of decorum around my young daughter.

"Thank you, Guy," I say, as warmly as I can.

"Have you packed Beebee?" asks Hatty, anxiously.

"He's in your weekend bag."

"Can I have him now?" she asks, tugging at the zips.

"Of course," I reply, digging him out by his floppy ears.

"Have you remembered my hair clips and my head band and my inhalers and my toothbrush and my little bag in case I feel sick?"

"Yes, I've put all those things in there," I say, looking through to double-check.

"And which book?"

"The purple *Worst Witch* book that you were reading earlier."

Hatty seems satisfied, which is just as well as we really need to dash now if we're going to get to her Granny's in my old banger before Philip appears.

Hatty runs up and gives Guy a hug, which makes me smile and leaves him beaming.

"See you later, Guy," I say, practically shoving Hatty into the car.

Just at that moment, Seb appears, waves to us, and gets into his camper van.

"Where's he off to?" I ask as I climb into my car, determined to get onto the narrow drive before he does.

"Some kind of New Age festival in the West Country, I think," says Guy.

"Not the Melksham Aquarius Festival?" I ask, checking my mirrors.

"Something like that," he says, raising an eyebrow. "How do you know about it?"

"I've got a friend who's going," I say as I click my seatbelt, remembering why Charlotte said I couldn't stay with her this weekend.

"Drive safely," Guy calls through the open window as I shut the door. "And don't forget, it's Friday night drinks on the Terrace. 6.30 sharp."

"Are you sure? I thought last week's invite was a one-off and I was supposed to stay below stairs from now on?"

"Don't be absurd… you're our guest, and I *want* you to be there."

"I'll do my best," I say, starting the engine and silently cursing that I'm going to turn up stressed and sweaty for Friday night *drinkies*, rather than swanning onto the gravel in plenty of time in a stunning sports car driven by a gorgeous man, who it turns out *actually fancies me back!*

As I put the car into gear, my heart skips at the realisation that I have *all weekend* with him, and Hatty's permission to enjoy it. I'm determined to give her my full attention for the next half hour, difficult though that will be, and I grin at the sight of Guy waving in the rear-view mirror as I pull away.

Chapter Ten

That night after I'd said goodnight to Guy I was awake for hours. I tossed and turned, troubled by strange dreams. I couldn't stop remembering Hatty's reaction to seeing Guy kissing me in the pool and wondering if I'd done right by her, although she did effectively give us her blessing, inasmuch as a seven-year-old is capable of making such a discernment.

Once she was safely ensconced at Granny's, Guy and I had shared many other kisses, sitting entwined in an arbour, heady with the scent of climbing jasmine. But that's as far as it went, and my body is aching for him now. I stretch out, feeling the cool sheets on the other side of the bed and wishing he could be next to me, holding me, waking me with gentle kisses. I'm shocked by my wantonness. I know I'm my own harshest judge, a kiss is just a kiss, after all, but isn't *wanton* a great word? I laugh at myself.

Knowing that Guy feels the same way and that we're both single (at least I'm pretty sure he is), I can't think of any more reasons to hold back – other than Mrs Powell's warnings, my natural reticence, a fear of being hurt again, and most importantly, the threat of losing what I have gained by standing on my own two feet. I've been managing fine on my own… haven't I?

I roll over in bed, reach for my phone and realise it's already nine AM and Guy has sent me a text.

> Morning, Sleepy. Don't want to disturb you, but when you're awake, there's somewhere I'd like to take you.

I grin, feeling a little thrill in my stomach, and reply.

> Hi. I can be ready in 20 mins. What shall I wear?

I drink a glass of water, and have a super quick shower. When I come out, the reply is:

> Comfortable shoes and a pretty dress, not too formal.

That's pretty much my staple wardrobe, so easy enough. I'm glad that he understands I might need some idea of what to wear for any given occasion. My ex could never fathom why I needed to know, so I'd turn up to barbeques dressed for a hike, the pub quiz in a cocktail dress, and once I had to walk from a quaint country church to the pub in the next village for a wedding: two miles of rough footpaths in strappy high-heeled sandals – which Philip considered 'a short walk'.

Now I know I'm appropriately dressed, but I'm still intrigued about where we might be going.

When I get downstairs, Guy is waiting. He takes me into his arms and kisses me tenderly, turning my insides to mush. I can almost feel little wings growing on my heels as I float onto the Terrace, where someone has laid a table for us with homemade bread, jam, home-grown strawberries, fresh orange juice, and a steaming pot of Darjeeling: my favourite kind of breakfast.

We're both strangely shy, and other than passing each other things and pouring drinks, we don't say much to begin with. What do you say to your new… I'm not even sure what to call him – my boyfriend? We haven't said anything about any kind of commitment – we've only kissed, after all – and *boyfriend* seems a silly word to use at our age.

Eventually, Guy breaks the silence. "I really enjoyed our evening together," he says as I take a sip of tea from a pretty bone china cup.

"Me too," I reply, replacing the cup delicately in its matching saucer.

"You're a very good kisser," he says, his eyes smouldering.

"Really?" I say, finding the pattern on the cup fascinating.

"You're very… passionate…"

If I am, it's only because of him and how he makes me feel, but I'm too shy to say so.

I try to take some butter from the dish with a fiddly silver butterknife, but I fumble it and get the handle covered in grease, and I don't know whether to wipe it on my linen napkin or just live with it. When I look up, he's gazing at me, like a collector captivated by a work of art.

"You remind me of a Pre-Raphaelite Stunner," he says, resting his chin on his hand like Rodin's *Thinker*.

"Ew!" I say.

"Oh, I'm sorry," I gasp, as I look up and see that his face has fallen. "I didn't mean to throw your compliment back at you. It's just… I'm not that keen on the Pre-Raphs. And…"

"Oh Alice!" he sighs with a wry smile. "Just take the compliment and don't *analys*e it!"

"I'm sorry…" I feel myself blushing again. I'm useless at this stuff. All my life, I've longed for a knight in shining armour to sweep me off my feet, but the moment he does I'm asking if he's done a health and safety risk assessment before mounting that horse. "…I'm just not used to people complimenting me. No one's ever said anything as lovely as that to me before."

"Not your ex?" asks Guy quietly. "Philip, isn't it?"

"I won't say he never complemented me, but it was always quite… straightforward and… bland. And very occasional. More about my clothes and presentation when I'd made a special effort, not really about me. I mean I'm sure that no one's ever called me a Stunner. I always thought I was quite plain."

"Anything but, Alice. You're a real English Rose."

"Really?" Hopefully he hasn't noticed my wonky nose and the very un-Pre-Raphaelite grey hairs round my temples. I'm still not sure what to do with the slimy butterknife. Guy holds out a side plate for me to put it on and gives me a clean knife, and I smile my gratitude to him.

"Yes, Alice. You're lovely."

I notice him blushing, so I stare into my teacup and my heart feels like a rose beginning to unfurl under his admiring gaze. But what if he's just saying that to get into my knickers? But does that even matter? What if I'm actually thrilled that maybe he wants to sleep with me, because I'm a single grown-up and I'd really like that? At the thought that I could just follow my desire and see where it leads, my stomach flutters with excitement. I can't finish my breakfast and I push my plate away.

"Finished?" he asks.

I nod.

"Then shall we go?" He plonks his napkin on the table and pushes back his chair.

"Where are you taking me?" I ask, doing the same.

"Wait and see," he says with a cheeky smile. "Are you all set?"

"I'll just powder my nose," I say.

"Very wise!" he laughs. He obviously knows what we mums are like after a pot of tea. "I'll see you on the front drive in five minutes."

"Do you need help clearing the plates?" I ask as I get up.

"Nah – Mrs P will do it."

I feel guilty leaving stuff lying around, but I guess that's how Guy's grown up. I'm not sure I'm entirely comfortable with that, but I hear him picking up the plates as I walk away, so he's obviously not leaving the whole thing for the servants, which relieves me slightly.

Minutes later, I'm easing myself into his Aston Martin. I'm not really a car person, but its sleek lines and luxurious interior finish make even me want to purr.

Guy strokes the steering wheel in a way that sets my pulse racing. "This car is my one indulgence. If I lived in London full time, I wouldn't have a car at all, but I need to get to and from home at the weekends and to meet specialist contractors. They're often in quite out-of-the-way places."

I think he cares even more about restoring Tillingford Hall than I do about miniatures. His passion for it warms me because it's so honest. Anyone can see from his dedication and the way his face lights up when he talks about the Hall that it's a life-long bone-deep love.

"I love the way you talk about your home," I tell him, putting my hand on his and looking into his eyes.

"You're the first person I've got close to who understands it," he says, leaning across the gear stick to kiss me deeply. Turning back to the wheel, he puts on his seat belt, starts the engine, and slips on a pair of designer shades. With a grin and a raised eyebrow, he asks if I'm ready. When I nod, he eases the car down the drive with a satisfying crunch of gravel.

The Hampshire countryside is smiling in the sunshine. The hedgerows and roadside oak, ash and horse chestnut trees shade us from the glare of the sun, fragments of light filtering through the leaves, strobing over our faces as the Aston shoots over the tarmac, clinging to the curves. I catch glimpses of full-grown lambs gambolling as though it were spring, and my heart sings.

I haven't felt this light-hearted in years.

The journey is over in barely fifteen minutes, but I'm charmed when we arrive in the village of Chawton, sliding into the carpark opposite Jane Austen's cottage.

"Oh wow!" I beam.

"Have you been here before?" Guy asks.

"Never – but I always meant to! I'm such a Jane Austen fan!" I squeal.

"I thought you might be." He smiles, cutting the engine and swinging his long legs out of the car while I glance, unusually, in the vanity mirror. I think Aston Martin must have perfected a beautifying filter on their mirrors as I seem to look alright today – pretty, even.

He takes my hand as we cross the road to the house. I can't decide if I'm more excited that I'm outside my heroine's home or that I'm here with Guy. We walk through the cobbled courtyard, festooned with drying laundry that looks like it's come off the set of a period drama. A gentle fragrance wafts from the sun-warmed herbs growing in large terracotta pots outside an outhouse. Beyond it lies a modest garden, mostly laid to lawn, with a few trees and herbaceous borders buzzing with happy insects. A black cat approaches us and winds herself round Guy's legs with a small mew.

"I don't know why cats always come for me," he says as he kneels to scratch its head. "I must stink of dogs! But I've always preferred cats, really," he admits as though this is somehow heresy.

"Me too. I'm not a dog person at all." The cat rolls onto her back, artfully tempting us to stroke her fluffy tummy. But we know better and just laugh at her.

Guy insists on taking a series of selfies of us at the kitchen door, each one worse than the last, and a few pictures just of me before we enter the house. It smells of herbs and furniture polish. The scrubbed oak table is arranged as though the cook is in the middle of making lunch, with plaster-cast pastries and a plastic pie in a wicker basket, as well as real dried herbs over the fireplace. There are facsimiles of Jane's 'receipts' (as she called recipes) on the table, and as I wonder what her favourite dish was, I'm touched by how close she feels.

We're greeted by a plump costumed interpreter who says she's Mary the Cook. She's wearing a modest calico gown, but a fluorescent pink bra strap at the shoulder and strands of blue hair creeping out from under her mob cap somewhat break the illusion.

"The misses Austen, Miss Jane and Miss Cassandra, live here with their mother and Miss Jane's best friend, Martha Lloyd. Between you and me, they're not very well off, so although they do keep me as their cook, they have to do a lot of housework themselves – laundry, sewing, and some of the cooking. I work every day and I only get Sunday afternoons off."

It sets me thinking as we thank 'Mary' for her interpretation and saunter into the next room. "You always think that people like Jane Austen and the Brontës were ladies with huge amounts of leisure time to write in," I say to Guy, "but they weren't that well off and probably quite busy doing housework and other chores. I suppose they had to fit their writing in around all their other commitments, just like I do. They probably did it because they were so bursting with ideas, they just couldn't help themselves." I'm touched to think that Jane Austen and I have this secret bond. "I'll never say I don't have time to do my PhD again."

"Tell me more about your PhD," says Guy.

"I've been working on it for over a decade," I sigh, as I gaze out of the window. "I wanted to do it full time, but I couldn't get the funding, and obviously Philip couldn't bankroll me, so I had to keep working at the gallery. It's been hard enough finding the tuition fees, let alone the time to do the research and the writing. But it's my passion and having a body of academic work behind me will be good for my career in the long run."

"Richard Cosway's quite obscure," he frowns.

"I know," I say, wrinkling my nose as I glance at an indifferent print of Steventon Rectory, "but when you get into something…"

"Oh, I understand!" he says, with a smile. "I'm just in awe of you finding the right person to supervise you and then sticking at it for ten years. I don't think I'd have the dedication and patience, and to be honest, I'm not *that* clever."

"Come on, Guy, you work in a hedge fund! You must be good at analysis and thinking on your feet," I point out.

"Of course," he says, coming to stand beside me and look equally indifferently at the print. "I had the best education money could buy, but I'm more of a doer than a thinker."

"I'm more of a thinker," I say, turning to the next picture. "But I've had to become a doer; thinking alone isn't enough to get a PhD done. You need to be dedicated and organised too, especially when you add children to the mix. And a fighter, if people around you don't support you."

"Your ex?"

"Yes, he always thought it was a waste of time," I say. "I've made more progress in my Hatty-free weekends over the past four years than in the previous six with him moaning about it."

"If my wife had a passion, especially something as valuable as adding to the sum of human knowledge, I'd totally support that," said Guy. "I'd be dead impressed if someone that clever wanted to hitch her wagon to mine!"

I laugh at his quaint turn of phrase, but he's looking at me so intensely that my stomach flips. For a moment, I allow myself to think he might have meant me, but that would be silly. He can't be thinking of me that way, not when we've only just met, though goodness knows I can't imagine anyone who would make a more perfect husband.

"So, why didn't things work out between you and Philip?" he asks, trying to look casual as he pores over some artefacts in a glass case.

I cringe. I don't really like talking about my ex – who does? – but I guess Guy has a right to know if we're going to get any closer. "Really, there's not much to say. We didn't want the same things in life… and he became controlling and manipulative, especially once we had Hatty. He decided I didn't really fit his image; he needed a partner who was more business-like and glamorous, which was fine by me, because I don't want to be some corporate robot. But it really knocked my confidence."

"I can imagine," says Guy. "The man was clearly an idiot to let go of someone like you."

"Oh look!" I say, desperate to change the subject, "I recognise that dress from the BBC *Pride and Prejudice*. I used to fancy Colin Firth as Mr Darcy," I admit sheepishly.

"Of course," says Guy with a smirk. "Which girl didn't? I'm sorry I'm not dark and rugged like Mr Darcy."

I let the comment pass as we walk into the drawing room. I can't think of anyone I've met in real life who is more handsome than Guy, but I can't really say that, can I? So I just slip my hand into his, and he gives it a squeeze.

In front of us is a mahogany bureau and bookcase belonging to Jane's father, next to a chaise longue and small 'square piano' made by Thomas Broadwood, the famous piano maker Beethoven so admired.

"Do you play?" asks Guy, squinting at the manuscript on the music stand.

"Not really – I did a few grades, but I was never much good. I wish I'd been better and had the conviction to keep it up."

"Me too," says Guy. "I tried guitar for a bit and had a terrible rock band at school with a few friends. We were called *Johnny*

Incorrigible and the Boiling Kettles. Seb was the drummer. We were pretty dreadful!"

I laugh and read the quotes from Jane Austen's letters posted along the walls, relating to the various items on show – the sewing table, the card table, a pair of white kid gloves.

"Blimey, this wallpaper's a bit garish," comments Guy. "It says here they found some fragments of the original wallpaper behind the shutters and commissioned a near-match, but I wonder how strong the colours really were?"

"Apparently they did like their wallpaper bright in the Regency," I explain. "I've seen similar styles in other houses, although I'm not sure what dyes they used that early – it wasn't really till the Victorian period they had chemical dyes. I could see if I could find an article about it on JSTOR…"

"That would be interesting…" he says.

"Really?"

"Well… a bit," he says with a laugh. "But if we found something like that at home, I'd definitely want to know more. My four-greats-grandfather, the second Baron Tillingford, made a lot money out of the railways – the line from Alton to London runs through land that used to belong to us. He did a complete refurb in the 1860s and no one after that could do much to the place, which is why the whole interior has a very Victorian feel to it. I'm sure under all the Victorian tat, there's some hidden Regency wallpaper or fabric from the time of The Admiral, or even earlier."

Above the piano is a portrait of Jane's brother Edward as a young boy. He was adopted by rich relatives and ended up inheriting the Chawton House estate, which is how he was able to give this cottage to his mother and sisters. Without that piece of good fortune, who knows whether Jane would have had the wherewithal to write at all.

"The Chawton estate marches with ours," explains Guy, "the part we farm ourselves, in theory – although our manager deals with almost everything. The Chawton estate is much smaller, of course. They were only gentry, after all, whereas we're…"

"Aristocracy…" I fill in.

Guy looks uncomfortable.

"Guy, there's nothing shameful about being born into a privileged family," I say. "What matters is what you choose to do with what you've been given."

"I'm glad you think so, Alice. I know there are people who think we shouldn't have the wealth and status we have. In any case, it's passing away with every generation. My father had a place in the House of Lords when I was a child – not anymore. To be fair, I'm not sure he took much interest in politics, so Tony Blair was probably right in *his* case." He rakes his hand through his hair. "But I would have been active in the Lords, given the chance. It would be so useful for my work with inner-city kids if I had a bit of political clout.

"I'll be honest with you, Alice, this life isn't what people think; the estate's not been in profit for over five years, not to mention the house, which is an absolute money pit, and that's my main concern right now. But can you imagine what the inheritance tax is going to be?" he sighs as we pass into the vestibule where the original door onto the street would have been.

"Here's Jane's family tree," I comment, not sure what to say. Guy's financial problems are in such a different realm to mine, they don't even feel real to me. After looking at the poster for a few moments I realise I'm not really that interested in who Jane's ancestors were, but two middle-aged ladies are having a very animated discussion about it with an elderly volunteer who says he's Jane's "five-greats nephew" and grew up in Chawton House and I can see that some people might feel that understanding Jane's ancestry gets them closer to her, especially with a living relative explaining it to them.

Guy is by the window, looking pensively at the High Street. "If we could ever get Tillingford Hall open to the public, I don't think I'd say much about the stories of my ancestors and who married whom. I think what people really want to know is: 'What was it like to live in those times? What did people care about? Was the life of my seven-greats grandfather more comfortable than mine? What about the servants? Their life must have been hard, but what would it have been like if they'd stayed in their villages and been farm labourers?' I sometimes think people forget that standard of living and quality of life are totally different things."

"That's so true," I say, coming over to join him. "I mean, Jane must have had quite a modest lifestyle compared to the wealthy people in her books – but even their standard of living would have been basic compared to what we're used to today. It must have been peaceful, though, not being at the mercy of mobile phones or call centres, not feeling you had to have the latest this and that."

"Although I suppose they had fashions and social anxieties just as people do now, but perhaps it was tempered by the knowledge that death could be coming for them at any moment," he says, turning back to me.

"That's a bit grim!" I say, laughing nervously. "But yes, people must have lived faster in those days," I say, pointing at the family tree. "Jane was only forty-one when she died. I haven't got long then…"

"Hey! Don't be silly," Guy says, squeezing my hand. "We're still young… we've got our lives ahead of us!"

And falling in love in this sunlit room, I'm starting to feel he might just be right.

The dining room, which I recognise from a scene in the film version of *Pride and Prejudice* with Keira Knightly, is decorated with leafy green wallpaper that's even more lurid than the one in the drawing room.

"Oh my goodness!" I gasp. "*Her writing desk!* Look, Guy, it says she wrote all six novels on it!" and it's all I can do to stop myself from reaching out to touch the sacred object.

"It's tiny!" he says. And really, it's more like a card table or an occasional table than a desk. There are a few facsimile manuscript pages and a quill pen in an inkwell on the table. Apparently, only the family knew what Jane was writing, and she used really small sheets of letter paper so she could easily hide them from inquisitive servants and visitors. I'm moved to think that in this place, this funny, clever lady created these wonderful stories and had to keep it all secret. My heart is full. I glance at Guy.

"Kind of awesome, isn't it?" he says, taking in my reaction.

I nod, not trusting myself to speak as my eyes start to brim.

On the dining table is a breakfast abandoned, with a scrunched-up napkin tossed carelessly aside and remains of toast on the plates, as though Jane and Cassandra had just been interrupted by a visitor.

"What do you think of that, Guy?" I ask, pointing. "Too contrived?"

"I don't know," he replies. "Maybe. I like it when they have authentic food to give you a feel for a place, but when it's too staged, it's distracting. I've been thinking for a long time how we'd do it at Tillingford Hall, and I'm quite sure I don't want dummies or waxworks."

"Ugh, no! They're usually pretty creepy and make old buildings feel even more dead. I like costumed interpreters, though – if they're any good, that is! What era would you focus on for Tillingford Hall?" I ask.

"Hm, that's a tricky one," he says as we start up the creaking stairs. "The main building is 1710s, and the big refurb was Victorian. The most famous baron, apart from the first, was probably my great-grandfather, the Brigadier General who served in World War Two. But he didn't do much to the house, so I don't know really. Probably a journey through the ages, though I wonder how we'd manage that geographically in the house."

As we arrive in the family room I say, "How about focusing on different eras at different times of year? A Victorian Christmas, a Regency ball in the summer, the World Wars around Remembrance Day? You could even have an eighties wedding, so you're not always doing the obvious things. You could theme it around that picture of your mother in the Portrait Gallery and get some people to dress up in puffy velvet-and-taffeta ballgowns from Oxfam. That way you could give your regulars – you'd obviously offer membership – things to come back for throughout the year."

Guy looks at me and takes my hands. "Alice, you're a genius!"

"I don't know ab–"

Before I can finish, his lips are on mine. His arms entwine around me, and my body comes alive as we melt into each other.

The chatter and tread of visitors on the stairs pulls us apart, but Guy takes my hand firmly and won't let go – to be fair, if he did, I might just float to the ceiling.

We somehow make it to the family room which focuses on the games the Austens played. There are some dolls and toys which actually belonged to Jane; a portrait of a fat clergyman, a distant relative, who was an inspiration for Mr Collins in *Pride and Prejudice;* and some miniatures, nothing special, of family friends. But I'm not really paying attention. Guy is so close we're practically breathing the same breaths. When the other visitors come into the room, he releases my hand, and it's almost a relief to have a break from the intensity of our touch.

And then we come to Jane's bedroom, which contains a single four-poster bed with a lovely green silk dress laid on it. Apparently, it was worn by Anne Hathaway in *Becoming Jane.*

"I don't think I bothered with that one – it sounded like a load of made-up tosh," I admit.

Guy laughs at me. "Oh Alice, you're such an intellectual snob sometimes!"

"I try not to be, but… Oh look! It's a reticule! Don't you just love that word, *reticule*? You only ever see it in Jane Austen."

"What on earth is a *reticule*?" asks Guy, bemused.

"That beaded handbag on the mantelpiece," I say, crossing the creaking floorboards to take a closer look.

Guy's clearly not too interested in this Regency fashion detail, but he seems to have developed a fascination with my hair, twining his fingers through it and stroking my neck as I gaze at the beaded bag for far longer than the artefact warrants. When I relax my head back to receive his affection, he draws me away.

"Come on," he says. "Let's keep moving, or I might just need to throw you on that bed and ravish you."

"Guy!" I say, slapping his hand. I'm shocked (and secretly thrilled), looking round to check there are no other visitors within hearing distance.

After a couple more rooms, where we briefly admire Jane's turquoise bracelet, and a topaz cross her sailor brother bought for her with his prize money from capturing an enemy ship, we descend the narrow stairs into the reading room. There are some of Jane's letters laid out for us to look at, but we don't linger as even I am starting to glaze over slightly.

"I almost feel I could reach out and touch her," I sigh as we come back into the daylight.

"I'm glad you enjoyed it," Guy beams, his arm around me. I look away so Guy can't see my eyes glistening. "Have you had your Jane Austen fix now?"

"We can't leave without exiting through the gift shop," I say.

"Of course not," he concedes. There is some lovely jewellery, including reproductions of the topaz cross and turquoise bracelet. Guy says they aren't as lovely as my oakleaf bracelet, and I agree, although I certainly wouldn't be upset to be given such a thing.

Guy insists on buying me a Jane Austen mug that reads *life seems but a quick succession of busy nothings* and a huge book for Hatty which folds out into a colour-it-yourself Regency doll's house. I insist it's too much, but he buys them nevertheless, along with a bag of humbugs, which he says are for him.

"Now how about some tea and cake?" he asks.

"Definitely!"

And so, we head across the road to Tilney's Teashop.

Chapter Eleven

"What will you have?" Guy asks as we eye up the homemade cakes on the counter.

"I'm torn between the coffee and walnut cake and the lavender shortbread," I say, my mouth starting to water.

"Have both!" he says.

"No way! I'll be round as a ball," I protest.

"You've got plenty of room for growth," he laughs.

But if I keep eating cake and Mrs Powell's dinners, I'll never be skinny like Sahara, I think.

"D'you know what you'd like?" the orange girl behind the counter interrupts, chewing her filler-puffed lips and fluttering her huge falsies at Guy.

"An Earl Grey, a double espresso, a slice of coffee and walnut cake, and the shortbread, please," he says.

"I'm not going to eat all that!" I say.

"I know – but I am!" he laughs.

I slap his wrist.

"You can have a corner of my biscuit," he says teasingly as the girl makes our coffees.

"But what did you really want?" I ask.

"I'm indifferent to cake," he says. "I like it all, but I'm really not fussed about which type."

"I can't understand how anyone could be *indifferent to cake*!

Teatime treats are one of the things that make life worth living," I say, my mouth now fully watering as I gaze at all the goodies.

"Shall we sit outside – if you're sure it won't be too bright for you?" he suggests.

"I need some light after a week in the Collections Room. Look, there's a table just under the awning that'll be perfect," I answer.

"Why don't you go ahead and save it, and I'll bring the tray?" Guy suggests.

So, I go over to investigate. There are a few crumbs left by the previous occupants, which I flick off with my hand before sitting down at the shady side of the table. Within moments, a robin is hopping about, eyeing me boldly. It flies off as Guy puts our tray down and sits opposite me, the gold of his hair highlighted by the sun.

"It's amazing coming round here with you, Alice," he says as he pours my tea. "You get it. And I know you understand why we desperately need to open the Hall to the public if we're going to keep it going, keep it in the family even."

"Of course!" I say, watching carefully as he breaks a corner off the shortbread and pushes the rest towards me.

"Sahara wasn't interested… at all," he says and takes a sip of coffee. "She had a vague penchant for contemporary art. She made friends with Tracey Emin – Dame Tracey, as we should call her now – when she sat for her and once she bought a stupid Mr Brainwash montage at a charity auction, but that was about it… Poor Sahara," he says, and although he's not praising her, the way he says her name sounds like the whisper of angels crossing starry desert skies: ethereal and exotic – everything I can never be.

It's a kick in the guts.

"She lived in the moment – " he goes on, casually snapping another corner off the shortbread, "never a thought for the past or the future. My heritage bored her, her past was a nightmare, and the future scared her. She hated making plans."

I don't want to be talking about Sahara, but she intrigues me in the same measure as she intimidates me. To know Guy and where he is now, I need to understand what this woman really means to him and what exactly happened between them, so: "Tell me about her, Guy," I say. "What happened between you two?"

He looks away, takes a sharp sip of his super-strong coffee, then puts down his cup and looks steadily at me. "It's a while back, Alice, but… I guess you should know. Check out the previous owner, as it were." His mouth twitches in an attempted smile.

Guy carefully divides the coffee cake and pushes the plate towards me. "It's a long story… you're going to need some sugar to get you through it," he says, handing me a fork.

"Seb was my best friend at Winchester. Sahara was only a year younger. Their mother had… issues. She died when they were old enough to understand, but too young to cope. They were packed off to boarding school too soon by a dad who had better things to do than comfort his distraught children. And they struggled – with a lot of things.

"When I first saw her, I was fifteen. I was just a boy, but at fourteen, she was already becoming a young woman. I was captivated by her. She was so beautiful and unearthly, like a naiad, and throughout my teens I just wasn't interested in any other girls. They all seemed too… solid, too real, too ordinary. Sahara was so… *fragile*. She got in my head and under my skin, and though I loved Seb like a brother, Sahara was an obsession.

"She started modelling at sixteen, and I worried for her. I wanted to protect her, but the world had other plans. She had her first Vogue cover shoot on her seventeenth birthday, followed by a massive party at a private club in the West End. Seb and I were off our tits on coke, giddy with her success and teetering on the edge of adulthood, but a couple of hours in, I realised I had no idea where she'd gone. No one else even really cared, but I had to find her. I…" here he cradles his coffee cup, closes his eyes, and sighs. "I… found her in one of the bathrooms in the club with Johnny Parker…"

I look blank.

"The lead singer of *The Stingers*?"

"Oh… him," I recall. "The one who dated Annie Whitehouse and they were always having public screaming matches?"

"Yeah. That little shit. They'd been chasing the dragon and…" he looks away for a moment, then takes a deep breath and carries on. "That was when I vowed I'd never go anywhere near hard drugs again. I spent the next five years chasing her through the mad labyrinth that her life had become, trying to protect her from herself. And the further she went from me, the more I wanted to help her – and the further she ran."

My heart clenches for him as he turns from me, blinking rapidly.

"And then she ended up at the Priory. It was Seb who finally persuaded her to go – she wouldn't listen to me. The first time I visited, I was mobbed by paparazzi. I couldn't even get my car through the gate, and then, of course, the media had us down as a couple, and suddenly I became her knight in shining armour.

The narrative suited her; I was no longer just the boy next door. She finally wanted me, and next thing I knew, we were engaged.

"She was clean – for a bit, while she lived at Tillingford with Mum and Dad. But she was bored by country life, and when she realised her anorexia had made her infertile, it wasn't long before the dragon came knocking again..."

He sighs and looks up through the wavering branches.

"And I hadn't accounted for James. I have him to thank, really, for saving me from her, in a way," he goes on. "I knew I couldn't marry her, not when I knew she didn't really love me *that* way. I guess it was inevitable from the start that I'd never be able to hold her steady, but it's not been easy watching her ruin her life. I always felt like I should have done more to help her."

I hesitate before saying anything, but I feel moved to reassure him. "It sounds like you did more than anyone could or should have done. No one should marry someone out of pity – I don't think that could make anyone happy in the long run."

His explanation hasn't really reassured me that he's over her.

He picks up his cup and, seeing it empty, says, "I think I've had enough, Alice… let's go and look at the garden."

I gulp down the rest of my tea and follow him back across the road in silence. He takes my hand and squeezes it, wordlessly.

We disturb dozens of fat, fuzzy bees as we brush past the lavender bushes outside the bakehouse door. "I love lavender. It's so calming," he says. "I want to make a lavender garden on that sloping lawn just below the Terrace, showcasing all the different varieties, maybe take back a few acres of the estate for lavender fields and make lavender-scented things, soap and stuff."

"That would be amazing! It has lots of healing properties, you know. You can use the oil for sunburn, and it's soothing for skin complaints. I made a concoction for Hatty with aqueous cream, lavender, and calendula oil, and it got rid of her eczema completely."

"We could make Tillingford Hall Hand Balm," he murmurs thoughtfully, taking my hand.

I look into his eyes and my stomach does half a dozen back flips.

Chapter Twelve

I'm getting that Sunday feeling – you know, when a lovely weekend is drawing to a close and the impending doom of Monday starts to hang over you. Knowing that Guy will be returning to London in a few hours with so much unspoken between us only makes it worse.

Yesterday afternoon passed in a whirl of exploring the estate together and sharing our hopes and dreams over dinner at The Tillingford Abbey hotel, a Michelin-starred restaurant. We kissed goodnight, but when he reluctantly left me at the door of my room, I was relieved and disappointed in equal measure.

I know it sounds clichéd, but I've honestly never felt this way about anyone before, and I admire Guy as a person as much as I fancy him as a man. That he is a gentleman who wouldn't take advantage on a first date is obviously a good thing – especially for someone reticent like me, I remind myself – but there's that niggling feeling that maybe he just isn't quite as crazy about me as I am about him.

We planned to go riding today, but since sunrise, the whole estate has been scarcely visible through sheets of rain. Guy agreed that going out in this might be a bit much – even for the horses, who are all huddling under the trees in their waterproof jackets – so he suggested a game of billiards. I've never played before, but he said he'd teach me, which is fine by me, not least because I still haven't got around to looking at the miniatures that should be in the Billiards Room.

It seems to have become a kind of box room for storing various random bits of junk – a couple of broken chairs, an old ironing board, a few packing cases. "Sorry about the mess," he says. "I've asked Seb to tidy it up and put these things in the cellar or get rid of them, but Mum always seems to need him for something else. She never comes in here, so she doesn't really care."

"Wow!" I can't help exclaiming as I glance around the walls. "I hadn't realised there were so many pictures in here. I should really have come in here earlier."

"I reckon there are at least forty in the display cases here," says Guy, grabbing the billiards cues from an inlaid mahogany cabinet in one corner of the room. "And I think there are some in the drawers of the card table too. They should really be in the Collections Room. The other pictures in here are just some hunting scenes by unimportant local artists, although this one is meant to be a Stubbs." He vaguely gestures to a picture of a glossy black horse called, uninspiringly, *Midnight*. "Now let me teach you to play billiards."

"OK, then!"

Old Alice would have found any kind of ball game very tedious, but Guy's verve and playfulness make it all much more worthwhile, and it's not like we've got anything else to do right now. Of course, I play games with Hatty all the time, but it tends to be board games, pretending games based on whatever book or story she's obsessed with in that moment, or her favourite, *Hairdressers*, which generally ends up with me having to cut knots out of my hair where her plaiting has gone a bit wrong.

It's nice to have some downtime with another adult for once.

Guy puts out just three balls – one red, one white with spots, and one yellow with spots.

"So, we use a full-size table like this one," he explains – as though I'd have a clue whether a table was full-sized or not. "Each player gets a cue ball at the beginning and plays with that cue ball throughout the game. Yours is white, mine is yellow. We use the cue ball to hit the other balls. The red ball is 'the object ball'.

"To see who starts, we perform what's called 'a lag' – we each hit our cue ball up towards the top cushion, so it bounces back down the table towards what's called 'the baulk', that is the first quarter of the table. Whoever's nearest gets to play first."

Luckily, I did play pool a few times in the Student's Union, so I have a rough idea of how to hold a cue, but Guy gently adjusts my hands, my shoulders, and my elbows to help me into a better position, which is hugely distracting, but very nice.

"So, you're going to play first," he says as, somehow, I manage to get my ball nearer to the baulk.

He puts the red ball on the spot at the top of the table. I try to hit it with my cue ball, which of course I don't, but Guy shows me how it's done, explaining various scoring options – a 'cannon', which is when you strike the cue ball so that it hits both the other balls. A 'winning hazard', where you hit the red ball into a pocket. And a 'losing hazard', which seems to depend on which order the balls get pocketed in. Apparently, you could get all three of these in one hit – in theory. I don't pretend to understand how, so I concentrate on trying to hit the cue ball at all.

After twenty minutes or so, I admit I'm getting bored, so I let Guy practise his shots while I look at the pictures. There's a large case on the wall adjacent to the door. It has a velvet lining in a kind of dull buff colour that looks like it could once have been gold. Embroidered on the background in dark gold thread is a stylised tree trunk with branches coming out, and attached to each of the branches with gold ribbon is a framed miniature. It's a kind of illustrated family tree. The names of all the Tillingford ancestors are written in faded copperplate on little paper scrolls under each picture.

When faced with this many pieces, I usually start at the top and work my way along, but I'm immediately struck by one in the centre: a handsome blond man who just doesn't fit. I can't pin down why. Maybe because he's blond and the others all have black or brown hair – or at the very least, they're somewhat mousy – if their hair can be seen at all (which it often can't, due to wigs, hats and bonnets). Or is it something about the frame, which is yellow gilt with an ugly chip out of it, rather than a dull antique gold like the others? Or perhaps it's the odd brownish patina that looks shiny, almost as though it's a glaze that's been painted on?

Is that why alarm bells are ringing? I remember the Cat Lady in the Collections Room. Except I feel like I recognise this face.

"Come and look at this," I say to Guy.

"Hang on," he says, his pert backside tightening as he leans over the table to reach a tricky shot, distracting me from my purpose. The three balls cannon into each other with a satisfying click. "Yesss!" he says, with a fist-pump. "I managed to do that thing where you pot all three balls in the right order and score ten," he says with glee. "I can't remember what it's called – a Jemmy or something…"

"Come and look at this," I reply, forgetting to comment on

his success as I'm constitutionally incapable of generating any interest in the outcome of ball games of any kind.

"It's a picture," he says, blandly, and I'm about to retort something about it being less tedious than billiards but bite my tongue.

"Look closely, at this one," I say. "Sir Nicholas Tillingford. What do you think of it?"

He glances at it then paces back to the billiards table. He picks up the red ball. "OK, you're obviously suspicious of it – you've already told me you think some of the pictures in our collection aren't quite right." He throws the ball up and catches it a few times. "The brush strokes are made with fox hair instead of sable. The varnish is pitch pine resin rather than rat oil, and the frame is clearly by a Wiltshire craftsman, possibly from the area around Devizes?"

"Mock away. Can't you see what's odd about it?"

He leans towards the picture, scrutinising it with a near-squint that's almost comical. Then he does a double take and looks at it more intently.

"I think it's a modern fake," I say into the silence. "And it looks a bit like you." I can almost hear the cogs whirring in his troubled mind. "Have you seen it before?"

"I think it's been here a while – look how dusty the cabinet is – but I've never really studied it. I didn't sit for it, if that's what you're asking," he says, his brow furrowing.

I look again and see that it only looks a bit like him, like an unflattering picture of how his brother would look, if he had one.

But it certainly doesn't look like any of the other Tillingfords in the case.

"Then who is it?" I ask.

"Don't worry about it," he says, putting the cues away. "Come on, let's go."

He throws the balls onto the table, and as I watch them ricochet off the sides, he's already turning off the lights and ushering me out.

Chapter Thirteen

It's ten o'clock at night, and the house is eerily quiet. I'm sitting in the Kitchen, which is lit only by the single bulb above the range. It seems daft to turn all the lights on when it's just me, but it does give the vast, crypt-like room a spooky look. I have a monster headache, and I'm feeling deeply sorry for myself, not least because I know it's all my fault. I'm too wired to sleep, so I'm trying to unwind with the classic old wives' remedy of a cup of hot milk. But really, I could do with a listening ear, so I decide to give Charlotte a try.

"Hey, Sister!" she replies chirpily. "Still up?" Charlie's hair is wet, and she admits she was just redyeing her 'rebellious streak'. "How did your weekend with Lord Farquhar go? Did he ravish you in the shrubbery?" she asks.

"No! Nothing like *that*," I giggle, scanning the mugs, "but…"

"Go on…."

"Well, he did *kiss* me," I admit.

She squeaks.

"And we did have a really lovely trip to Jane Austen's house at Chawton," I say, remembering that I've got my new mug upstairs. But it's a long way to go for a mug, and I don't want to wake Hatty up.

"Aw, bless! Was that your idea?"

"No, his," I explain as I grab the old Jane Austen mug, the one that says *…but indeed I would rather have nothing but tea.*

“Aw. That’s so sweet,” she sighs. “He’s got you sussed, hasn’t he?”

Indeed, as I reach for milk from the fridge, I think he might have.

“So, what happened next?” she insists.

“Well,” I say, pouring the milk into the mug and putting the bottle back in the fridge, “he took me to a lovely restaurant on Saturday night, and afterwards we kissed, but nothing more. Today it was raining all day, so we just kind of mooched around, and he taught me to play billiards, and it all got a bit boring. Then I needed to pick up Hatty, and he offered to come with me. But I didn’t want Philip to meet him. You know how Philip’s always looking for ways to wriggle out of his responsibilities; I was worried that if he saw me with another man, especially a drop-dead gorgeous one with a sports car worth more than his entire annual income...”

“What on earth kind of car is it?” Charlie interrupts.

“An Aston Martin.”

Charlie gives a low whistle. “Blimey he really must be loaded…”

It would take too long properly to explain Guy’s financial situation right now, so I put my mug in the microwave and carry on: “I was worried that if Philip saw Guy, he’d jump to conclusions and use it as an excuse to give me less support, and I was sure Hatty would rather see me alone first. So I told Guy that it wasn’t necessary. And then he got slightly huffy – he didn’t say anything, but I could tell he was a bit offended.

“And then, when I picked her up, Hatty was disappointed that

I'd come in my car because she wanted to go in Guy's 'fancy James Bond car' as she calls it. It turns out she had told Philip all about Guy and his car anyway, so there was no need for all the cloak and dagger, and then *she* was in a huff that Guy hadn't turned up. And she started asking me all sorts of awkward questions on the way home, like, 'Did he kiss you?'."

"Aw, isn't that sweet?" says Charlie.

"No, it isn't!" I retort. "She's seven years old! She shouldn't be asking things like that! It's all this ghastly modern tweenie girl culture that she's absorbing by osmosis despite my best efforts to keep her away from the internet and TV by making her read nice wholesome books like *What Katie Did* and *The Secret Garden*!"

"And endless Disney films!" Charlotte points out with a laugh. "Hello… Earth to Alice! It's the twenty-first century. Most kids have seen porn by the time they're eleven. And besides, you should be pleased that Hatty's happy for you. Imagine what a nightmare this would be if she'd taken against Guy or wasn't willing to share you, like so many kids."

"S'pose…" I admit, grumpily, getting my milk out of the microwave and stirring it. "But it gets worse. When we got back, Guy had already gone – he didn't even text or leave a note or anything. And he and I both completely forgot that he'd promised to have a TV supper and watch a Disney film with Hatty, but *she* hadn't. She was gutted.

"Luckily when his mum saw how upset Hatty was, she offered to watch *Frozen Two* with her while I unpacked Hatty's bag and organised her supper. Considering we haven't really seen much of Maxine and she seems to think I'm the new scullery maid, it was really nice of her. Although Hatty did say something funny…"

"Oh, what was that?" Charlie asks.

"She said that Maxine reminded her a bit of Elsa, except she wasn't magic and was old with short hair, so not very much like Elsa at all actually, but I think I know what she means – Maxine's certainly a bit of an Ice Queen," I say with a giggle.

"But at least it sounds like the rest of the weekend was nice."

"Yes," I sigh. I test the milk and cast my mind back to the good bits of the last three days. "I had a wonderful weekend, but one of the things I like about him more than anything else is how he's handled Hatty. He's been so kind to her, and he seemed genuinely interested in her as a person and knew exactly what she'd like. At Chawton, he chose this lovely make-your-own-doll's-house book for her, which I know she'd have loved.

"But now he's blown it by forgetting his promise to spend time with her (which I know was as much my fault) and dashing off without saying anything or even remembering to give her the book."

"He doesn't sound like a complete duffer though, Alice."

"No, he's not. But I can't help thinking he's just toying with me. I don't understand why he went all funny on me and didn't even say *goodbye* – it's almost like he couldn't wait to get away..."

And I remember it was the precise moment when I showed him the picture of Sir Nicholas Tillingford that things changed, but that's way too complicated to share with Charlotte. I sit down and take a sip of my milk.

"Just take it easy," says Charlie. "Get to know him a little better, find out what kind of man he is."

"I really fancy him, Charlie. I'm worried that's going to cloud my judgement. He's so lovely, and we had a beautiful time together, but obviously, someone like *him* – an aristocrat, for goodness' sake, with a super-model ex-fiancée and an American property heiress waiting in the wings – won't be seriously interested in a tired bluestocking divorcee from Morden. He's probably just stringing me along. I'm such an idiot."

"Don't be so hard on yourself, Alice. Maybe a little fling with someone gorgeous is what you need right now. But also, remember you've got a lot to offer, too. Perhaps he's just never met someone quite like you before. Maybe this *could* be the Real Thing. You can't have all the answers just like that – you've got to wait and see."

She's right, of course, and it makes me feel slightly more at ease, and I eventually wind down enough to climb the stairs to bed.

Chapter Fourteen

The next day I get up with fresh determination. While I admit I've got a monster crush on Guy that I'm well aware probably isn't going to go anywhere, especially after the way we ended things on Sunday, I do also feel a deep respect for him as a human being and a desire to support him in what he's trying to do here. This secondment already matters a lot to me as something which will help me further my career, but my admiration of Guy and his values imbue my work with new meaning. I want to do my best work because I really care about this project on so many levels.

I know for sure that some of the pieces in the collection are fakes, but I don't know what it all means. I need to check the cabinets in the Billiards Room and see if that golden-haired imposter has a catalogue number, but I haven't got to that bit of my schedule yet. I'm still working on my traffic-light system, and I'm not due to cross-check the artefacts in that room until next week at least, but for once, I decide to be spontaneous. I take my massive bunch of keys down to the Billiards Room and try to find the right one for the cabinets. None of them fit. Are my hands shaking from excitement, or too much coffee? I take three deep breaths and try each key slowly.

No, not a single one fits.

I go to the kitchen to look for Mrs Powell. She's making pastry with Hatty.

"It's going to be a pie!" explains my daughter, her face streaked with flour, her hair sticking up in snowy tufts.

"What sort of pie?" I ask, getting myself a glass of water – I really don't need more coffee.

"Chicken and ham," says Mrs Powell.

"Sounds delicious! I can't wait," I say. I suspect Hatty won't like it (like most kids, she hates her food being mixed up), but I'm hoping I can separate out the chicken and ham pieces so that it looks more palatable for her, and there's a chance she might nibble on the pastry. I turn back to Mrs P. "Mrs Powell, I was wondering… do you have keys to the display cabinets in the Billiards Room? I need to have a closer look at them, but I don't think I've got keys in my set that fit."

Mrs P straightens up and looks at me. "You have the master set," she says. "That should have one copy of everything on it."

"I've really tried all of them," I say.

"Maybe His Lordship might be able to help," she suggests. "He does have copies of most things, but it's possible something like that cabinet would only have one key. Or Herbert could probably get into the cabinet – I can't imagine the lock's very secure."

I resist the temptation to roll my eyes. It's all so… haphazard. How can anyone store twenty valuable artworks in a cabinet with just one key? And yet somehow, I'm not surprised.

"I'll ask Lord Tillingford, then."

I thank her, give Hatty a squeeze, and ask her to be a good girl for Mrs P, and then go in search of Giles.

Should I tell him what I've found so far? I know that some of the miniatures are fakes, but the question is, who's been faking them and why? And that goes way beyond my professional experience and certainly beyond my remit. Maybe Guy's spoken to him already.

I'm shaking as I make my way up to Lord T's study. I don't know why I'm nervous, but I can hear him speaking, and his voice is fierce but quiet like he's having a bit of an argument with someone on the phone. I don't want anyone to think I'm eavesdropping, but what should I do? Knock and interrupt or come back later?

I take the coward's way – or the polite way, depending on how you look at it – and decide to come back.

I walk into the garden and let the problem spin round in my mind. If I can, I need to get the keys off Lord T or ask Herbert to help me open the cabinet and get a good look at Sir Nicholas to see if there are any clues on the back of the picture. As for the rest, I need to speak to Desmond. Not only is he my boss and the country's leading expert on miniatures, but he's also a kind and wise man. I'd adopt him as my uncle if I could.

I walk towards the Shrubbery to make the call so I won't be overheard. As I select Desmond's number from my contacts, I become aware of people on the other side of the hedge – low voices and a throaty giggle. I recognise Maxine's nasal tones – but who's with her? Perhaps this isn't the best place for a private phone call after all.

I start to move away, but I can't help myself; I want to know who the man is. I know I should respect their privacy, but now I'm in Super Sleuth mode and fired with curiosity. Something is going on at Tillingford Hall, and I'm determined to uncover whatever it is. Perhaps this will be a clue.

So, I creep forward and glance through the hedge. There, by the pool, Maxine lies face down on a lounger, her bikini top unclasped. Sebastian in bulging budgie smugglers is rubbing sun cream slowly along her legs, massaging it into her skinny thighs in a way that is definitely not in his job description.

I shudder. Ugh. Poor Giles. Does he know? Should I tell Guy? How on earth do you say to someone, "By the way, do you know that your mum is fooling around with your best friend?" But what *should* I do? Take a photo for evidence? Ew! I can't do that!

I take a step backwards, trying to wrest my eyes from the scene.

I've not been employed as a private detective, and the way Seb and Maxine are acting, while certainly disturbing, is absolutely none of my business. My urgent priority now is to get away so they don't know I was here and then wash my eyes out with soap and water!

I all but run back to the Collections Room, where I take a deep breath and bury my aching head in my hands. I need to get that key, but I can't face Lord Tillingford just now. And I need to speak to Desmond, but I'm not sure I won't blurt everything out. I'll have to forget what I saw. Hopefully I can just pretend it never happened.

When I eventually go back up to Lord T's room, all is quiet. I wipe my palms on my floral cotton dress, then knock tentatively on the door.

Silence.

I catch my breath. Come on Alice, be brave, I tell myself, knocking louder.

"Come!" says a gruff voice, and I walk into the study. "Ah, my miniature lady," Lord T says with a beaming smile as Bailey and Bertie, the beagles, gather round for a good sniff and Algie the Great Dane yawns, stretches, and breaks wind. "Lovely to see you, do come in," Lord T says, oblivious.

"Thank you," I say, easing the door shut behind me and noticing gratefully that the window is open. I don't know why I was nervous. I give Algie a pat as he gets up to investigate me.

"Take a seat," says Lord Tillingford. "What can I do for you?"

I'm unsure where to start – and what to include. "Lord Tillingford…" I begin, as I sit down opposite him in a carver chair with a sagging burgundy velvet cushion.

"Giles, please…" he corrects.

"Giles," I say shyly, aware of the slobber dribbling out of Algie's jowly mouth onto my hand. "I'm sorry to disturb you, but there've been some developments that I think you should know about."

"Oh. *Developments?*" he says, leaning his elbows on the desk, pressing his fingers together, and looking at me over the rim of his glasses, like an old professor. "You're not leaving us, are you?"

"Oh no, nothing like that!" I assure him. "I've just found some… irregularities, and I think I'm going to need backup." I explain the anomalies in the catalogue and how I think we'd better get Desmond to come and see what he thinks.

"Having seen your CV, Alice, I have every faith in your abilities, but," he says, getting up and walking to the window, "I agree some additional expertise would be very useful if things are as bad as you think. Charming fellow, Desmond. I met him, of course, when he came to assess the collection in the spring. It would be an absolute pleasure to see him again. He must come as our guest over the weekend."

And then I explain about the cabinet key.

"You'll be surprised to learn, Alice, that I do actually have a key-holding system and copies of most things," he says with a smile.

I laugh nervously, not wanting to give away too many of my presumptions.

He pulls out a blue hardback notebook from a shelf and runs his finger down the list. "I don't have anything listed here that could be *that* key," he admits, "but I do have a Box of Shame if you'd like to look through that? There might be an orphan there who would be pleased to be returned to his rightful place. Maybe your little girl could try a few of them around the house and see what they do?"

"She'd love that!" I say. "It turns out she likes making herself useful – here at least."

"Hatty's a real charmer now she's becoming a bit less shy. She's a credit to you," he adds, making me glow with pride.

"That's really kind of you, Giles. I've done my best to bring her up properly," I say, sounding a bit like Mary Poppins, although Algie keeps drooling on my hand, which I'm sure would never have happened to the famous nanny.

"And you've done a good job. It can't be easy managing it on your own."

"It has its challenges," I admit, relieved that Algie's got bored with giving me a free shower and is now snuffling his way toward his bed. "I really do appreciate you allowing me to bring her. I don't think I'd have been able to come if you hadn't agreed to that. And being here is so good for her. She's getting so much fresh air and exercise. She wouldn't have paddled in fords, climbed cedar trees, or made pies if she'd stayed in London this summer.

It's been wonderful."

"I'm glad to hear it. I only wish more children could enjoy our home and grounds. They're so underused at the moment...," he says, gazing out of the window. "Now, I realise Hatty is very young," he continues, "but it seems to me she'd be perfectly capable of testing these keys if we gave her the responsibility, and it would do me a favour. I'm not going to get around to it myself, but it would be useful if someone could. I'd be happy to give her a bit of pocket money for it," he says, sitting back down, which seems to be a cue for Algie to flump onto his bed.

"That really won't be necessary," I insist. "You're already doing so much for us."

"Not at all! What is life if we can't share what we have with others? Anyway, here's The Box," he says, handing over a beautiful mahogany casket inlaid with brass, which is full of keys of all shapes and sizes. "See if you can find what you need and then give it to Hatty to try all the little keyholes around the house. I think they're all small keys for cabinets and suchlike, so there's no need for her to bother with any of the room doors, I don't think – and obviously ask her to stay away from people's bedrooms; we do need a *bit* of privacy."

"Of course! We'll see what we can do," I say. Algie gives a little *snoof* as he settles his head down on his paws.

"And Alice?" he adds, as my hand reaches the door handle.

"Yes?" I say, turning back.

"Make sure you keep this between you and me until we're sure what's going on."

"...of course," I agree, the back of my neck prickling. I'm getting the feeling there might be more mysteries to be uncovered;

certainly, not everything at Tillingford Hall is what it seems.

With a kick in the stomach, I realise that maybe Guy isn't the person I thought he was either. I resolve to be more professional and keep my distance from now on (although it might be a bit late for that, what with all the kissing and stuff). My heart aches as I remember last Friday night and our magical time in Chawton.

It's not far off lunchtime, so I rush down to my desk to call Desmond while I've still got time.

"Alice, my lovely!" he croons in his faint Trinidadian accent that never fails to make me feel better about… well, everything. "How are things down in darkest Hampshire?"

"Dark," I reply.

"Oho, tell me more," he says, his accent coming through more strongly as he gets excited. I can hear a strange snuffling, sucking sound, which is probably his wrinkly little pug, Mr Biggles.

"Well, Desmond, I don't know quite how to put this, but I think we might have a Country House Mystery on our hands."

"How *thrilling*! Is it the Vicar in the Library with the Lead Piping?" he asks.

"No, not that sort of mystery," I giggle. "At least, I don't *think* so, but there's definitely something odd going on. There's a substantial number of pieces missing or miscatalogued, and worse, I'm pretty sure we've got a few fakes, including some copies where originals should be and some which seem to be completely made up. Lord Tillingford wants you to come and take a look."

"We'd be delighted to, wouldn't we, Biggly?" he says, addressing the dog, who goes everywhere with him.

"Could you come this weekend? The Tillingfords would be very happy to have you as their guest, and I'm sure Mr Biggles would enjoy the fresh air. Their son, Guy, could maybe give you a lift from London – although I think your MG would look beautiful on the drive," I add, knowing that this pleasing aesthetic in itself might be enough to entice him away from the city lights.

"Ooh yes, why not? It's a while since we've been the guest of aristocracy – and we did have such a lovely time when we came down to discuss the project a few months ago. What do you think, Mr Biggles? It'll be very exciting to have a trip to the countryside – all those lovely smells!" The snuffling at the other end gets louder, and there's a tiny bark. "Done. Mr Biggles and I will come down on Friday night. With the MG. And then we can look for that lead piping," he says, chortling. "I can't wait."

"Thank you, Desmond."

"No, thank *you*, Alice, for keeping me up to date and giving me the chance for a little break from London to see the lovely Tillingfords again. Mr Biggles and I very much look forward to it. See you on Friday." And with those gracious words, he hangs up.

I heave a sigh of relief. Knowing that backup is on the way eases my mind and makes me more determined to sort out the catalogue. I have to get as much done as possible before Desmond gets here, so that I have some specific examples for him to check out.

I look at my watch. As if on cue, there's a mousy knock on the door, and my dear daughter's head pokes round. "Mummy, it's nearly lunchtime."

"OK, Little One, I'm just coming."

I put my computer on sleep and follow Hatty downstairs. "I'm looking forward to that chicken and ham pie," I say to encourage her.

"Me too," she says, licking her lips. She would normally say that anything mixed up with sauce was yucky, so I can't contain my curiosity.

"Have you tried it?" I ask, as she puts her little paw in mine and fairly drags me down the stairs.

"I had some of the inside goop before it went in the oven. It was super yum. Mrs P made sure there was a bit of ham, a bit of chicken, and a little bit of creamy sauce so I could taste them together, and I ate them ALL UP!" she says with an exaggerated lip smacking and a tummy rub.

"Good girl!" I'm about to make some comment about trying new things but decide to leave it at that. I'm so glad I brought her here to have all these new experiences. I don't know many seven-year-olds who would both make *and eat* chicken-and-ham pie with creamy sauce. I certainly wouldn't have put myself through the aggravation of trying to cook something like that for her back in Morden.

Herbert and Giles are already sitting at the table talking about rose blight when Hatty and I arrive. I apologise for being late, but they don't seem bothered, especially as Mrs P is still fussing around with potatoes and vegetables. Hatty puts on a child-sized apron that has appeared from somewhere (I can't help wondering if it was once Guy's) and helps Mrs P serve up.

"Will Her Ladyship be joining us?" asks Mrs Powell.

"I doubt it," replies Lord T.

Maxine doesn't normally appear for lunch – she's skinny as a rake, so it's probably part of her regime to skip it. As someone who needs regular feeding, I can't understand a woman who doesn't eat lunch.

"Although," chuckles Herbert as Giles gets up to refill the water jug, "I expect Sebastian won't be far away. I never see him miss one of your pies, Mrs P or," he adds to me under his breath, "be too far from the Wicked Witch of the West."

The ghost of the scene from an hour ago flashes before my eyes, and suddenly my pie doesn't look that appealing.

After a few seconds though, realising how hungry I am, I manage to shake off thoughts about Seb and Maxine and tuck in. The pie is amazing, and I congratulate Mrs P and Hatty. Mrs P shakes off my compliments, insisting it was Hatty's careful chopping and measuring that made it so good. Hatty is gleaming with pride, shovelling grown-up food into her mouth like Oliver Twist.

"Hello, Maxine," says Giles as his wife appears in the doorway, her cheeks flushed. "Come and have some of Mrs P's delicious pie."

"I'll just have salad," she replies, holding Coco very firmly, as the minuscule mutt looks determined to jump on the table and lick everyone's plates.

A few seconds later, too soon to convince anyone they arrived separately, Seb makes his appearance, looking somewhat tousled.

"You'll have pie, won't you, Sebastian?" says Mrs P, indicating he should help himself, which he does with the appetite of a man who's had an energetic morning.

He sits next to me, the heat emanating off his body, and I catch the faintest trace of his driftwood cologne. My skin prickles. I don't want to be attracted to Seb – not one bit of it, and especially not after what I saw this morning – but Guy has awoken something in me, and it's responding to Seb's unwitting signals.

"Just to remind you, it's my afternoon off," Mrs P tells me, "so you'll have to mind Hatty yourself, I'm afraid."

"Oh yes, of course," I reply, showing Hatty how to scoop up her peas without touching them with her fingers so I can angle myself away from Seb.

"And don't forget *we're* going out this afternoon, Darling," Lord T says to his wife. "I have to see a man about a dog."

"Another beagle," says his faithful retainer to no one in particular, his head bobbing in a quiet chuckle.

"Really?" sighs Maxine, clinging to the fridge door with a look of despair.

"I'm just having a look…" Giles says, like a child with his face pressed to a toy shop window. "But I need you to come too because, if you remember, after I got Bertie, you said you'd have to help me choose the next one so I wouldn't come home with another maniac!"

"Absolutely," says Maxine, rolling her eyes.

"We'll be gone for some time," says Giles, winking at me.

The sun has gone in, and large raindrops are starting to strike the windows. With the house empty, this will be the perfect time to go through the Box of Shame with Hatty.

Chapter Fifteen

"Come on, Hatty," I say as soon as I hear Lord T's Range Rover swish out of the drive, windscreen wipers on overdrive. "Let's try and find the key for this cabinet."

"Can we invite Lily and Poppy to help us with the key hunt? They'll think it's lots of fun," says Hatty.

"I'm sure they'll be doing something else today, and anyway, Lord Tillingford said you were just the girl for the job! I don't think he'd want any old girls to take charge of the Box of Shame, do you?"

Hatty agrees this might be true. "But I want to play with them," she whines.

"Well, maybe they can come over at the weekend for a pool party," I say, remembring how Guy said we should feel free to invite them and hoping that's genuinely OK.

Hatty satisfied, we wend our way to the Billiards Room with The Box. Hatty hands me the first key, which is way too big.

"It won't be that one," I say.

"It might be a *magic* key," suggests Hatty.

"It could be," I sigh. This is going to be a long afternoon, but it's raining, and Hatty has nothing else to do, especially as it's Mrs P's afternoon off. Besides, I must get into the cabinet, so hey ho.

The next key looks more promising, but while it fits into the lock, it won't turn. It's probably for a similar-sized cabinet somewhere else. The third key is ornate brass and slightly too large, with a velvet tassel. I drop each of the discarded keys into a plastic sandwich bag we've brought with us, so we don't get mixed up. The fourth key is tiny, like one of those ones you get for a diary or a jewellery box – far too small. Then there's a little gold one, a modern window key which can't be for any window in *this* house, a rusty iron one, and an ivory one that I'm worried about breaking, so I wrap it in a tissue before gently putting it in with the others.

After a while, we've tried thirty-eight different keys, and none of them work. So we tip them all back in the box, except the ivory one, which I place very carefully on top. I need to ask Herbert to find another way to open the cabinet, but Hatty's determined to try every key in every lock in the house, and I do need to keep my little girl entertained for a while, so I go along with it. Even with her insatiable curiosity, she's going to run out of steam eventually.

We look around the room and find that the billiards scoreboard is actually a cabinet that can be shut and locked. Trying the keys, we find one that fits but agree it would be best to leave it unlocked, so we put the key in another plastic bag, and Hatty, using a Sharpie, puts *billards scor bord* on it in her best handwriting. I breathe deeply, trying not to think about the key I'm actually looking for. I'm desperate to get that cabinet open.

"Tell you what, Hatty. Let's go and see Herbert – he can get this one open for us while we test some other keys."

Thankfully, Hatty agrees this is a good idea. We put the Box of Shame back in the Collections Room as it's rather heavy, pull on our rainwear, and go down to the Potting Shed, which is always the first port of call if you want to find Herbert.

We knock quietly but there's no response. Hatty gently pushes the door until it creaks. Through the crack, we see the grizzled old gardener napping in a deck chair.

"Oh dear," I whisper. Bearing in mind he's seventy-five if he's a day and that we've just had lunch, I tell her we'd better not wake him up as he probably needs his sleep.

"What shall we do?" says Hatty.

"We'd better come back later," I say, almost crashing into a bearded man-mountain who seems to have appeared out of nowhere.

"You gave me a fright, Seb!" I gasp. "What are you doing here?"

"I came to get some tools," he explains.

"Herbert's having a nap in there," says Hatty. "You can't disturb him."

"I need to do my job," he says bluntly.

"Of course. You just gave us a fright, creeping up like that."

I'm about to ask him if he can help us open the cabinet, but something stops me. "Come on, Hatty, let's go." I take my daughter's hand and pull her and frowny little face back to the house.

"Let's go and look at some more locks," I say brightly. We take off our wet things in the Boot Room and pad up to the Collections Room in our socks. The door's closed but unlocked. I swear I locked it. As I enter, I can sense something's different, but I can't pin it down. My laptop's open – I usually snap the lid shut, but I could easily have left it open, especially this morning, when I was a bit keyed up. The Box of Shame is on the desk, how I left it… I think. I can't put my finger on it, but the hairs on the back of my neck are standing up.

"I wonder if there are the same number of keys in The Box," I ask Hatty in a jolly voice. "Can you remember how many there should be?"

"Thirty eight!" she chimes.

"*Are you sure*?" I ask, teasingly.

"Yes! Thirty-eight, thirty-eight, thirty-EIGHT!!!" she shouts.

"If they *are* magic keys, maybe it might have changed. Shall we count them just to check?"

Hatty's eyes widen, then she tips back her head and laughs. "Silly Mummy! Alright then, let's count the keys."

There are thirty-six, including the *billards scor bord* one in a bag. "It must be magic!" I say, trying not to sound hysterical in my attempt at jollity, when actually I'm having kittens. Did Seb have time to come in here and grab some of the keys before running across the garden? Or did I lose some? Why did he come to find us if he was busy nicking keys? Was he trying to give himself some kind of alibi? Or is there someone else in the house? We definitely counted thirty-eight keys before and there are definitely thirty-six now.

Hatty, laughs, mystified. "Did *you* hide the keys, Mummy?"

I don't want to frighten her, so I go along with it. "I might have… or maybe… it's *magic*!"

She giggles.

"Let's go and see if we can open any more!" I say brightly, firmly locking the Collections Room door. I can't be sure if anyone's interfered with the laptop, but I'm glad I keep the external hard drive with an extra backup in my bag or my room and not on my desk.

We spend a good hour trying locks all over the house. We find a secret drawer at the back of a huge black lacquered Chinoiserie chest that opens with the little gold key. The red-tasselled key fits a glass bookcase in the Library, and the piano can be locked with a small brass key. None of the other keys seem to fit any of the other locks. Believe you me, we try *all* the keys in *all* the locks we find; Hatty can be surprisingly methodical when she gets into something. (At least I know where she got that from.)

And three keys accounted for is better than none. I'm sure Giles won't be dissatisfied.

We go back to the Collections Room and deposit the Box of Shame on my desk. I lock up carefully, and we go to find Herbert. The rain has eased off, and the sun's coming out so that a million diamonds seem to be falling from the trees while a rainbow starts to form against the receding clouds. Herbert isn't in his shed, and this time there's no sign of Sebastian, but I can hear the sound of clipping coming from the Rose Garden.

"I can see you're busy deadheading," I say once we find Herbert hard at work with rusty secateurs, "but getting this particular cabinet open is actually a bit urgent. I don't suppose you could..."

"No problem, gurl. I knowed you wanted to ask me at lunch-time, but with the Wicked Witch in the room..." he trails off as he starts to shuffle towards the shed. "Let me just get some tools."

Suddenly we hear, "Herbert! Come over here quick and help!"

"Oh, man!" sighs Herbert. "I better see what's up."

Seb comes loping towards us. He's spilt a whole tin of paint on the limestone tiles by the pool. I can't help wondering if this wasn't an accident. Was he creating a distraction to keep him and

Herbert busy this afternoon?

I offer to help, but Herbert says we should leave it to the men, so we do.

"Oh bother!" says Hatty, exactly echoing what I feel. "Now we won't get into that cabinet!"

Unless….

It's not Fort Knox, I think. It's an antique display cabinet.

We run up to the Collections Room, scarcely stopping to throw off our wellies in the Boot Room. I snap open my laptop; YouTube is bound to help. And so we watch all kinds of videos of people breaking into things, which we both find absolutely fascinating and faintly disturbing (I must get the lock on the patio doors checked when I get back to Morden). Eventually I feel confident that, armed with a hairpin, a screwdriver, and my trusty Victorinox Swiss Army Knife with twelve attachments that I was given when I was a Girl Guide, I should be able to break in. *Desmond, forgive me!*

Hatty's getting nervous and excited, so I make her go to the loo first, then realise I need it myself. Then, we creep down to the Billiards Room, and I put Hatty on watch at the door. She's hopping from foot to foot, occasionally fiddling with her knickers so I'm still convinced she's going to wet herself. I try to calm her down, making out that breaking into a cabinet full of priceless art works is a normal part of my job, but she's picking up on my nerves.

My hand is shaking as I insert the hair pin into the lock, wiggle and twist.

"Oh."

"What?" says Hatty, hopping up and down.

The cabinet swings open. "That was easy," I say, lifting the portrait of Sir Nicholas out and closing the cabinet.

"Well, that's good!" says Hatty, relaxing a bit.

But it isn't! The security in this place is absolutely dreadful.

"He's coming!" she squeaks as footsteps echo down the corridor.

I'm all fingers and thumbs, and I don't know where to put anything. I'm not doing anything wrong, I'm just…

"Herbert! You nearly gave me a heart attack! Why didn't you tell me which 'he' it was, Hatty?!"

She just gives a little, overexcited squeak while I laugh, slightly hysterically, which relieves my tension. Eventually Herbert joins in.

When he's gone, I decide Hatty needs to do something quiet – and I need time to look at Sir Nicholas. So I ask her to do a page of her Frozen colouring book with Beebee and Mousy while I examine the miniature, which has been knocking around in my pocket all this time. If it were an antique, I never would have treated it this way, but I knew as soon as I picked it out of the cabinet that it was no older than me.

Looking at it now, I'm puzzled. It's modern, but not brand new. It has a patina of age on it, but not hundreds of years – maybe twenty or thirty. I wrap it carefully in a tissue and put it in my pocket for later examination. If this piece is as old as I think, then someone's been tampering with the collection for a long time.

I'm debating whether to tell Guy. But right now, there's nothing to say. I'm no further on than I was before. I need to chew it over with Desmond.

Chapter Sixteen

It's Friday afternoon, and I'm almost dropping off at my desk when my mobile goes.

"Hey, Alice, how's things?" asks Charlotte.

"I'm tired," I admit, stretching back in my chair with a yawn.

"Lord Farquhar been keeping you busy all night?" she asks.

"I told you he works in London all week, and anyway, it was just a kiss…" I say tetchily. If truth be told, he *has* been keeping me awake – but only because I have no idea how to behave around him after last weekend's mixed signals.

Charlie starts humming *As Time Goes By* while I try to drown her out, explaining that I've been starting at five or six every morning this week, getting in a couple of hours' work before Hatty wakes up and doing another two or three every evening once she's in bed – as well as a full day's work in between. Knowing that Desmond will be here to check up on me at the weekend has really put me under pressure.

And I don't admit it to Charlie, but I don't want to let Guy down either. I know it's a bit pathetic, especially as I barely know him and have hardly heard from him this week, but I'm desperate to impress him. I want him to know that I can work as hard as he does and that I care about things as much he does.

"My brain's fried," I admit, flicking to the start menu so I can shut my laptop down. "I'm going to knock off early and just chill by the pool for a few minutes before I get Hatty from Mrs P. Desmond's going to be here soon."

"OK, I'll let you go, but give me a ring – I want to know all about it."

I really want to tell her about the mysteries of Tillingford Hall and mull over the Guy situation with her and try to work out whether he's really interested or not. But right now, I'm just knackered, and I can't wait to see my little girl; I've been almost ignoring her this week. I need a bit of downtime first, especially as I don't think I'll get any time off this weekend, so I hang up and promise to call Charlie soon.

It's a lovely warm afternoon, so I climb up to our pretty little room in the eaves, slip on my swimsuit and kaftan, and go down to the pool. I flop down on one of the teak loungers, yawning.

I don't know how much time later, I'm woken suddenly by the unmistakeable growl of a classic sports car. My boss has arrived! I jump up, all of a dither. Is anyone watching? Am I sunburnt? I can't go out to meet him like *this*: possibly looking like a lobster and dressed only in a swimsuit and kaftan… regardless of how elegant it is. I fly onto the Terrace and into the house through the Ballroom so I can avoid the Kitchen, where I'd have to spend ten minutes hearing about Hatty's day as well as explain why I'm running through the house in my swimsuit.

But – *Oh no!* The Ballroom leads straight to the Entrance Hall, of course, so this is precisely the *worst* place to be as the door clicks open! Then I remember there's an Antechamber between The Ballroom and the Salon, so I scurry across the icy marble floor to hide in it. As I fling open the door I'm arrested in my tracks.

Maxine and Seb are bent over a Chippendale card table, Seb is holding a credit card and Maxine is using a rolled up £20 note to hoover a line of white powder up her nose.

"Oh!" I gawp. "This didn't just happen."

Maxine stares at me through dilated pupils. "No, Sweetie, it definitely didn't."

Seb doesn't lift his head, credit card still poised. I back out of the room, but even in that split second, I notice a squat little cabinet in the corner of the room made of very dark wood. It's beautifully inlaid with savannah wildlife in ivory and I make a mental note to check it out in the morning.

Voices echo from the Entrance Hall. Desmond is being warmly greeted by Giles, who is making the most tremendous fuss of Mr Biggles, as are Algie, Bertie, and Bailey by the sounds of it. I make a dash for the Terrace, hoping the door to the servant's stairs will be open.

It is, and I get safely up to my room, wondering why I didn't think of that in the first place.

I need to calm down, check out my sunburn, clean up, and cool off. I hop in the shower and try to wash away the memory of Seb and Maxine snorting coke, but it's seared onto my mind.

When I make it downstairs twenty minutes later, I'm wearing my black linen dress, but this time it's accessorised with a cerulean chiffon scarf and black court shoes. I hope I look professional for Desmond, alluring for Guy, and understated for Maxine, although, as I catch sight of myself in one of the massive baroque mirrors in the Entrance Hall, I realise I look more *air hostess circa 1990* – but it's too late to worry about that.

I go down to get Hatty, but it turns out she's very happy helping

Mrs Powell. They're making some 'chicken nuggets' (although they look more like home-made goujons, thankfully) and potato wedges so that Hatty doesn't have to eat with the grown-ups and can watch Disney+ instead, which is obviously no great hardship. Mrs P really is a star.

I follow voices up to the Terrace. Desmond and the Tillingfords are sitting with huge gin and tonics, chatting and laughing, their dogs dancing together and sniffing each other's bottoms with great delight. Mr Biggles is a very popular dog, and Maxine's Bichon Frisée in particular clearly thinks he's, well, the dog's bollocks.

Maxine is laughing, slightly manically, I think. I try my best not to stare at a tiny spot of white under her nose. Sebastian is nowhere to be seen – he never is at formal occasions, I realise.

"My dear," says Desmond, thankfully breaking my line of sight as he stands up to give me an extravagant air kiss. He's looking very dapper in a cream linen suit and, despite the heat, a red silk waistcoat and gold cravat that complement his dark skin. "I hear you've been a whirling dervish this week, slaving all hours to create piles for work for us this weekend!" He has such a chirpy demeanour and such a huge grin that I can't help but smile when I see him.

I'm really lucky to have him for a boss, I think as I sit on one of the shabby-chic wrought-iron chairs grouped round the similarly distressed table.

"I'm sure it's not all for Desmond's benefit, is it, Alice?" pipes Giles as he delicately picks up a slice of lemon with a set of tiny silver pincers.

I must look confused as he drops the lemon in a glass with a flick of the wrist.

"You can't deny you've taken Tillingford Hall and its denizens very much to heart," adds Giles, handing me an unasked-for but much-wanted G&T.

"Oh, do tell," says Desmond.

I take a deep sip of my drink and try not to sigh too loudly. Whatever the weather, there's nothing quite like a G&T to get the world in perspective, I always think. "I assure you it's all very professional," I say, grabbing a handful of nuts.

"We can all see you're crazy about Guy," tuts Maxine, "but he's only playing around with you, Alice. You're obviously not Lady Tillingford material, are you?" She laughs hysterically. "Oh dear, what's that?" she says, bending down towards her dog. "Coco says that sounded very rude!"

Before I can blink back the moisture pricking my tired eyes, Maxine picks up her dog and stalks off, muttering something about, "Damn these people…"

Giles looks mortified. "I do apologise for my wife," he says, giving me a sympathetic glance as he flops into a chair. "Sometimes I've had enough of her menopausal melodramas."

"Have we done anything to annoy her?" Desmond asks, and although he's looking in my direction, I'm grateful to him for saying 'we' and taking my side.

"Of course not, please just ignore her. I'm very happy with Alice's work and the way she's fitting in here. I for one would be delighted if things work out between you and Guy, Alice. He seems pretty keen on you too, and you're just what he – what *we* – need. He's a good man, and he's been lonely for a long time.

"But as for Maxine, you have to understand, she is very

private," says Giles. "That's why she's not happy about our plans to open the Hall to the public. She doesn't like people snooping around her private affairs, opening the cupboards and finding the skeletons. All families have them, after all. Perhaps ours more than most."

"Oooh," says Desmond, scooping up Mr Biggles. "Tell all!"

"Another day," says Giles, playfully tapping him on the knee.

Desmond puts his hand over Giles's and the men's eyes lock. "I can't wait! We'll be all ears, won't we, Mr Biggles?" He reaches his hand into his pocket to find a dog treat for his fat little pug and the other dogs gather round.

Giles jumps up as Guy springs onto the terrace, flushed and tousled.

"I am so sorry," gasps Guy, raking his hand through his messy hair, "there was some kind of snarl-up on the A3 round Surbiton. Police, ambulances, everything – it's taken me an hour longer than usual."

"Oh dear." Giles frowns. "I hope no one was too badly hurt. But at least you're safe, and here now," he says, enveloping Guy in a bony hug.

Desmond catches my eye and nods discreetly towards Guy with an approving glance, flooding my face with heat.

"Hi Alice," says Guy softly, giving me a gentle kiss on the cheek. *Is he just tired, or embarrassed? Or has he cooled off a bit since last weekend?* I wonder. I can't help sighing as my whole body responds to him, longing for more. I wish we'd had a chance to meet alone before facing the audience.

"Where's Hatty?" he asks.

"Having an early supper in the kitchen," I say, "so we can all have a grown-up dinner."

"Oh." He looks disappointed. "Fair enough. I was hoping to give her this." He holds out a massive bag from the Disney store.

"Oh Guy, you really shouldn't have," I say. "I'm sure she's spoiled enough already!" Although Guy knows Hatty isn't spoiled at all, and really she doesn't have all that much stuff for a little girl of her age. She will be utterly thrilled with whatever it is that he's brought, and I'm so touched he thought of her that I almost want to cry.

Maxine reappears, her nose now clean. "Hello, Darling," she says to her son, holding her cheek out for a kiss. "Mrs P says dinner can be served now, or we can wait a few minutes if you want to have a super quick shower, Guy."

"I'm famished," he says, flapping his shirt a bit to loosen it where it's clinging to him. "So I'd love to eat now, as long as you don't mind me glowing a little!"

"I like a young man with a bit of a glow," says Desmond, with a naughty chuckle.

"Then let's go in," says Giles. He throws some treats onto the lawn, shouting, "Chow down, Dogs," as he ushers us through the French doors, which he thankfully shuts behind us to keep the dogs out while we enjoy another a magnificent dinner in the fabulous Dining Room.

Chapter Seventeen

Dinner ends up being quite a laugh. I give Desmond the credit for that; he always enlivens a social occasion. With all the chatter and laughter, we've only just finished the main course by Hatty's bedtime, so I say I'll skip pudding so that I can put her to bed. Guy insists on coming with me so he can give her the bag from the Disney Store.

Inside is a wonderful Aurora's Cottage Playset, complete with a miniature Flora, Fauna, and Merryweather. I'm actually a bit envious! And such a lovely distraction means bedtime is going to take at least half an hour longer than usual.

But inside the Disney bag, there's also a present for me: a gorgeous Jo Malone candle, which I know is a really generous gift. But I'll admit I feel disappointed at first that it isn't something more personal; it feels more like the sort of present you'd give your aunt or sister than a token from a lover. But then again, should I have expected something more?

Guy lights it there and then so I can enjoy the alluring perfume, rather than just put it on a shelf and admire it (or save it to give to someone else, as I usually do with expensive gifts). The delicate *English Pear and Freesia* aroma makes my little half hour with Hatty and her new toy quite magical and totally makes up for missing the pudding… and Guy.

I don't sleep well, and I wake up stupidly early on Saturday morning feeling tired but wired about the day ahead. Sunlight is streaming through the curtains, and I decide I'm better off going for a walk than ruminating in bed. So, I get up really quietly so as not to disturb Hatty, slipping on my pink sneakers (the ones with ribbons for laces) and a cotton dress with a tiny bumble-bee-and-ladybird print. I grab a cardy – it's only a little after six in the morning, so it won't be hot yet – and go outside.

Creeping down the servants' stairs now, I remember Hatty drifting off to sleep muttering something about Guy being like Prince Philip. I was puzzled until I realised she meant the Handsome Prince in Disney's *Sleeping Beauty,* not King Charles's late father!

A smile plays on my lips, but I sigh as I open the back door. The sun shines directly into my eyes so I can scarcely see, but I'm acutely aware of the heady perfume of the sun-warmed rambling rose around the doorway. Its aphrodisiac scent heightens my physical longing for Guy, battling with my natural reticence and anxiety.

I know he *likes* me, but I really don't know whether he *fancies* me, nor how serious he is. I'm scared how I'll really feel if he wants to take things further, and whether he'll be disappointed when he realises how boring I am in bed. (I mean, I don't know if I am, I just guess I probably am; Philip and I never really spoke about sex; we just sort of got on with it.) And I've got stretch marks and cellulite, not to mention needing a wax. Worse, I'm terrified I might turn out to be just a distraction between Sahara and Chelsea. I'm not sure I could accept just having a fling; I've always believed a relationship should be meaningful and long-lasting. But Brave New Alice is wondering, just wondering, if she could let go of that this one time and just see where her feelings lead her.

As I step out onto the Terrace, I'm expecting the dogs to bark at me, but someone must have been up and fed them already. The gravel crunches behind me, and then two strong arms encircle my waist, and Guy's neat beard is tickling my neck as he kisses me, sending shivers down my spine.

"Hello, you," he says huskily.

"Hello," I reply as we turn to face each other, still entwined. He's wearing a white polo shirt and jodhpurs and smells faintly of horse. I pick a bit of straw out of his hair, and he laughs, grabbing my hand as it passes his mouth and kissing the inside of my wrist. I don't need to ask whether he's just come from the stables.

"Up already?" he says.

"I couldn't sleep," I admit. "Once it's light, that's usually it for me."

"I'm the same; I just don't get enough sleep in the summer, especially when I've got things on my mind," he says, "and no one to distract me from my own thoughts."

Then why don't we just sleep together? I want to say.

"Lovely Alice, you're so… good," he says. He kisses me softly, but I respond as passionately as I know how, so that he's in no doubt about how much I want him. When we finally pull away, he looks at me with smouldering eyes.

He takes a deep breath and exhales loudly, as if trying to regain some sense of self-control. "You're amazing, Alice," he breathes huskily in my ear, and a little bit of me that's been waking up these last two weeks is thrilled that I can turn him on. He leads me to a nearby bench surrounded by lavender and marguerites, the flowers wide awake and dancing in the morning sunshine.

He beckons to me to sit down, looking directly at me. "Alice, you're... wonderful," he sighs. "I'm bowled over by you...."

"But?" I say, my eyes pricking. "I can sense a *but*..."

"I... I think we should take things slowly," he says carefully.

My stomach, which has been fizzing with desire, thinking maybe we could go up to his room to share the last moments of the morning before the house is awake, plummets like a stone.

"I don't want to cock this up," he says. "I don't want to burden you with my baggage – and seriously, there's a shitload of it. *You* see the lovely house, the fancy car, and you think it's all rainbows and unicorns and happily ever afters..."

My eyes are starting to mist with tears. Is that what he really thinks? That I think he's some kind of fairy-tale prince come to rescue me?

"...I don't think you really understand just how much work – how much of a headache this all is," he carries on.

But I *do*, I want to say. I can feel my chin wobbling, and I don't trust myself to speak.

"Work's a load of crap, and the shit's about to hit the fan at home..."

This time I do speak. "What do you mean?"

"I can't explain now, Alice, but I'm starting to get a hunch... oh never mind," he says, leaning his elbows on his knees and raking his hands through his hair. "It's all too complicated!"

"Try me..." I say, putting my hand on his shoulder.

But he just looks at me out of the corner of his eye without moving his head, like it's really none of my business. "I can't, Alice. I'm not even sure what to think myself, and I don't want to burden you with my crap. You deserve better."

"I can't think of anyone better than you," I manage to say, and his look softens.

"Lovely Alice," he says, taking my hand and playing with the silver oak leaves on my wrist, "you hardly know me," he says, putting my wrist down, "and I hardly know you."

But sometimes you *just know*, I want to say.

"I think we could have something special," he says, looking me in the eyes, "but we've both got a lot of problems and a lot of responsibilities and a lot of history, and I don't want either of us to get hurt. So, let's just take our time."

You're hurting me now, I say with my eyes. And maybe he's right, but time is what we don't have. I'll only see him for a few hours every weekend, and I only have four more weekends after this one – and then it will be back to how it all was before, and this will all just be a dream.

His phone rings, and he swears as he picks it up.

"*Where the hell are you?*" I hear the person on the other end saying, as Guy stands up to take the call.

"At home, trying to have breakfast," he replies tetchily. "What do you expect on Saturday morning?"

"*What about the Tokyo call?*" says the voice.

"You can tell Tokyo I don't give a toss," Guy says. "It's Saturday, and I happen to have a life."

"*If you don't get on Zoom this second, we're going to lose this whole bloody deal.*"

He sighs. "OK. Then tell them I'm on the line to Zurich about the Magnetum project and that I'll join your call in two minutes," Guy says, looking at me sadly as he hangs up.

"I'm sorry, Alice," he says. "You see what it's like?

It's half six on Saturday bloody morning…" he mutters as he stalks off towards the Library, fending off a beagle.

Left behind on the bench, I rip flower heads off the lavender bush and crush them, trying to find some comfort in their soothing perfume.

Chapter Eighteen

The Kitchen is bustling as we all chip in to prepare salads, marinades, and all kinds of delicious BBQ food for Sunday lunch. I'm hoping the busyness will take my mind off our encounter on the Terrace yesterday morning, but every time Guy passes, I itch with longing. And Hatty starts to get on my nerves, poking her sticky fingers into dips and nicking the crisps, so I send her up to our room on a spurious mission.

Just as we sit down to coffee on the Terrace – like I need any caffeine, I'm so wired already – we hear wheels on the gravel, and Guy and I scoot round to the front of the house to meet our guests. Elizabeth is cutting the engine on a beaten-up classic Land Rover. Mike helps the twins out of the car while Elizabeth jumps down, dressed in a fitted navy-and-white striped swimsuit, tiny white shorts, a wide-brimmed straw hat, oversized sunnies and strappy espadrille wedges. How she drove a Land Rover in those, I cannot fathom. She looks amazing.

"I need to wear these or I can't reach the pedals," she says to me in her tinkly voice, as she notices me staring at her shoes. She turns to Guy. "Sorry we're late… Fr Matthew's sermon went on a bit!"

"Nice wheels," says Guy as Algie lopes over to investigate. "I had no idea you drove a Series One."

"I don't normally," she admits with a chiming laugh.

"I only take Bertha out for special occasions. She was my father's. We drove her across the Sahara a few times. She's an absolute pig to drive and breaks down every ten minutes, but I'm too sentimental to get rid of her. My dad died a couple of years ago, so..."

"I'm sorry," says Guy.

"Oh, don't be," she says, waving a hand in the air as Lily and Poppy dash past, chasing and being chased by Bailey and Bertie. "He was eighty-eight and had the most fabulous life. I miss him like hell, but not in a sad way. I keep Bertha so I don't forget to 'keep buggering on', as he would say."

"Where's Hatty?" Lily shrieks as Bailey chases her past me.

"Look up there," I say, pointing at the window of our room, where Hatty is waving.

"Why don't you see if you can work out where her room is?" asks Guy.

What a genius way of keeping two boisterous seven-year-olds busy, I think. He really does have an instinctive way with children.

"Will they be OK?" asks Elizabeth. "Won't they get lost?"

"Only a bit," Guy reassures her. "The house isn't THAT big! They'll be perfectly safe. Let me help you with that, Mike," he says, as the girls' dad appears, struggling with two matching unicorn backpacks, a bag of beach gear, flowers, and a huge Waitrose bag. "You didn't need to bring anything."

"Oh, don't be silly," says Elizabeth, taking the Waitrose bag and handing it to Guy. "We're going to eat you out of house and home, the least we can do is bring a few bubbles."

A couple of bottles of Veuve Clicquot Champagne clink in the bag amongst some Godiva chocolates and, oddly, a giant bag of Maltesers.

A few hours later, I flop onto a Chesterfield in the Salon, releasing a plume of dust motes into the shaft of sunlight that cuts through a chink in the curtains. Elizabeth and I agree it is simply too hot to stay outside, and we are taking full advantage of the men finally agreeing it's their turn to watch the girls.

"I'm stuffed," I admit to Elizabeth.

"Me too…," she agrees, "and I definitely shouldn't have had that last Pimms," she hiccups. "But it's not often that Mike offers to drive home."

"And I don't even have to go anywhere," I sigh, blissfully.

"Lucky you!" agrees Elizabeth, still with her enormous hat and shades on, arms flung along the sofa back, looking for all the world like a fifties Vogue cover model.

"There's always room for a Malteser, though." She passes the bag to me. They're all melty and sticking together. "I love them like this," she says, licking her fingers.

I like Elizabeth. She's clever, sassy, and a dedicated mum, and her self-confidence really rubs off on me. We sit in companionable silence for a couple of moments, mesmerised by the drone of a lone housefly slowly circling the room.

"There's something between you and Guy, isn't there?" she says, taking off her shades to eyeball me.

"Is it that obvious?"

"Maybe not from you, but it's totally obvious he adores *you*. You do realise that he's Britain's twenty-ninth most eligible bachelor?"

"What! Says who…?" I ask, baffled as to how she knows this.

"*Tatler's Little Black Book.*"

"Which of course I read *every* year," I scoff, slightly ashamed

I even know what she's talking about.

"According to them, he comes number twenty-nine, right after the Marquess of Granby."

"You meant there really *is* a Marquess of Granby?" I ask. I should probably inform myself more about the current state of the English aristocracy if I'm going to be involved with Guy.

"Apparently… although *he's* behind Tornado at number twenty-seven."

"Tornado the *rapper*?" I ask incredulously.

"You mean you've heard of him?" Elizabeth says, turning to me with mock surprise.

"Yes… I am at least *vaguely* aware of what goes on in the world of popular culture."

"Tornado's hot property – he's rich, *single*, and well… *grrrrr…*" she growls, making her hands into claws. "Have you seen those muscles? Although I can't imagine I'd be *his* type." She says, with a theatrical sigh as she gets up to peer at some photos on a table. "But Guy…" she studies one of the photos intently. "I can't deny he's a fox. You'd make a lovely couple."

That Barbie pink colour is rising in my cheeks again. "You think so?" I ask, getting up to look at the pictures with her.

"Why not…?" she says, picking up a silver-framed portrait of Guy in a gown and mortarboard.

"He's way out of my league," I say, taking the picture from her and feeling that usual thrill as I look at him. He was handsome and self-confident even at twenty-one, when some men are still gawky.

"I wouldn't have said so, Alice. You're a graceful, fantastically well-educated woman. You're just the kind of person who could stand by Guy's side and help him run an estate like this," she says, peering at a photo of Lord Tillingford and the late Queen.

"So… I'm fairly clever," I say, putting down the graduation picture. "But I'm not very glamorous…"

She scrutinises me, her head to one side. "Glamour's only skin-deep, Alice. It's nothing a good haircut and a couple of shopping trips couldn't sort out."

"I don't mean my clothes, I mean… I don't have any… *mystique*."

"*Mystique?*" she scoffs.

"You know what I mean!" I say, reddening.

She pulls a face.

"I *mean* I'm not like Sahara Seaton-Smyth."

"Well, who is? And why would it matter anyway?" she asks, clearly exasperated.

"They used to be engaged," I explain, picking up a picture of Sahara, Sebastian and Guy as teenagers dressed in riding gear, all hugging a big black horse.

"Did they?" says Elizabeth. "But she's engaged to James now – supposedly – although the gossip in the village is that *HELLO!* misreported it. I mean, you can't pin James down. He might be living with Sahara, but he's definitely having a thing with Laura from the shop. And I found him in the storeroom at the shop with Darcy the shop assistant the other day. And Laura's friend Nadia was all over him..."

"I think Guy's still in love with Sahara," I interrupt, tears pricking my eyes.

"Everyone's in love with Sahara! How can you not be?"

"That's what I mean, Elizabeth... *mystique*, *charisma*, that certain *je ne sais quoi*." I pick up another photo of Sahara that looks like it comes from that infamous first Vogue cover shoot, but when I thrust it at Elizabeth, she just shrugs.

"She's only seventeen in that picture – have you seen her recently? And anyway, the next Lady Tillingford needs to be a rational, hard-working woman with a good head on her shoulders," says Elizabeth, flomping back down on the sofa. "Not some spoiled, dreamy, drug-addled loon."

I'm speechless. Elizabeth certainly doesn't mind telling it like it is.

"It must be rather lovely spending the summer holidays somewhere like this!" she says, stretching her arms along the sofa and throwing her head back.

"Yes, it really is," I say, thankful to her for changing the subject. "Although obviously it's not a holiday for me," I say, picking up a photo of Maxine with Darcy Bussell and three tiny little ballet girls. I momentarily wonder where our children are, but I remind myself they're in good hands.

"I know you're working," says Elizabeth, "but it's still a break from London. And you've got the weekends. It's the closest any of us will ever come to actually living in a house like this." She gets up again and wanders round the room, studying the furniture and paintings.

"I wonder who this handsome fellow is?" she asks, pointing to a faded colour picture on the piano of a gorgeous blond man hugging a teenage girl. I'm about to say it's Guy, when I realise it's someone different, older. I pick up the picture and look closer; his face is so familiar. I'm wondering where I've seen him before.

"I think it must be an uncle or a cousin of Guy's," I say.

Then it comes to me.

He looks just like Sir Nicholas Tillingford in that fake Regency portrait from the Billiards Room.

Suddenly, the girls come crashing in, still in wet swimsuits and flip-flops. So much for the men keeping an eye on them.

"Mummy, Mummy!" says Hatty, holding up a small, clear plastic bag. "We found some sherbet. Can we have some? I haven't had sherbet for ages. There's some Haribos too."

"Sherbet?" I ask, taking the packet from her.

"It *looks* like sherbet," she says.

Elizabeth snatches the lurid packet of sweets from Hatty and examines it closely. Then she turns to me with a look of terror.

They are not Haribos, but 'eddies'. I only know this because the police sent a circular about the hash-laden gummies to all the parents at Hatty's school, and it looks like Elizabeth knows this too. And I'm pretty sure the white powder is not sherbet.

"Where did you get these?" I ask, trying not to sound hysterical.

Hatty looks at the other two, slightly shifty. "In a box."

"Where?" I demand as Elizabeth looks on in disgust.

"You know that little room near the Ballroom, there's a box with animals on it. We were playing with the Box of Shame, and we found a new key that fits the Animal Box. Inside there were some sweeties and some sherbet – and some money, but of course, we left that there. *Please* can we have some? You never let me have sweets! *Please*, Mummy."

It's true I'm a bit mean with sweets and this is only going to compound Hatty's low opinion of me in that department. "Why don't we go to the Kitchen and get you some biscuits?" I say. "And there might be some ice cream, too."

"Oh *pleeeeease*," says Poppy, while Lily grumbles that they want *sweets* and Elizabeth ticks them off for being rude.

"These ones are out of date and might give you a tummy ache," I pronounce, congratulating myself on my quick thinking. "We've got some much nicer things in the Kitchen."

The girls reluctantly follow us downstairs where I put the offending articles on a high shelf and start to rummage in the freezer, while Elizabeth does an impression of a cat chewing a wasp.

"Oh, *there* they are," says Guy as he walks in.

"*You* should have been keeping an eye on them," Elizabeth snaps.

Guy looks questioningly at me.

"I'll explain in a minute," I say with a scowl. "Elizabeth, why don't you take the girls in the garden with their ice cream, and I can speak to Guy?"

"Actually, I think we'll go home, if it's all the same to you," she says in a slightly wobbly voice.

"Nooo, Mummy! *Pleeease* can we stay?" Lily pleads.

"No, Girls, it's definitely home time."

"What's happened?" Guy mouths at me.

"I'll tell you later," I hiss.

And so, our party comes abruptly to a close as Elizabeth and Mike rush their daughters away from the den of iniquity that is Tillingford Hall.

"It's not Hatty's fault," I plead with Elizabeth as she shoves the kids' bags into the back of the Land Rover.

"Of course not!" she says tetchily. "And I know it's not yours either, but I don't feel it's safe for Lily and Poppy here – too many hazards and hidey-holes and places for them to get lost. We'll have Hatty over to ours, where I can keep an eye on them…" she slams the hatch shut, "*when* I feel up to it. And I'll make sure I've got some sniffer dogs on the doorstep to check her out." She attempts a smile, but her eyes are blazing.

I know she's trying to lighten the situation, but I'm distraught, and I'm sure it shows.

"I'm not blaming *you*," she tuts crossly. "See you soon, no doubt."

And they're off in a spray of gravel.

"Why did they go so quickly?" says Hatty in tears. "Did I do something bad?"

"No, Hatty. It's not your fault. In fact, you were a very good girl. You were absolutely right to ask permission before trying those sweets." I'm torn between wanting to preserve her innocence and keeping her safe by educating her. "I know they looked like sweets, but they're actually not what they look like and could have made you very sick."

"Are they those bad gummies the policeman told us about?" she sniffs, wide-eyed with shock.

"Yes, Hatty," I say, folding her into my arms.

"But why were they *here*?!" she wails. "Who do they belong to? Are they Guy's?"

"What are you talking about, Hatty?" says Guy as he approaches, dismayed to see her in tears.

"I'll explain in a minute, Guy." I turn to Hatty. "No, I'm sure they're not Guy's. They were locked away by someone who wanted to keep them secret – and safe from little girls who shouldn't have been snooping around. Now, how about you have a bit of quiet time in front of the TV?"

Hatty agrees to this, and I grab a tissue to wipe her snotty nose. Guy sets her up with *Sleeping Beauty* in the Snug, while I go and find her a dress and some squash.

Chapter Nineteen

When Hatty's safely ensconced in the Snug, dressed and sipping a drink, Guy closes the Kitchen door firmly behind us and says crossly, "Will you now please tell me exactly what just happened?"

I look over my shoulder, go over to the high shelf, take down the baggie, and hand it to him. "Tell me what this is."

He eyes me suspiciously and dips a finger in the white powder. "It's coke," he says.

I hand him the gummies, but this time he looks puzzled. I explain what 'eddies' are. Apparently, City financiers don't particularly go for them; they're aimed at younger – and less well-heeled – clientele.

"So, you've decided to follow Sahara into the drugs scene?" he says, handing them back to me.

"Guy, that's not even funny!" I shout, slamming my hand into the table. "The girls found these in that inlaid African cabinet in the Antechamber, where they were playing when *you* were meant to be supervising them."

He's clenching his teeth and a vein twitches in his neck as he faces me across the scrubbed oak. "Do you really think I can keep track of three tiny beings in this massive place?" he grumbles, waving his arms around in exasperation.

"Well, yes, actually, that *was* the idea," I say, wondering –

probably unfairly – whether this man is going to find any parenting skills when he needs them.

"But what were these… things… doing in the African cabinet?" he asks, then "Herbert…" he mutters under his breath.

"Oh my God, Guy! Talk about unconscious bias! They're your mum's!"

"What the…?" he swears.

"On Friday evening, just before you got home, when we were having drinks on the Terrace, your mum was a bit… *lively.* She had white powder on her nose, but she must've wiped it off just before you arrived."

"And you didn't think to tell me?" He's genuinely angry now, but I need to stand up for myself; none of this is *my* fault.

"Why would I? I'm an art curator not a police officer! It's not really my place to say, *Oh hello, Boss, your mum's doing coke!* Is it? Is that what you would've done in my position?" I'm also not going to mention Seb and make things even more complicated.

But Guy looks angry enough to lash out, and I don't have to say anything for him to draw his own conclusions. "Damn Sebastian!" he spits… "I bet he knows about this. Those little girls could have died! He's bloody well going to pay for this!" He stomps off.

"Guy! Wait…" I put my hand on his arm.

"What?" he says as he spins round.

"Please, just calm down and hear me out! Hatty got into that cabinet because she was showing the Box of Shame to the Twins."

"What's the Box of Shame?" asks Guy.

I promised Giles I wouldn't tell, but this could get very

messy if Guy doesn't understand what's going on. "It's a box of orphan keys that your father gave me to try out around the house. He encouraged me to involve Hatty, to give her something to do, but he asked me to keep it a secret. I didn't think Hatty would go off and snoop around with the Box on her own. She doesn't normally do things like that; she was just showing off to Lily and Poppy. But if you go to your mother about this, at best she'll make it difficult for me to access all areas of the house – at worst she'll tell Giles to sack me! So please stop and think!"

At least that gets him to pause.

I take a deep breath and go on: "I think these things might all be related: the fakes and forgeries, the drugs, the..." I'm about to mention Seb and Maxine fooling around in the Shrubbery but decide to spare him that one... for now. "But I don't know how. Maybe I've been watching too many police dramas, and I'm just imagining things. I need more time to work things out before we go round accusing people."

"OK, but I still need to talk to Seb," says Guy, a bit calmer. "He can't stay here if he's getting involved in all this stuff again. I can't have him anywhere near Sahara if he's not clean."

"So, this is all about protecting Sahara..." I say, sitting down and gripping the table.

"Of course not!" he insists, sitting opposite me. "It's about everything – Hatty's safety, my mum's well-being. It's about my family's reputation!" He runs his hands through his hair.

"Why do you keep helping Sebastian, when he's so much trouble?" I ask.

"Because he is... *was*... my best mate. He's a kind of second son to my mum and dad."

Whatever your mother thinks of him, it's not that, I think.

But how can I possibly tell him?

"I loved him once, and I pity him now," he says grimly. "And it's safer to keep him where I can see him."

Guy walks out of the Kitchen and stalks towards the trees where Neville is usually parked. I follow because I have to know what he's going to say. I'm terrified Maxine will use this invasion of her privacy to send me and Hatty home, and I can't bear to leave Tillingford Hall in shame with my work half done.

When I catch up with Guy, he's standing by an oak tree, staring at Neville the camper van. It's bouncing up and down in a way that suggests Seb is either practising his Scottish country dancing or…

"He's back at least," Guy says grimly. "He's usually in Bath at the weekends."

"Guy, just leave it," I say, putting my hand on his arm. Leaf shadows flick patterns across our skin.

"Who's he with?" Guy asks me.

"Do you think I know?" I ask.

Guy hesitates just long enough for me to hear a small, dry tap as an early acorn falls to the ground. "Yes," he says bitterly. "I think there's a lot you know that you haven't been telling me."

"Some things are best not known." I whisper.

"*Do* you know?" he asks, his eyes boring into me.

I purse my lips. "I've got a pretty good idea, but I don't want to say."

"It's Mum, isn't it?" he says, looking up into the canopy of the trees.

"I can't be sure… maybe he's practising his kung fu in there.

But they were being very intimate by the pool the other day, so it's a distinct possibility," I admit.

Guy picks up his phone.

"What are you doing?" I ask as he speed dials someone from his favourites.

From inside the van, a tinny version of *Wake Me Up Before You Go Go* starts up.

"She's in there all right. Shit!" says Guy, leaning back against the oak and staring up into the canopy. "Alice, I'm sorry. I've had enough." He gets up and starts heading back towards the house. "I'm going back to London."

"OK," I say, scurrying to keep up with his frantic pace.

We go into the house through the door by the Library, and Guy turns to me with a deep frown. "Look, Alice, this isn't your fault, but I've got a lot of shit to sort out."

"I can see that," I say, aware of how inadequate that sounds, but keen for him not to get away until I've answered more questions. "This may not be the best moment, Guy, and I understand that you need to go, but there's something I really need to ask you. I don't know when I'll get another chance."

"OK…" And at least he sounds intrigued, if impatient.

"It's about a picture in the Salon…" I lead him through to the Salon and point out the handsome blond man in the picture on the piano who looks like Sir Nicholas Tillingford. "Who's this?" I ask.

"That's a family friend, Brad Masters," he answers, "with his daughter, Chelsea – you know, the one Mum said is coming over soon. Why do you ask? What are you thinking?" he questions urgently.

"Oh, nothing… I just… "

"Alice, please stop hiding things from me!" His eyes are boring into me.

"I just thought they might be your cousins or something," I say, putting the photo down.

"No, no relation," he says, rubbing the corner of the cabinet with his finger, his frown deepening.

"How uncanny," I say. "He looks just like Sir Nicholas Tillingford."

Guy suddenly looks very tired.

"Are you OK?" I ask, reaching out to touch his hand, but he rakes it through his hair before I make contact, his other hand firmly in his pocket.

"Alice… my life is falling apart," he says. "Can you tell me why, wherever I look, the walls are crumbling down and you seem to be standing there with a sledgehammer?"

But before I can even begin to think of framing an answer, he's already left.

Chapter Twenty

That night, I have vivid nightmares about three little girls on hospital trolleys with drips in their arms, surrounded by medics while I'm trapped outside, looking through the windows, unable to get in. A doctor who looks just like Sir Nicholas Tillingford turns round and stares at me through the glass. And I wake up with a start, sure that Guy will never speak to me again and that Elizabeth must hate me.

When I come down for breakfast, I'm surprised to see Desmond there with his pug in an otherwise empty kitchen. My heart lifts slightly.

"Good morning, Desmond. I thought you'd be back in London by now," I say, slumping down at the breakfast table with my cereal.

"I'll be going up later this morning – I'm due some leave and I didn't want to rush. Giles has gone out to walk his dogs while Mr Biggles and I take our time."

"Well, it's nice to see you anyway," I say, truthfully. Here at least is someone I haven't annoyed… yet.

"My dear Alice, you look like you've lost a pound and found a penny. What's the matter?" he says, pushing a freshly poured mug of tea towards me before giving Mr Biggles a titbit of jammy toast.

I decide to tell him, not least because I'm worried Maxine

might have me sacked, and I think it's best he's forewarned.

He listens quietly and without judgement.

"I wish I wasn't the one digging up all these skeletons," I conclude as I take my empty bowl over to the dishwasher.

"The truth was bound to come out eventually," he says, carrying more crockery over to the sink. "Maybe you've done him a favour in the long run."

"I doubt he'll see it that way *now*. He seems to be blaming *me* for everything, and if Maxine finds out, that might be the end of our project." I grip the side of the sink and take a deep breath.

"Don't worry, Alice, I'll see that doesn't happen," he says, putting his hand on my shoulder. "And, about Guy, anyone can see he's crazy about you."

"If he was, I don't think he is now," I say, picking up a J-cloth. "He walked off yesterday with barely a backward glance."

"He had a lot on his mind by the sound of it," says Desmond.

"And what about Sahara?" I ask, wiping the table.

"What do you mean?"

"Sahara Seaton-Smyth. You know, the supermodel? He used to be engaged to her. And there's Chelsea, this American heiress who's visiting soon. I thought she might be a cousin, but it turns out, she isn't related to him at all and so could easily be lining up."

"And what about Philip?" asks Desmond.

"What do you mean?"

"Think about it," he says. "You see your ex every couple of weeks, speak to him most days on WhatsApp. *You* know how you feel about Philip, but does Guy? Do you think it's easy for him having Hatty and your ex on the scene?"

"But we're divorced…"

"You've *both* got baggage, Alice, but maybe you can help each other carry it," he says, picking up Mr Biggles who lets out a little fart. "I need to get back to London now, but I hope you'll come with me to Christie's on Wednesday? It's seventeenth- and eighteenth-century portraiture, and Angus has given me a budget of £150,000. We could pick up something nice. The lots I'm interested in will come up around three, so let me buy you lunch before that. Sounds like you need a bit of a distraction."

I hesitate, wondering about Hatty and whether I can face the travelling. "Thank you, Desmond. I'd really appreciate that; it'll be a good opportunity to pop into the Gallery and catch up with a couple of people."

Once he's gone, though, I can't concentrate on my work. It's muggy, and I'm tired and upset. Around ten, there's a knock, and Mrs Powell pokes her head round the door. She's holding a large bouquet of flowers which she's arranged in a vase.

She doesn't look too pleased. "Where do you want these, Ducky?"

"Who are they from?" I ask, but with a skip in my heart, I know the answer already. The note reads:

> Sorry about yesterday. Looking forward to this weekend. Love, Guy X.

I detach the card, knowing I'll want to read it again and again throughout the day.

"Seems our Honourable really has taken a shine to you," Mrs P says, pursing her lips.

I try not to look too pleased, but my heart is doing a mad tattoo in my chest. "They are lovely," I say, "but I'm not sure it's a good idea to have them in here – what if the water spills? Would you enjoy having them in the Kitchen?"

"Not particularly, dear," she says crisply.

"Then I'll have them in my room," I suggest.

"Right, then," she sighs, obviously not relishing the trek up to the garret on the top floor.

"I'll take them up myself."

"Don't trouble yourself, Ducky," she replies, "I'll take them up."

So, I leave her to it, feeling awkward and thanking her profusely.

After that, my morning goes a bit better. I make myself concentrate, promising myself that I'll re-read his card and think more about what it means when I've done another hour. It's a strategy that works – if only slightly.

Just before I go down to have elevenses with Hatty, I look at the card again. He's looking forward to the weekend. He knows it's a Hatty-free one, so presumably he's looking forward to spending it with me. He signed off with *love* and an *x* – both indicate affection, but perhaps nothing more. And he apologised, even though he had good reason to be cross.

All good enough, I suppose, but I'm longing for him – and for the reassurance that he feels as passionate about me as I do about him. My very soul aches at the thought that I might never have that.

But during the week, Guy calls a few times. He apologises for the way he spoke, and I apologise for… well, *everything*. And then we talk a bit about what happened to the girls. He says it's testament to my excellent parenting skills that Hatty asked whether she could have the sweets, rather than just taking them and doling them out like many children would have done. What might have happened is unthinkable – it was the good discipline I'd instilled in Hatty which saved their lives. I am so grateful to him for turning it around and making me look good.

And he hasn't mentioned sledgehammers again.

Luckily, Elizabeth says something similar when she phones a couple of days later, so we're all good, if still shaken. Elizabeth wants to tell the police, but I explain as discreetly as possible that it really wouldn't help my position here and if she could please let Guy deal with it in his own way, that would be much more helpful.

I was so shocked about what could have happened to the girls that I haven't really thought about the wider implications, from Guy's perspective, of all the other things that happened last weekend. But Elizabeth and Guy's votes of confidence have allowed me to move on from the horror of what could have happened and to start thinking about how you'd feel if your best mate was having an affair with your mum.

I mean, *ew*.

Admittedly, Maxine is very young for a mum. I think she was only twenty when she had Guy – and I can definitely see how she could be in the MILF category, but still… poor Guy. And poor Giles.

And then there's the whole Sebastian question – did *he* get Maxine into drugs? I point out to Guy that she may well have been taking drugs before Seb was even born. He admits that it's more than likely – for all we know, it might even have been the other way round. At that point, the possibility that this has been going on for years dawns on us, and that thought really doesn't make either of us feel any better.

I hate that I'm the one who's opened this can of worms, although I know it's not really my fault. But I'm grateful that Guy is confiding in me and using me as a sounding board, even though he sounds guarded, like there's still a lot he's not telling me.

It's always really hard to hang up because our little chats become increasingly intimate as we drift off to sleep with our phones in hand, albeit I'm very careful about what I say with Hatty in the bed next to mine, even if she is asleep.

Chapter Twenty-one

So, when Friday comes round and he arrives a bit early, I'm not too surprised. He comes into the Collections Room around four and, once we've disentangled ourselves from each other, tells me I should take Hatty to her Granny's myself. Apparently, he's got something he needs to do, but he's looking forward to spending the evening with me.

I always find it hard to drop Hatty off with her dad. I know I should be glad that he wants to be involved, but I'm so used to having her around that it's a wrench when she goes. And sometimes she grumbles that he's strict with her, which is saying something, because I'm not exactly laid back. Hatty also implied that last time, he didn't actually get there until Saturday lunchtime. Granny's already told her the same is going to happen this weekend, so she's spending more time with Granny than her father.

When I get back to Tillingford Hall, supper is in the Kitchen as Maxine is in London and no one can be bothered to eat in the Dining Room when she's not around. It's just Guy, Giles, and me. The atmosphere is subdued and tense. Guy seems impatient and I'm certainly desperate to get him on my own, while Giles seems thoughtful.

But now, finally, Guy is leading me into the garden, my hand in his, and a couple of glasses of chilled Sancerre have relaxed me. He stops, takes my wrist, and looks at my oak-leaf bracelet.

"You wear this all the time, don't you?" he says.

When I nod, he says how pretty it is. "There's a beautiful folly the other side of the lake," he says. "Have you found it yet?"

I admit that I haven't.

"Pan's Pavilion they call it," he says. "Legend says that if you dance naked in the Pavilion at midnight on Midsummer's Eve, your true love will appear before your eyes."

I laugh. "That doesn't sound like a real English country tradition. It sounds like a recent invention. I mean, sleeping in the Pavilion with seven different wildflowers entwined in your hair sounds feasible, or at least it's the kind of whimsical notion some romantic poet would have made up in about 1820. But dancing naked sounds far too Bacchanalian – not the sort of thing nice Hampshire maidens would do!"

"It *was* a recent invention," agrees Guy, brushing his hand against a lavender bush with a bemused smile.

"You just made it up, didn't you?" I say, giving him a shove in the arm.

He smirks, handing me a stalk he's broken off the bush.

"Anyway, it's the end of July, not midsummer," I point out, relaxing as I inhale that beautiful fragrance.

"Sometimes, Alice, I think you're way too analytical," he says, laughing. We stop to admire a rose bush and he squeezes my hand.

"It has been mentioned before! I probably just spend too much time staring at pictures of dead people. I know I need to get out more. That's why I came here."

"I come here to get away," he says, burying his nose in a swirl of red petals.

"Then we meet in the middle," I say, laughing. He beckons for me to smell the rose too. It might be the most deeply perfumed bloom I've ever smelt, or is it the magic of being in love on a warm summer's evening?

We arrive at the Lake, and Guy grabs the oars of a slightly rotten-looking skiff, beckoning for me to get in.

"Is this safe?" I ask, prodding it with my foot.

"There's no water in the bottom of the boat," he points out, "so we can assume it's sound. As for safe..." he waggles his eyebrows roguishly, "well, who's to say?" Catching sight of my face, he says, "I'm just teasing, Alice. The lake is no more than four-foot deep. Do you want to row, or shall I?"

"I'll enjoy watching you," I say getting in. Did I just say that out loud?

"Oh yeah, I'm so dench…" he says in a Multicultural London English accent as he takes up the oars.

But he *is*: muscular and handsome. I used to think a man's physicality meant nothing to me, but now I'm older, more confident as a woman, watching Guy's muscles ripple under his well-fitting shirt as he rows turns me on.

But it's not just that – he's such a gentleman, so sweet and kind, and funny, too. I'm aching with longing as I think how much I want him, and although we've been getting really close this week, I'm not sure how slow *going slow* is going to be. Worse, after the way he spoke last weekend, I wonder whether we'll ever really get our relationship off the ground, and my inner being almost breaks in two at the thought.

It's not long before we touch down on the opposite bank. Guy ties the boat to a dodgy-looking jetty with a frayed painter and helps me out. The jetty creaks and sways as we walk along it, and the damp scent of bulrushes and pond weed waft around us.

"I'd love to get this fixed someday," he says, "but the roof is my priority this year. Long-term, my dream is to have a glamping site and make this a wild swimming pond for the campers. It always was a dipping pond but it was difficult to keep up without the staff, and my mother hated it, which is why we had the new swimming pool done. This one doesn't have a natural filtration system like it should, so it's slimy at the bottom, just like the Ornamental Pond," he says, looking at me with a smile and a raised eyebrow and I colour, remembering our first meeting.

Beyond a thicket of laurels, in the gathering gloom, is a circular folly, like a tiny Roman temple, lit by dozens of fat candles in storm lanterns. Guy must have come down to light them all while I was dropping Hatty off. The effect is magical.

In the grove outside the temple is a statue of the cheeky god, Pan, playing his pipes, with one of his little goaty legs flipped up in a dancing pose. As I step closer to gaze at him, I hear a pop.

"Champagne?" asks Guy.

He pours a glass from a dark bottle dripping with water fresh from an ice bucket. I've already had two glasses of Sancerre, but who could refuse such an offer?

"Come and sit," he says, handing me the crystal champagne flute and indicating the carved stone seats, made comfy with silk cushions and half a dozen cosy throws. We take a few sips of champagne in silence.

"Alice," says Guy, clearing his throat. "I've got you something." I'm intrigued as he takes a small rectangular velvet box out of his pocket and hands it to me. "Open it," he says.

Inside is a silver necklace with an exquisitely detailed acorn pendant. "It's lovely!" I gasp as I reach out to touch the cool metal the colour of moonlight.

"It goes with your bracelet," he explains. "Let me help you put it on."

I lift my hair, and his warm hands brush my neck as he does up the clasp. I put my hand to my throat and feel the little knobbly acorn there; I want to wear this every day. As Guy moves back to face me, the look in his eyes sets a fire burning in me.

"Alice," he says, taking my hand. "I don't think I can…"

"What?" I say, dismayed at those words crashing into this perfect moment, willing him to finish the fateful sentence that he's hesitating over.

"I don't think I can go slow anymore," he says at last. "I've realised why you're there as my old life's crumbling apart."

"What, Guy? Tell me, explain what you mean!"

"I need you, Alice. All my life I've been looking for someone just like you, and just as everything else is changing and I don't know what the future holds, there you are."

Then he takes my hand and kisses it, sending bolts of electricity coursing up my body. He traces the line of my arm with his lips until our mouths meet in the deepest, sweetest kiss I've ever experienced.

Eventually, we pull away, and through the tears of sheer joy gathering in my eyes, I see his eyes are brimming too.

"Be my future, Alice," he says, and my heart is so full, I can't reply.

As the stars gradually turn overhead, there's more kissing and more champagne. Our hearts entwine to the song of the summer evening: a nightingale's melody, soft rustling in the woods, the call of an owl. Our names are whispered to the wind, our bodies close, sharing warmth as the cool of the night creeps upon us.

Hours later, I wake, shivering and slightly confused. In the guttering light of the candles, I search for something to put on. Guy stirs beside me and pulls me towards him. "Beautiful Alice," he murmurs, kissing my shoulder.

"Cold Alice," I say.

He replies huskily, "I can warm you up… but, yes, maybe we could go to bed?" We dress quickly, fighting the instinct to take everything off again. He says to leave the glasses – he'll tidy them up in the morning – but wraps a big plaid throw around me and helps me into the boat. I feel like the Lady of the Lake escorted by her Knight. And I laugh at the thought that, officially, that's exactly what he is – or at least what his ancestors were.

Chapter Twenty-two

Late the next morning, I ease awake, suffused with a sense of wellbeing. And then the realisation that I'm not alone in bed steals over me.

I dare not breathe as I bask in the heat emanating from Guy's body, afraid of waking him and ending this moment, but then I hear him stir. I can't resist rolling over to look at him. He moves at the same time, and we come face-to-face, gazing at each other goofily.

"Hello," he says gruffly.

"Hello." I whisper, my smile stretching from ear to ear.

We lie and stare at each other for a few moments, before he reaches across and kisses my forehead. "Alice."

"Guy."

"You're beautiful," he says.

"Thank you. And you're the most gorgeous man I've ever known." I say, with complete sincerity.

His face crinkles with a self-deprecating smirk, but he must surely know how handsome he is.

"Guy?"

"Yes?"

"What happened to 'I think we need to take things slowly because we've got so much baggage'?"

"Ah, yes, well… about that…"

I prop myself up on my elbow so I can look at him properly.

"I *have* got a shitload of baggage," he says, "more than I ever realised, apparently, and you're not exactly unburdened are you, Darling?"

I shake my head.

"Yet here we are," he says.

"Yes, indeed… here we are."

"So, I guess we'll have to carry it together." He reaches for me, enfolding me in his strong arms, and our lips meet in a passionate kiss. Our bodies simply *fit*, and I've never felt more safe or right. That little *but what if?* voice has gone quiet for now, and I manage to inhabit this moment fully, so certain of Us being A Good Thing. For now, it works. I don't need to think about *forever*.

I don't need to think at all.

When we wake up again, it's full daylight, but sunshine isn't bursting through the curtains. When Guy lets me go, I get up to look out of the window and see rain pelting down over the estate.

"Fancy a ride in the rain?" asks Guy, stroking my back as I sit down.

"Is that some kind of euphemism?" I say, coyly.

"No, I literally meant that the horses need exercising. Do you want to ride with me?"

"I've never ridden a horse before," I say, rolling over. New Alice would definitely be up for a ride, but even New Alice isn't sure this is the weather for it. "I don't mind walking in the rain, or even swimming. But I think my first horse ride should be on a nice, sunny day, don't you?"

"Fair enough – they'll just have to get fat. Mum won't be pleased, but she knows if she wants to keep the bally things, she has to look after them. She can't expect Herbert and Seb to do everything, and we can't afford a full-time groom."

"Oh poor you…"

He throws a pillow at me. "I know how that sounds, but there used to be a staff of nearly a hundred people running this house before the Second World War. That should give you an idea of how much we've cut back having just three – including Seb, who hardly counts. I'm not sure how much he actually gets done… apart from entertaining my mother..." he says bitterly.

He's right, of course; I wonder how they do manage to keep the Hall ticking over. The cleaning alone would take a full-timer, especially as a lot of it ought to be done by specialists. I guess that's why so many corners of the house are dusty or shut up – and why most of the garden isn't quite as manicured as it could be.

"Anyway," says Guy, his beard tickling my neck as he kisses me behind the ear. "I can think of plenty of other ways to spend a rainy Saturday morning."

Eventually he creeps downstairs to make us some breakfast while I run us a bath, and we enjoy toast and tea surrounded by luxurious bubbles. I feel totally blissed out and never want this magical moment to end. I try to ignore the little clock in the back of my mind that's telling me that in just over a day, he'll be leaving for London, and I'll have to wait five days to see him again.

Only this time, I won't have him to myself because Chelsea will be visiting. I'm desperate to know more about her, not least to reassure myself that she really is just a family friend and that there's no history there, but now isn't the moment to ask.

When the water's turning chilly and I'm wrinkly like a prune, Guy helps me out of the bath. We dry each other slowly, exploring each other's bodies, hungrily claiming possession of this new territory.

Now I feel like I really know what making love is. Sex with Philip was merely functional, and before him, I had a few awkward fumbles with my first boyfriend. But last night, for the first time in my life, I felt true passion, and it scares and delights me in equal measure.

Scares me because Guy has said so much and yet so little. I have no doubt about his attraction for me, but as for his intentions, his commitment – I can't be sure, and I don't know if he even knows himself. If I've thrown myself away on a fling, a momentary passion, I don't regret it; our time together has been blissful.

But I *am* scared about how I'll deal with the rejection, the loneliness, if this isn't for real, because I already know I am deeply in love with Guy. It's not just the chemistry, his looks, his status (though who can't forgive Lizzy Bennet for thinking differently about Mr Darcy when she sees Pemberley for the first time?), but the very soul of this man who shares my passion for beauty and history; his work ethic, his kindness. I know there's a lot I don't know about Guy, but what I do know, I have come to love, to adore, in this short time.

I'm utterly smitten, and I'm scared of how I'll cope if this turns out to be just a holiday romance.

Chapter Twenty-three

It's Friday again, and I haven't seen Guy since four on Monday morning, when he tore back to London to get to the office at his usual ungodly hour of six because he said he couldn't bear to leave me until he absolutely had to. I've missed him so much, but now that I feel secure in the knowledge that we really are together, I want to do everything I can for him. That means doing my best to finish the catalogue so we can see exactly what's going on.

I'm utterly spent, what with late nights facetiming Guy and early mornings working before Hatty gets up. So, when I get a text saying Guy's coming home early, I shut down my PC and get ready to meet him by the pool. Somehow, whether because of Guy or my daily swim toning me up, I feel body confident enough to abandon my kaftan and lie on a lounger by the pool in just my swimsuit. This time I put on plenty of sunblock and allow myself to drift off, only jerking awake when I hear someone approach.

Guy's got two drinks on a tray, with ice, lemon, and even little cocktail umbrellas. My heart lifts as I see him, handsomer than ever, bringing me a little treat, just to show how much he cares, even though he's just driven for hours to get here. I sigh and sit up, butterflies in my tummy.

He puts down the tray and kisses me wordlessly and deeply. As he pulls back, his look burning into my eyes, he says, "Alice, my darling Alice, I've missed you so much."

"And I've missed you," I reply.

"You look gorgeous… and very hot!" he says with a mischievous smile, grabbing an ice cube and dropping it down my cleavage.

I jump up, shrieking and laughing.

"You bastard!" I squeak as I slap him, wriggling as I try to get the ice cube out. "Get it out, get it out!" I shriek, bending over to see if gravity might help.

"OK," he says with a Sean Connery smile, shoving his hand down my swimsuit. I'm bending over with his hand inside my cossie, cracking up with laughter, when a tall blonde woman with oversized sunglasses and a fluorescent pink sarong stalks towards us. Guy's beside himself with laughter as I straighten up and try not to squeal as the ice cube wends its way further down my body.

"Guy!" the woman screams in a raucous American accent, a look of shock and disgust on her face. "What the hell are you doing?! And who's *this*?" she spits.

Guy draws a sharp breath. "Chelsea, this is my girlfriend, Alice."

"*Girlfriend*?" she squeaks. "Guy! *What the*…? When you said you wanted to talk, I thought you'd finally…" she hesitates, looking between me and him with a look of anguish on her face. "I thought we understood each other, Guy – I mean, I'm like your girl-next-door," she says, pushing her huge sunglasses up into her blonde coiffure.

"From *Boston*?" he laughs bitterly.

"You *know* what I mean, Honey! We've been so close for so long…"

Guy looks at me momentarily with a mixture of panic and apology in his eyes.

"I thought we were… you know. I mean, I thought we were…" she gabbles, tears springing into her eyes. "I love you, Guy!" she wails.

"I love you too, Chelsea," he protests. "But not *that* way," he adds firmly.

"Oh my God!" she says, the tears are streaming down her face now. "When you messaged me about us having 'a closer bond', I thought you meant…" she gulps. "You said we had an important appointment in London tomorrow, I thought you were…. *about to propose*! That's why I got an earlier flight and came straight here, so we could finally spend an evening together."

"*Propose*? Shit! I'm sorry, Chelsea… nothing could be further from my intentions than that…"

"What the crap *did* you mean?" she says, slapping him.

She's crying properly now, and Guy enfolds her in a hug and she leans into him as he comforts her. I'm wishing the ground would swallow me up.

"I'll just… go and get Hatty," I mutter, creeping away.

"Yeah, Bitch, why don't you just take a running jump – whoever the hell you are?" spits Chelsea over Guy's shoulder.

"Chelsea, calm down!" Guy orders, then mouths 'Sorry' at me and pulls an apologetic face as he gently rubs Chelsea's back.

I can't leave fast enough, but the ice cube is still wending its way down my body, making it very hard to move in a dignified way. I squeak as it hits its target, raising what sounds like a small snarl from Chelsea.

I thought Guy was collecting Chelsea from the airport

tomorrow, and obviously so did he. So, I guess he thought he could get away with playing us off against each other. What a bastard! Was he really on the verge of *proposing* to her? At the very least, whatever he said to Chelsea must have given her that impression.

Guy has got *a lot* of explaining to do!

My mind is going into complete meltdown. I find myself stumbling not towards the Kitchen, but towards the Shrubbery, to be alone. Ready to retch, I sink onto a bench, my chest heaving, oblivious to the cold stone against my skin. After an age – it could be half an hour or more – I hear Hatty running through the grounds calling me:

"Mummy! Mummy!"

Though I can't face anyone right now, it's not fair to drag my little girl into this.

"Over here," I call weakly.

"Mummy! *There* you are!" she says as she bursts into the Shrubbery, looking relieved. "Are you OK? I didn't know where you'd gone! It's almost dinner time, and Mrs P and Giles told me to call you, and Desmond's here now."

"Oh! That's nice," I lie. "I didn't know Desmond was coming this weekend. Is Guy with them?"

"No, he's cuddling the Piano Lady by the pool. The Piano Lady is crying a lot."

"The *Piano Lady*?"

"You know, there's a picture on the piano of her with Guy."

With Guy? But that's… Brad Masters, I think. She is clever, my daughter – even she has spotted an uncanny resemblance between Guy and the Masters family. But what does it mean?

"Oh yes…" I croak. "The Piano Lady. Her name is Chelsea."

"Are you OK, Mummy?"

"I will be, Little One. I just felt a bit sick. Maybe I got too hot by the pool. I think I just need a few moments to get ready for dinner. I certainly need to get changed, don't I? I'd look pretty silly having dinner in my swimsuit."

Hatty giggles. "Yes, Mummy you would look *very* silly."

But not half as silly as I feel: utterly, completely stupid, in fact.

"Are you happy staying with Mrs P, or do you want to come and read a story to Beebee while I get changed?" I ask.

"I promised Mrs P I'd chop the parsley," she says. "If you don't mind?"

"Not at all," I say. At least my daughter's becoming more self-confident. "Chopping parsley is a very important job. Maybe you could save a few leaves for Beebee?"

She looks at me witheringly. "He's a toy, *Mummy*… I don't think he'll be needing any parsley."

"Quite right," I say. "Silly Mummy."

"Silly Mummy," says Hatty with a little wave, dashing off towards the house.

Ten minutes later, Silly Mummy is ready for dinner. I walk down the Grand Staircase, not sure if we're eating on the Terrace or below stairs. Generally, when Maxine's not around, we're below stairs, but who knows what the arrangements will be this evening?

As I reach the bottom of the steps, I hear a buzz. Guy's mobile is about to vibrate itself off the Louis XIV console table in the Entrance Hall and smash on the marble floor. Besides possibly being terminal for the phone, that would probably leave a nasty nick in the marble, so I pick it up to move it, my eyes going automatically to the screen. The call is from some place called the New Life Clinic. I quickly press the off button and replace the phone exactly as it was, but the words are seared onto my brain.

A moment later, there's a single buzz. I can't help myself; I take a quick glance round to check I'm alone, lift the phone, and look at the screen again to see a text from New Life scrolling past:

> New Life: this is a reminder of your appointment at 2.30pm tomorrow

Chapter Twenty-four

Giles and Desmond seem unnaturally jolly at dinner, which is thankfully in the Kitchen. None of the dogs except Mr Biggles are allowed down here, so we can eat in relative peace, ignoring the scratching, whining, and occasional howl at the Boot Room door as the Tillingford hounds protest their exclusion. Mr Biggles has a very smug look on his face as Desmond and Giles feed him titbits.

Without Guy there, I feel awkward, as though Hatty and I are intruding on a *dîner à deux*.

Guy does eventually appear as we're finishing the starter: garlic mushrooms garnished with the parsley which Hatty so carefully chopped, as she's reminded us a couple of times already. In her new adventurous state, she's tried them, but she says they're like stinky slugs and she'll wait for the main.

"Sorry about that," Guy says to no one in particular, taking off his glasses and cleaning them with his shirt. "If only I'd known Chelsea was coming this afternoon, I'd have gone to get her at the airport. As it is, she had a terrible journey, and she's a bit over-wrought. So she won't be joining us, I'm afraid."

But he doesn't even look at me. I don't know what to think or say, and I keep my eyes on my plate.

The cheerful art world patter from Desmond and Giles and Hatty's occasional interjections keep the table from sullen silence, but Guy and I say barely a word. I can hardly get my food down.

Desmond glances at me questioningly as he hands me the potato salad, but I don't respond. It's sweet the way he looks out for me, but I can't really start sending smoke signals across the kitchen table, can I? He'll have to stay in the dark for the moment.

"Alice, will you come for a walk?" Guy asks in an undertone while we're clearing up afterwards.

"OK," I reply unenthusiastically. I know I should at least give him the chance to explain. "Let me get Hatty settled."

The evening is muggy and overcast, and Hatty, like the dogs, is restive. She looks tired but says she doesn't feel sleepy. Luckily, she doesn't mind me going for a walk with Guy; she almost seems to expect it now. So, I set her up with an audio book and a sketch pad so she can draw pictures to go with the story. She decides she does want Beebee after all and sucks his ear, a disgusting habit I've tried to discourage, but I don't say anything about it this evening, promising I'll be back in an hour.

"Who is the Piano Lady, Mummy?" says Hatty as I stand on the threshold.

"She's a friend of Guy's." I reply, as I try to start the audio at the chapter she wants.

"Is she Guy's girlfriend?" she asks, flipping through her sketch pad to find an empty page.

"I'm not really sure, Hatty."

"Because I thought *you* were Guy's girlfriend now…"

So did I… "Don't worry about it, Hatty. These things get a bit complicated when you're as old as Guy and me – I mean, I've still got your Daddy, haven't I?"

"I guess," she says, unconvinced. "But you don't like each other very much. That's why you got divorced."

"Your dad's alright – and he loves you lots," I say, firmly pressing play so Roald Dahl can take over before this gets any more difficult.

I go down the servants' stairs and out through the little door by the Library. Guy is waiting for me by a wrought-iron bench, fiddling with his phone. At this time of the evening, the heady perfume of the overblown tea roses and climbing jasmine is thick and cloying.

"Alice…," he says, dropping his phone back in his pocket. He tries to take my hand, but I don't give it to him.

"I think you need to tell me what's happening, Guy."

We wander silently down the pathway towards the Lake, the atmosphere between us as loaded as the heavy summer evening, brewing for a storm. Last week when Guy brought me here, the Lake seemed to shimmer with magic and romance. Pan's Pavilion was filled with candles and decked out in rugs and cushions. We drank each other in with our champagne and spent the most blissful night of my life together.

We should have taken another path tonight, because now as I approach the water, those memories pierce my heart, and all I can think about is how Chelsea has exploded into my life. Guy is pensive and distant. He's obviously brought me here because 'we need to talk' and the ice is in my veins.

As we approach the Lake, pushing past the overgrown bulrushes in the twilight, we walk through a cloud of tiny flies and I have to swat them away from my face. Guy reaches for my hand, but it doesn't reassure me. I'm trying not to second guess what he's going to say. It's obvious that I let my guard down too soon, and now exactly what I feared has happened.

What we had was nothing more than a fling. A one-night stand, in fact.

I feel sullied. The silence hangs heavy between us, but I really have nothing to say. What is the point of small talk? It won't make the parting less painful. My mind races, trying to work out how I'm going to get through the next two weeks with this awkwardness overshadowing us.

"There's a light in Pan's Pavilion," I say, glad of the distraction as I notice a faint glow from the folly. "Who could it be?" I whisper.

We instinctively crouch behind the bulrushes to look without being seen. Guy's brow furrows. "Your guess is as good as mine," he growls. "Maybe trespassers…"

We're close enough that I can feel the muscles in his arm tense, and I'm shot through with unwanted desire.

"I'm going to have a look," he says, squeezing my elbow.

"Wait! There's someone coming out!" I whisper.

A tall, pale, gangly figure in a robe and flip-flops emerges, followed by a shorter, darker, rounder one.

Guy relaxes. "It's just Dad…"

"… and Desmond," I add.

"Ew," I say when I realise that they've jettisoned their robes… and there's nothing underneath. I screw my eyes tight shut.

Guy, smirking, puts his hands over my eyes. "No one should ever have to see their boss naked, particularly not if he has a physique like Desmond's," he whispers, stifling a laugh.

There's a gentle swoosh and then a loud splash as the two men plunge into the water, each in his own way. I squeak.

"Oh, Alice," Guy whispers warmly. "You're so funny."

He turns me towards him as though going in for a kiss, but his face suddenly changes – ashen in the twilight. I follow his gaze to see that the men haven't swum more than a few strokes. They're standing chest deep in the water, embracing and gently kissing.

Now it's me turning Guy's face away. He curls up, clinging to me. "Dad…" he whispers. "…now it all makes sense." He looks at me, his eyes awash with pain.

"Let's go," I beg, and he nods mutely.

I struggle to help him to his feet; his body is a dead weight. He mechanically puts one foot in front of the other, following me. I walk away, far away, not really knowing where I'm going until we find ourselves by the Ornamental Pond where it all began.

I remember that shaft of sunlight that came between us when I first saw him. It made him look like a Greek god, but now in the gathering gloom of twilight, I see a sad, confused human. We sit in silence on the stone benches as Guy sighs and draws himself together.

"Did you know? Did you have any suspicions that your father was gay?" I ask, eventually.

"None. He and Mum always seemed to get on as well as most people's parents. Maybe he's only just realised?"

"Don't torture yourself, Guy."

"And Mum? Or maybe she's known all these years. Seb probably wasn't the only guy she…" he goes quiet. "Of course there were others," he says after a moment. "There was a time she spent the whole winter in London and that polo player who was always over here a few summers ago. And the photographer who did the famous picture of me, Seb, and Sahara with Helmut. I'm so dense! At the time, I couldn't understand why these guys were around here so much, but it's all starting to make sense."

He turns away. "I've got a lot of thinking to do," he says, and we start back for the house in silence. At the bottom of the stairs, he gives me a peck on the cheek. "Go to bed, Alice. I'll see you in the morning."

"Guy. Stop. What about *us*? What's going on with Chelsea?" I ask, tears in my eyes.

"A misunderstanding, Alice. But it's complicated, and I need to sort it out," he says, his jaw clenching.

"Surely I deserve at least some explanation?"

"You're right," he says, looking weary. "Come on…"

Chapter Twenty-five

I almost run to keep up with him until we reach the Portrait Gallery. I'm shaking as I place myself gingerly on a Chippendale chair, looking up at the only man who's ever genuinely made my heart race. Is he going to apologise? Is he going to explain?

Is he going to dump me properly?

He's framed against the midnight-blue curtains. They are damasked with delicate leaves in gold, the perfect backdrop for Guy and his dark blond hair, as if the entire scene has been set up by an artist. He looks down at me sorrowfully and turns off his mobile. Its beep echoes down the gallery, a startlingly modern sound in this dusty, creaking, wooden place.

"Alice," he says, drawing up the chair's twin and turning it so the back's facing me. He sits astride it, his arms resting on the back. "Your research… your hunches… all of it got me thinking," he says, looking over his glasses at me.

I'm annoyed that he's talking work; I've been psyching myself up for hearing about Chelsea, how he's always loved her, for him to dump me officially. But instead, he's given me that half-arsed failure of a conversation by the lake, and now here we are chatting art.

"It was when you showed me that portrait of Sir Nicholas Tillingford, the only one with blond hair, the one that looks suspiciously like me, that I started doing my own research. It's not a copy or a forgery. It's just completely made up."

"What do you mean?"

"There never was a Sir Nicholas Tillingford in the early 1800s, and there's never been a blond Tillingford. Ever. Just look at all the pictures around us."

"Your Mum's blonde…" I reason.

"Not as much as she looks," he says with a bitter laugh. "And anyway, it's a recessive gene. Forget the hair, Alice. I don't look *anything* like them!" He stands up and paces the creaking boards.

And it's true. All the Tillingfords for generations have had long, thin faces and big foreheads, and they're all, without exception, chinless wonders with a bit of an overbite. Most of the gents have widow's peaks (it's hard to tell with the ladies). They're not particularly blessed with good looks, in fact. Guy has a strong jaw, a Grecian profile, and a straight, moderate forehead. His floppy golden hair parts naturally in the middle. He's unbearably handsome.

And he doesn't look a thing like any of them.

"Giles Tillingford isn't my biological father, Alice. Whoever commissioned that fake portrait wanted to persuade the world that I belong here… but I don't. I'm a changeling. A cuckoo in the nest."

What on earth do you say to someone who's just realised they're not who they thought they were? Especially when they thought they were the future Lord Tillingford, heir to a beautiful house, a priceless art collection, and a considerable estate in Hampshire (even if it is losing money hand over fist)? What can I possibly say?

"Alice, I'm sorry. I'm not really a Tillingford at all. I might not even be the heir to Tillingford Hall, legally. I'm just Guy, a boring hedge fund manager who loves beautiful things."

He snaps open the curtains and stands in the cloud of dust, looking out the window. The moon has risen by now, and it bathes the whole estate in an eerie light. I get up and stand beside him, looking out at the extensive parklands that will never fail to delight me, even in the moonlight.

"Guy, you don't know that for sure. It's a hunch. You can have a test done," I suggest, fiddling with the silver acorn pendant and wondering what's coming next and whether I should be giving it back to him.

"We know what it's going to say."

"Giles loves you, Guy! Anyone can see that. Even if you're not his biological son – and you don't know that for sure – he probably knows already and long ago accepted you as his own. And if he doesn't, what's he going to do if – and that's a big if – you tell him? He's not going to cut you off. Tillingford Hall means everything to you," I say. "But at the end of the day, it's just a house, isn't it? And a liability."

"Alice, you of all people should know it's not like that!" he barks. "This house isn't just our home; it's our identity, our blood, our very DNA." He hesitates, fiddling with the curtains. "And the last fifteen years, I've been working my arse off to keep the place up. I've spent my twenties and early thirties – when most people would be partying and travelling and shagging around and finding themselves – pouring my life blood and millions of quid into this place. And now it turns out it's not even mine.

"And you know what I've also realised…?" he says, steel in his eyes. "It's thanks to *you* – your *research*, your *hunches* that this has all come out!" he snaps the curtains shut, enveloping us in a cloud of dust and he doesn't sound thankful at all. "It's thanks to you that Desmond's here."

"That's absurd! Your father met Desmond months ago. I came here because of him, not the other way round." I say, eyeballing Guy as best as I can, given that he's a foot taller than me. "But anyway, you don't need to worry about any of that. There will be no more research, no more hunches, because *I resign!*"

"What?"

"I'm going to take Hatty back to London tomorrow," I say. "I was excited about this secondment, the chance to work on such an important collection. I thought it would give me and Hatty a break from our grotty flat, get me out of my dusty underground archive, and give me a chance to shine." And now look: I've found a collection full of fakes and broken two hearts. With nothing left to lose, I take my crushed heart in my hands and put it on my sleeve. "Instead, I fell in love with you. But clearly what I thought we had wasn't real at all – just like those portraits."

The pain in Guy's eyes is searing.

"Alice…" he whispers, "don't do this…" He turns away for a moment. "Please, Alice. I'm sorry – I'm just confused and upset. I knew we should have gone slow, but you're everything I've ever dreamed of, ever needed. You're so unique, so loving, and I wanted you so much, I couldn't help myself. I know I've screwed up everything, but please tell me you'll forgive me. Can you forgive me?"

"What for?" I cry.

"For messing you around," he says, trying to take my hand.

"I don't know. I don't even know what we are now!"

"I have no idea either, Alice. I don't even know *who* I am anymore, let alone how I feel about anyone or anything."

But I know how I feel.

I know that I love him.

After Philip hurt me so much, I didn't want to let my guard down and let anyone in. I just wanted to be there for Hatty and focus on her. But I've never met someone like Guy. He broke me right open and found his way to the deepest part of my heart.

"Tread softly…" I say, my eyes moist.

He holds my hands. "…for you tread on my dreams…" he says, finishing the quote in a tearful whisper.

I realise then that however much I'm hurting right now, he must be going through hell on earth trying to process everything. And because I love him with all my heart and he's told me he wants to try to work through this, perhaps there's still a chance for us. I'd rather live this hopeful crucifixion than cut myself off from him forever from some kind of misplaced pride. So, I dig deep and say, "Take the time you need to work things out, Guy. I hope, somewhere at the end of this road, there will still be some space for me."

"I hope so too, Alice. I know there's something special between us, but I don't know what to do with that right now. I know this is going to hurt – hurt you, hurt both of us – a lot. I wish everything wasn't so messed up. But it is, and I have to work through it."

"I understand," I say. But inside my heart is screaming, like it's about to break in two.

He kisses me deeply and passionately. "Stay with me, Alice. Spend the night with me again."

"Guy, you can't ask me that," I say in anguish. "Not with you like this and me not knowing what you're really thinking or where Chelsea fits into all this."

"I promise you, I don't love her the way I love you. I told you it's all a misunderstanding, and I'm going to sort it out. Give me time, Alice. I promise I'll explain when I've found out the truth for sure. And please promise me you'll stay and finish the work you started? Tillingford Hall needs you – this family needs you."

"You're asking a lot, Guy," I say as my hand grasps the silver acorn at my neck.

His eyes are filled with pain. "I am. That's what love is, isn't it, Alice? Giving and asking everything of each other."

It seems right now that he's doing all the asking and I'm doing all the giving. And I feel my heart start to seal over, just so I can cope, everything that he awoke inside of me shutting away again like a butterfly climbing back into its chrysalis and wrapping itself up in silk once more. I've been in that dark, enclosed place before and I don't really want to be there again but I don't know how else to stay safe.

Apart from my daughter, my professional pride is all I've got now. "OK," I say. "I won't resign."

"Thank you," he says, holding me tight. I can feel him shaking, his tears dripping onto my neck.

"But in two weeks, I *will* go back to London," I say.

"Maybe two weeks will be enough time to make this better, so I never have to let you go again," he whispers.

Chapter Twenty-six

When Hatty and I look out of our window on Saturday morning, we see Guy leaving with Chelsea. She's leaning into him for support, him caring and solicitous. There's no kissing, no sexy hands on her waist or arms around her neck. Her shoulders are rigid, her head drooping, as though trying to hold it all together. She doesn't exactly have the look of a radiant victor in love. They seem so close, and yet so distant. It's as confusing for me as it must be for them.

No wonder Guy needs time. But even now, I don't understand why he can't explain to me what he's going through, why he won't let me help him shoulder his burden.

"Where are they going, Mummy?" asks Hatty.

"Chelsea isn't well, Darling, and Guy's taking her to hospital," I say with a sigh.

"That's very kind of him, isn't it Mummy?" she asks.

"Yes, it is," I say, although I'm actually confused as hell about what he is really up to.

Then she scrunches up her forehead, wrestling with a thought. "But I'm sad he won't be here to play with me this weekend."

"Me too," I admit, truthfully.

After breakfast, I put Hatty in front of a cartoon in the Snug, while I sit at the Kitchen table with a fresh brew in my new Jane Austen mug and look up the New Life Clinic.

It seems to be a fertility centre, which only sparks more questions. Is Chelsea pregnant? Is Guy the father? Maybe that's why she thought he was going to propose – but then surely to goodness he'd just have admitted that to me last night? Or maybe the father is someone else, and he's just supporting her as an old friend. But then her expectation of a proposal made no sense at all. And surely, if she was pregnant, *she'd* have made the appointment or just seen someone in Boston?

Or is this something to do with what Guy told me last night? That he's realised that he might indeed have 'a closer bond' with Chelsea than they ever realised.

Maybe they're going for the test we'd talked about?

I'm praying that's what they're up to, but I wish he'd actually *explained.*

I'm just wondering what to do with Hatty today and contemplating finding out what Elizabeth and the twins are up to, when Desmond comes down, with Mr Biggles in his arms and a twinkle in his eye, followed by Giles, who seems dreamy and thoughtful.

I help them get their breakfast together.

"Mr Biggles is enjoying Tillingford Hall so much that he'd like to stay another few days," he says.

"I'm so pleased!" I say.

It's lovely to see him happy, even if it reminds me of how utterly miserable I am. But I don't begrudge him his happiness; he's been through a lot too, and he really deserves this.

"I can help you with the collection," he points out. "We could do a bit this morning, if you don't have special plans."

"Not really," I say. "I guess Hatty could watch a movie, which will give us an hour or so, and I can take her out later."

Hatty's more than happy with this plan as she's looking forward to watching *Tangled*.

It's certainly helpful to have Desmond around – his expert valuations will save me loads of research time. There's still a lot to do, and he's also really helpful when it comes to checking the attributions and provenance of the pieces. We agree to make a sub-catalogue of dodgy pictures, at least twenty of which appear to be by the same unexceptional modern artist. Some are probably copies of what should be in the collection, while others are completely made up.

"Sir Nicholas is particularly vexing me," I say, handing Desmond the miniature. I decide to say nothing further and see what he makes of it.

"That's Brad Masters," he says immediately. "This is obviously a fairly recent novelty portrait done at some tacky Regency cosplay event – or something equally horrible – by someone utterly talentless, like a market-stall caricaturist or an A-level art student."

"It's pretty dreadful, but how do you know all that?" I say, taking it back.

"Giles showed me a photo of Brad when he was explaining who Chelsea was yesterday evening. *Sir Nicholas* is the spitting image of him."

"That's the photo on the piano, isn't it?" I say. "I need to look at it again."

Desmond and I rush up to the Salon, inasmuch as Desmond can rush anywhere with his stout body and the additional weight of an obese pug in his arms. We take the picture of the Masters, father and daughter, off the piano. As I thought before,

Brad looks just like the man in the fake portrait – and both Chelsea and Brad look so much like Guy.

"I'm not an expert on genetics," says Desmond. "But physiognomy – faces – yes; these people are Guy's family."

"What do you mean?" I ask him, although by now he's just confirming something I've been reaching for in the back of my mind for the past two days.

"Let's take a stroll in the gardens," says Desmond. "Mr Biggles needs his wriggles."

We stroll past the herbaceous borders, and I wince as the pug wees on every third delphinium. As soon as we're out of earshot of the house, I say, "They look so similar. You'd think they were cousins. But if they are, why not just say so? And why would someone do this portrait and actually take the trouble to slot it into the family tree?" I have *Sir Nicholas* in my pocket, and I pull him out to have another look. "It's like someone's trying to persuade the family that they had ancestors that look like this. Do you think Brad could be Guy's father?"

"That's exactly what I'm thinking," admits Desmond as he digs a poo bag out of his pocket.

I tell him about the New Life Clinic in Harley Street. "When I saw they had an appointment there, I wondered if she was pregnant, but I mean, he wouldn't have got his own sister pregnant, would he?" I feel physically sick.

"Not unless… he didn't know she was his sister," he says, stooping to deal with Mr Biggles' offering.

A bell is ringing in the back of my head. "But I remember Guy telling me that he hadn't seen Chelsea since her mum's funeral this time last year." It's a small straw to clutch at, but a straw, nevertheless.

"Perhaps the centre does DNA testing too," he says.

I'm feeling weak, so we sit on a bench under an oak tree, and Mr Biggles plonks himself underneath, as though his 'wiggles' were all a bit too much effort. I bring up the New Life Clinic website on my phone to check again what services they offer, and there, under all the fertility stuff, DNA Testing and Genetic Conditions are listed.

It still doesn't explain why Chelsea thought Guy was about to propose.

"It's a bit of a tangle, isn't it Alice? But a few things are starting to make sense to me," says Desmond, as a light breeze dislodges a few prematurely brown leaves.

They flutter to the ground at our feet. We sit in silence for a few moments as we process it all. Mr Biggles begins to snore.

"Alice," Desmond says turning to me. "You are a lovely lady."

From any other boss, this would be a bit creepy, but Desmond and I have been working together for such a long time that I know exactly how he means it. "I feel we've got to know each other over the years, so I hope you feel you could trust me with personal matters."

"If I had to. I've never wanted to burden you with my private life; we both know it's been messy enough. But yes, I feel I could tell you anything."

"That's good," he says as I pick up a leaf and begin to shred it, "because actually, I need someone to talk to right now. Mr Biggles is a great listener, but his understanding of human psychology is somewhat limited and his conversation skills a bit lacking. So I hoped you'd be a listening ear for me too."

"Of course," I agree, turning towards him, allowing the leaf crumbs to slip through my fingers.

"I haven't really had anyone I could speak to about matters of the heart since Federico died," he says, adjusting his cravat.

"I'm sorry, Desmond. Federico was lovely. I can only begin to imagine how much you must miss him." I look out across the parkland, noticing it's started to take on a dusty, autumnal look. "Is this about Giles?" I ask.

"How did you know?"

"Guy and I saw you in the Lake on Saturday night," I admit.

"Good Lord!" He throws up his hands. "The poor boy! I bet that was a bit of a shock." Desmond is quiet for a moment. Then he sighs. "Giles is a lovely man," he says. "He's always known, you know, from a very young age, but we grew up in the seventies, when the way we are still wasn't accepted. And a baron needs an heir, even in this day and age – or in the eighties, at least. Maybe things would be a bit different now. But back then, his parents were pressuring him to find a suitable wife. He thought Maxine would be the kind of girl who'd be happy to do her best with him and then, you know, find other amusements."

"Well, she's certainly done that," I point out.

"You mean, apart from Brad?" asks Desmond as Mr Biggles lets out a dreamy whimper under the bench.

"Seb?"

"No!" He turns to me with wide eyes. "He must be twenty years younger than her! How did you know?"

"I've seen them together… I mean, not actually *in flagrante* as such but, you know…"

"I don't think Giles knows about that," says Desmond.

"But Guy does… and he thinks there must have been others."

"Not for Giles…" Desmond muses.

I feel sad for Giles, that he's lived in this complicated marriage for over thirty years. I don't know what it all means for Guy, but I do hope Giles finds what he's looking for now.

"I've been so lonely without Federico," Desmond admits.

"I do understand. It's not easy to find yourself suddenly on your own," I add ruefully, knowing exactly what that's like. "It seems like Giles has been lonely too. Sometimes it's lonelier being in a relationship that's wrong for you than being on your own."

"Indeed. Do you think it would be so terrible of me to steal him away from his wife, knowing what you know about them now?" Desmond has tears in his eyes.

"Desmond, that's not for me to judge. What I do know is that this family has some serious issues, and I think we – and they themselves – are only just starting to realise that." I sigh deeply, my heart knotted in confusion. Have I done something wrong by leading Guy to the truth about himself, something which I now realise could tear his family apart? He asked me to wait while he solved the riddle, and I can't see I've got an option if I ever want to be close to him again.

"I don't think we have a choice but to leave them to sort it out for themselves," I tell Desmond. "I think we have to give them time, and it will all come right in the end," I add with more conviction than I feel.

"A wise head on young shoulders," says Desmond. "I always thought so."

"You're too kind. I like the *young* bit," I say, heaving a sigh as another autumn leaf drifts from the canopy above us.

"How old are you now, Alice?"

"Too old…"

He pulls a face that says, 'Come on, now!'

"I've just gone thirty-seven."

"Then of course you're not too old."

"Don't be silly!"

But at that moment the tiny seed of desire that's been dormant inside me starts to germinate. *Guy's baby. My child, an Honourable.* My breath catches in my throat, astonished at myself for even having such a thought. But what if Giles *does* cut Guy off when he finds out the truth? What about Sahara? Chelsea? My head is about to explode.

Desmond takes my hand. "The world is your oyster, Alice. You're still young."

I smile back at him.

"But *I'm* not," he adds. "I'm sixty-eight, you know. I'm retiring at Christmas."

"No!" I exclaim in dismay.

"Yes. Time's come to hang up my magnifying glass and enjoy myself while I still can. You should apply for my job."

"But…"

"You're more than qualified, Alice. You should have applied for it last time round."

Desmond would definitely have got the job last time round even if I *had* applied for it, but it's sweet of him to say so. "Well, I'm glad I didn't," I say. "Otherwise, I wouldn't have had you for boss."

He smiles. "Give it some thought, Alice. You'll be a shoo-in, and you deserve it."

"Let's get on with the catalogue," I say. I need to get back to work and distract myself from all this.

Chapter Twenty-seven

At last, I'm on my way to Bath, having dropped Hatty at Granny Janet's in Basingstoke. So much has happened since I booked this weekend with Charlie, back when I first started at Tillingford Hall, that it feels like years have passed. I've been really looking forward to it – a little light on the horizon. I think I've only been to see Charlie once since she started her job as curator of the Bath Physick Garden, and that was before Hatty was even born.

When Desmond and I got back from our walk-and-talk on Saturday my laptop wouldn't start. Eventually, in desperation, I managed to get hold of Elizabeth, who arranged for Father Matthew to take a look. He told me there was some spyware installed on my machine which had deleted everything. He wondered how it had got there, as I had good antivirus software.

Luckily, I had all our files backed up on the external hard drive, which I religiously take up to my room each night, and we were able to restore everything. I was just so relieved that Matthew had got the PC back up and running that I didn't give any further thought to it at the time. But now I'm wondering if it was anything to do with the software Seb put on my machine.

When Desmond went back to London on Wednesday, he left with a smile on his face and a reminder that he was going to be handing in his notice of retirement the next day.

And so, to add to my mental burdens, I've been agonizing about whether I want Desmond's job. I told myself I'd use this journey time to worry through that dilemma. His job was, I suppose, always my end goal, but I'm starting to wonder whether I really should spend the whole of my life stuck in the basement of the London Portrait Gallery. What if I could be something more, someone more 'out there', changing lives with what I do and bringing the joy of art to the kind of people who might not normally visit a museum? But I also need to think about having enough time and energy for Hatty.

As for Guy, I still haven't heard anything from him, so I'm none the wiser about Chelsea and the clinic. I understand that what he's going through is complicated, but I can hardly bear the uncertainty. Will I have to seal up my heart, pretend it never happened and try to heal? Or leave my flame for him burning for in case he decides to return? Sometimes I'd rather know it's all over so I can get on with the business of nursing my broken heart. And yet the hope of what we could have, if only we gave it a chance, burns me up and refuses to be quenched.

When I did weaken and try to call him, I got an international ringtone. If he can't even tell me where he is or what he's up to or why, I've decided that I'm better off forgetting the whole thing. I try not to think about it, but I can't help wondering what happened to our beautiful romance. I know I was a fool to jump in feet first like that, especially when I was already so wounded.

I'm counting down the days to the end of my time at Tillingford Hall, and when the secondment is over, I'm going to leave Guy Tillingford in the realm of holiday romance and knuckle back down to work in London, but his handsome face swims into my imagination and almost makes my heart stop.

It's not going to be that easy.

Hot tears prick the back of my eyes, but I take a deep gulp of air and pull myself together; I can't let my eyes mist up while I'm driving. I put on Absolute Radio and try to shake off my self-pity with a bit of rock, but it just gives me a headache. I dare not put on Classic FM because there's probably going to be some huge sentimental piano concerto or a big aria from a tragic opera that will start me thinking I'm the romantic heroine in the film of my own life.

I'm certainly looking forward to spending time with an old friend, particularly a plain-speaking one like Charlie. Apart from a few cups of tea with Elizabeth, occasional quick chats with Mrs Powell, and the odd Facetime with Charlie, I haven't had a good deep-down, face-to-face girly natter with anyone for months, and I miss that.

The countryside round Bath is so lovely bathed in the slanting evening light that it lifts my spirits as I drive towards the city. I long to live somewhere like this rather than Morden. One day I will, but right now, my work is what sustains me, and I have my support network in London. But the busyness and greyness and the lack of a view in the Wandle Valley really isn't great for me. Sometimes I get the 93 bus up to Wimbledon Common just so I can turn my back on London and look out towards the North Downs, even if Croydon does take up most of the middle ground.

After the usual parking nightmare, I'm finally climbing the stairs to Charlie's flat. It's a real poet's garret with little dormer windows that offer a view out over the Georgian crescents and squares of Bath, but only if you stand on a box and stick your head out the window. Climbing six flights of stairs to get there with a weekend case is the last thing I want, but luckily Charlie's come downstairs to help me. I gratefully let her take my case up as I'm so tired.

"Gin and Tonic?" she asks as we get through the door.

"Absolutely," I gasp, already refreshed by the sweet sound of those three little words.

"Do you realise I actually haven't seen you for *three years*?" says Charlotte, opening the fridge.

"No – it can't be that long." I move a pile of dirty laundry (for which Charlie apologises, explaining it belongs to her flatmate) off the grubby patchwork throw which covers the only easy chair in the room.

"Yes. I came to see you in the house in Wimbledon the summer before you divorced," she says. Lemons, tonic, gin, and glasses all emerge chilled from the fridge.

"Then that would be four years ago," I say as she hacks at the ice cube tray to release it from the iceberg that's gathered around the icebox.

"Four years! Where have you been hiding?" she says, getting out a chopping board and knife.

"Just working, trying to keep my daughter from starvation, and licking my wounds," I say, pulling my knees up to my chest.

"It's not your fault, Alice," Charlie says. She slices viciously into a lemon. "He was a tosser."

"So everyone keeps telling me."

"You should move on," she says, throwing ice and lemon in the glasses. "So how is Lord Farquhar?" The tonic bottle exhales with an excited gasp as she twists the cap.

I take a G&T from Charlie explain that Guy's got some difficult family business to attend to and that's why he's hardly been in touch this week. As a result, Charlie decides that Guy sounds like a tosser too. That makes me sad. I know love is blind, but there's something in Guy that is good and sincere. He's simply struggling at the moment with something that doesn't leave any space for an early-stage romance.

"We need to take your mind off him!" says Charlie. So we go out to a Turkish restaurant and stuff ourselves with hummus, baba ghanoush, imam bayildi, and other vegan delights, washing them down with a very cheap bottle of dubious Ruritanian red and catch up on all the juicy details of the past four years, including Charlie's complicated love life. She's been through another two actual boyfriends in that time and a few other, briefer dalliances. Right now, she seems to be going steady with a carpenter from Twerton who works elsewhere during the week but makes up for it at the weekends.

Afterwards we go back to the flat, Charlie tells me about her day job.

"I've been at the Bath Phyzick Garden for ten years now," she says wearily. "I've been looking for years for something else which will stretch me more, but nothing's come up at the right level. Historic gardens is such a small niche."

"Fancy a camomile tea?" she asks, pulling a jam jar of real camomile flowers off a shelf while she starts to tell me about her basket weaving, for which she cycles forty-five minutes twice a week to a workshop in Monkton Farleigh. "I'm not sure how I'm going to get the baskets home, though."

"I can take you in the car if you like? It would be interesting to see the workshop."

"It doesn't make any sense to do a special journey; I'll ask the teacher to drop them off next time she's coming to Bath farmer's market. She has a horse-drawn cart. I have to say, even by my standards, she takes being eco-friendly to extremes, but she's also canny. She's realised that the customers – especially the children – love stroking her horse, so she sells more baskets to the yummy mummies that way!"

Soon, under the influence of the camomile flowers, which seem much more potent than the dusty stuff you get in tea bags, we're both nodding off. Charlie insists I take her bed while she sleeps in her flatmate's room, which smells badly of the remains of a takeaway she left there before going away for the week.

I'm puzzled how the chintzy girl I once knew, whose parents called her Tottie and who used to dream of living in a Georgian Rectory with a classic Jaguar on the drive, can live like this. But I guess she's changed, like we all do.

As I settle down for the night, I reflect on how much I've missed the company of good friends. I haven't had a chat like this with someone close to me for years. I've been so focused on Hatty and getting through things. The bedsheets are cool as I slip into them, and despite the warm evening, I feel an icy gap on the other side of the bed.

Suddenly I feel so alone.

I'm not sure whether I should text Guy. The only one I sent this week went unanswered, and I don't want to crowd him or seem too needy.

I pick up my phone and decide to text him anyway, when I see there's one from him. All it says is:

Missing you xxx

That's all I've heard from him for seven days. He misses me – but not enough to actually phone.

Chapter Twenty-eight

"How did you sleep?" asks Charlie the next morning.

I don't want to tell her about the text. She'd just call Guy a tosser again, and whatever he is, I'm sure it's not that.

"Not brilliantly, to be honest," I say, fingering the silver acorn dangling at my throat. "I think the Turkish food disagreed with me a bit. My guts are too delicate for all that roughage." I grimace.

"You get used to it," she says brightly. "I've got so much energy since I turned vegan. What would you like for breakfast?"

"A bacon sandwich?"

Charlie makes vegan pancakes with soya milk and baking powder instead of eggs, and serves them up with soya yoghurt, blueberries, and maple syrup – and they are delicious.

"Do you remember I said there's this Regency tat stall I wanted to show you?" she asks.

So, we traipse across Victoria Park and down through the middle of Bath to the Green Street Market. Distracted by organic fruit and veg, home-made cakes, game and free-range sausages (which I sample, unapologetically), and the Tea Emporium with teas from every conceivable plant and part of the world, we almost forget what we came for.

"Oh, here she is," says Charlie.

Between a milliner displaying hand-made velvet hats and a dodgy-looking stall selling Bob Marley T-shirts, bongs, novelty cigarette lighters and tobacco pouches (many emblazoned with a fronded hash leaf) is a stall framed by muslin drapes tied back with purple chiffon ribbons selling Regency-style silhouettes and miniatures.

A framed notice in copperplate script says:

Regency Silhouettes in 15 minutes

£15 single, £25 double

The woman manning the stall is dressed in an empire-line muslin gown that wouldn't look out of place on the laundry line at Jane Austen's House, albeit her ample breasts are nearly popping out of it, and the draped fabric hangs oddly over her substantial midriff. Her dark auburn hair, piled up under a frilly bonnet, falls in little ringlets around her face. She's playing with a fan while she talks to a couple of Chinese tourists, trying to persuade them to sit for a silhouette, but I can see they don't really understand the art form. They take a selfie with her in her costume and move on to the hat stall.

Charlie moves in. "Hello Debbie," she says.

"Nice to see you, Charlie m'lover," says Debbie with a West Country twang that belies her Regency get-up. "How's things?"

"Not bad, Debbie," says Charlie.

I'm staring at a ghastly selection of miniatures of Jane Austen characters (I only know who they're meant to be because of the copperplate inscriptions – Mr Bingley, Captain Wentworth, and so on – underneath each one), which I couldn't see before because the tourists were standing in front of them. The portraits are blotchy and crude, and the frames are garish in their newness. In fact, they remind me rather of…

"I'd like to introduce you to Alice," Charlie says, looking between me and Debbie. "She's a friend of mine from Uni and, guess what? She works at the London Portrait Gallery!"

"Ooh that's nice," coos Debbie. "What do you think of *my* portraits?"

I'm caught like a rabbit in the headlights. "They're… wow. Well, what a brilliant place for a stall," I say. "You must get so many Jane Austen fans here in Bath. What a great idea!"

"Well, yeah," she says, obviously miffed that I'm side-stepping giving her a compliment, "that's why I started doing this kind of piece. I used to do large-scale abstract canvases using my own bodily fluids, inspired by Mark Quinn and Helen Chadwick, but I never hit the big time like them. I was getting pissed off by the shit reviews and needed to make a living, so I started doing these. I've built up quite a clientele, especially in America. I've even got celebs and aristocracy who like my stuff."

"Oh fascinating… like who?" I say, to see if I can get some intel out of her.

"I'm not at liberty to say," she says with a wink.

I'm instantly suspicious. Most artists are only too happy to tell you who buys their work – no one signs a non-disclosure agreement when they buy or sell art, do they? So, either she's lying (which given how poor her stuff is, could well be so) or there's a reason why she won't tell…

I smile sweetly. Cogs are whirring in my brain, and I need to get her onside and pull as much information out of her as I can without arousing her suspicions. I point to a miniature. "This one's brilliant. It really looks like a Romney," I lie.

"Oh yeah, that's a copy of one in the Holburne Museum," she says, putting her hand into her top to adjust her bosom. "These corsets…" she tuts under her breath. "But these others are of friends of mine in the same kind of style. I usually copy Thomas Lawrence – look, here's one I'm working on now." She picks up a tray from behind the counter, where she's in the middle of turning a grisly snapshot of a gurning bloke wearing a faded Iron Maiden t-shirt into a miniature of a Regency squire with a frilly stock and a grey wig. "This one's my dad" she says, proudly.

"He looks most distinguished," I say, with reference to the miniature, not the original photo. I need some way to keep in touch, to investigate further who she is and what she does. "I'd love one of my daughter," I say, thinking fast, "but she's not here now. How much would you charge to do one from a photo?"

"Well normally it'd be a hundred and twenty-five quid… but seeing as how you're a friend of Charlie's, let's make it a hundred."

"Oh really? That's very reasonable. Yes, I'll go for that."

I can't really spare the money, but I'm reckoning it might be worth it in the interests of research. We faff around with our phones for a bit while I text her a photo of Hatty and transfer £100 to her bank account. I have a feeling her details could come in handy.

"How long will it take?" I ask.

"Let me check," she says, scanning down a list in a notebook. "Shall we say second week of September?"

"Is there a chance you could get it done a bit quicker?" I ask, putting my phone back in my bag. "It's my mum's birthday next weekend, and I'd love to give it to her."

"Aw. That's nice," she says, pushing some stray curls into her bonnet. "I guess I could, as you're a friend of Charlie's."

"Thanks, that would be amazing," I say.

"Give me your address, love, and I'll post it to you."

I give her my parents' address in Hemel Hempstead so as not to arouse any suspicions, shake her hand, and wish her a nice day, which she returns with a warm smile.

"Let's get some food," says Charlie, heading towards a nearby stall. "You'll love this! And Cobain's so dreamy."

"Cobain?" I ask as she points out a young guy with fair, chin-length curls, who looks like he'd be more at home on a surf-board in Cornwall. "Is that his real name?"

"Yeah, Cobain Coltrane is his actual name. I've seen his driver's license."

But I'm not convinced. Charlie is a bit of a tease; she once persuaded me that our Renaissance Florence lecturer, Kevin Richards, was the brother of Keith Richards of The Stones, which turned out not to be true of course, knowledge gained by means far too embarrassing to relate right now.

We've bought falafel wraps and very green juices that look pretty much like someone's liquidised Kermit. As I seat myself on a bench a few minutes later I conclude, slightly too late, that a pure vegan diet just isn't for me.

"That was a bit weird," says Charlie.

"What was?" I ask, assuming she's referring to the little eruptions that emanated from me as I sat down.

"You buying a crap miniature from Debbie," she explains, to my relief.

"Isn't that why you took me there?" I ask sweetly, to try to put her off the trail.

"*Noooo*!" she replies, looking at me incredulously. "Do you even have a hundred quid spare to spend on a piece of tat?"

"Well, I'm not on the breadline, Charlie… but no, I admit it's quite a bit more than I'd normally spend on a birthday present for Mum. Don't you think it's a sweet idea, though?" I take a sip of Kermit Juice and grimace – it tastes the way I imagine the slime from the Ornamental Pond at Tillingford Hall would.

"Well, it is a nice idea, Alice, but I mean…"

"What?" I bite into my wrap, and a rock-hard falafel escapes and bounces onto the ground.

"I mean, I only took you to meet Debbie because she's funny and I thought you'd enjoy bitching about her stall with me later." I kick my loose falafel under the bench where a beady-eyed pigeon is already waiting to have a peck. "I didn't think you'd actually buy anything. Surely you can see that Debbie's stuff is utter crap?"

"Of course, it's dreadful!" I agree, looking grimly at my wrap containing five more indigestible chick-pea balls.

"Why buy it then?" asks Charlie.

I'm not sure whether to tell her. I look around conspiratorially, lowering my voice. "So, you know how I'm cataloguing the miniatures at Tillingford Hall?" I say.

"Yes, of course," she replies. "I had gathered that!"

"Well, the reason they got me in is because there's something fishy going on."

"Oh?" says Charlie, perking up in interest. "What kind of fishy?"

So, in headline form (and swearing her to secrecy), I tell her about the missing pictures, the dodgy-looking ones, the ones that look like poor copies of what should have been there, and the ones that are plain downright fakes, none of which I'd mentioned to her last night. By the time I've finished, Charlie's finished her wrap and is scrunching up the paper.

"I think Debbie might be responsible for some of the fakes," I explain. "I recognised her style." I'm so glad you didn't mention Tillingford Hall – it might have put her on her guard right away. Although, of course, she might not be directly involved. Maybe she doesn't know anything about it, but it's possible she's deeply embroiled in whatever's going on. I have no idea who's getting these fakes made or why. I thought I could find out more about her without arousing her suspicions if I commissioned a portrait. That way, she has to give me her details – even her bank details, which could be useful if the police get involved – and I can keep in touch with her."

"Cunning," agrees Charlie, lobbing the paper at the bin and grinning when she gets a perfect shot.

"Yes, I was quite pleased with myself for thinking on my feet," I admit. "I don't normally have to make quick decisions in my line of work." I take a big bite of wrap and this time manage to get my teeth into a falafel. "So how do you know Debbie?" I ask after a bit of chewing.

Charlie hesitates. "Well, you know, when I'm getting together with a few friends and want to get mellow, she'll, you know, well… she knows where to get stuff."

"She's your *dealer*?" I ask, horrified.

"OK," she huffs. "Yes."

I don't know many people who didn't do a bit of dope when we were students, but Charlie knows I think it's irresponsible. I never liked the whole scene, but now I can't help thinking of Sahara and Seb, who probably started that way, or the boys Guy's mentoring, or of what could have happened to Hatty and the twins. It makes me shudder.

"She only sells dope," she says defensively. "She gets it for her mum, who's got MS, and she sells a bit to me and a few friends to cover her trouble. Anyway, where's the harm? Not all of us have your responsibilities," she counters, seeing the look on my face. "And it's safer than alcohol..."

"I'm not judging you," I say, lying through my teeth. I can't believe she's bothered to wheel out that old chestnut. I can't help wondering what Sahara would say to that, and as I think of Seb and Sahara, somewhere in the back of my mind, my synapses are making connections, but I can't quite follow them.

When I've got down as much of the food as I can manage, we head towards the Roman Baths. Charlie pops into Tesco's to get a couple of bits, and I tell her I need to phone Hatty. Philip and I have an agreement that we're never in touch when he has Hatty unless there's a problem, so we can all relax and not interfere in each other's weekends, but the excuse buys me a few minutes to check Debbie out.

She's got an active Instagram feed, and her website is surprisingly well put together (and mobile responsive). Despite the quality of the site, the pictures are terrible. She's got some Austen characters and a few pictures of her real-life sitters as silhouettes as well as miniatures, but I can't see any sign of the Tillingford Hall ones. That doesn't mean she didn't do them, though. It makes me all the more suspicious that she knows exactly what she's embroiled in.

But maybe she didn't do them at all, and I'm barking up the wrong tree, in which case we still have a mystery on our hands, and I'll have wasted £100. But I'm thinking that when the picture of Hatty arrives, there might be some distinguishing mark, something in the frame or the way the picture is mounted, that might give it away or at least add a pointer.

But what if there's something at Tillingford Hall – a letter, an email, a bank transfer – that could incriminate her? Of course, it's not like you can go snooping around people's desks or filing cabinets looking for receipts or cheque stubs these days; everything's digital and locked away behind firewalls and passwords. Even if I were a computer hacker, the chances of being caught and the possible consequences would be pretty severe. It's not really a route I can go down. And I don't know anyone who could help me.

But I'm pretty sure the Tillingfords won't want to involve the police. Not yet, anyway. If this got out, it would definitely go viral and none of us, including me, would be untouched by the scandal.

Chapter Twenty-nine

"So, where are we meeting these friends of yours?" I ask Charlotte as we walk out of her flat, away from the fabulous Georgian town centre, through a barely lit park, and down an alley full of graffiti to a less pretty part of town.

"The George and Dragon. It's a bit rough – some people call it 'The Chase'."

"Why?" I ask as Charlie presses the button on a pedestrian crossing.

"Like 'chasing the dragon'…?"

"You mean mainlining heroin?" I ask, not noticing the green man has flashed up until Charlie starts to walk and pulls me along with her.

"No… mainlining's when you inject it," she says as we reach the other side. "Chasing the dragon is when you heat it up and inhale."

I'm aghast. "Same difference! Why are we going to a place like that?" I squeak.

Charlie rolls her eyes. "It's a joke. People don't actually do drugs *in* the pub – well, not class A ones, anyway." She's smiling, but I'm not. I'm about to start telling her about Sahara when Charlie says, "Look, the people I hang out with these days are a bit… alternative. They just don't fit in at All Bar One or Gin Genie. People like us aren't really welcome in places like that.

Whereas at the Dragon, we feel right at home."

"Fair enough," I say, but I'm now dreading the evening ahead. I'm sure I won't fit in at all.

From the outside, the pub looks traditional, half-timbered with a black-and-gold sign. No sign of any dragons, real, mythical, or metaphorical. As we walk in, a warm, beery wave of laughter and chatter washes over us. It's dimly lit, with a classic sticky, swirly carpet – do they sell them pre-soaked for pubs? I wonder – and that stale beer smell, with small packs of KPs hanging off cardboard strips behind the bar, just like you'd expect. When I was a kid, there would have been a busty blonde in a skimpy swimsuit on the backing board, but thankfully it's just plain blue now.

Two of Charlie's friends are here already. A tall guy with dreadlocks the colour of a dead mouse, who introduces himself as Tristain, greets Charlie with a kiss on the lips, although I'm sure she said he was just a friend. He enfolds me in a massive hug that makes me almost gag on the odd herbal smell of his multicoloured knitted hippy jacket.

And then there's Ama. She has a pale, heart-shaped face and green eyes, and her auburn hair is braided with coloured thread. Ama is an eco-activist who organises protests against road bypass schemes. She tells me her name means 'water' in Cherokee and that her mother is a shaman (despite, Charlie whispers to me, coming from Budleigh Salterton and rejoicing in the name of Trisha).

Ama says I have an interesting blue-green aura and wonders if I work in the arts – but doing something analytical, or detailed. I don't want to tell her she's right because it's just a bit too spooky.

Tristain claims to be an artist, although he won't show me any pictures of his work. He says that photographing his art robs it of its spirit, but he has some I can see in his camper van if I want to come by later. I think I might be giving that a miss.

A few minutes later, a woman with light-brown hair and big blue librarian glasses, sporting a bright African print dress, comes into the pub and walks over to us. She's vaguely familiar, and I remember we were at university together. She's called Emily and grew up in Devizes. She works for a charity called Water Support on engineering programmes in Africa, and she's just back in the UK for a few days to check in with head office and see her parents. She says she's desperate to get back to Zambia, where her fiancé, Masimba, is the chief engineer on a water project.

Charlotte's new friends are not the kind of people I usually hang out with. For the last three years, I've only really interacted with Desmond and other colleagues and a few school-gate mums. I haven't had time for a social life of my own. I'm actually finding them pretty interesting. They're the kind of people that Philip with his tidy urban ways would have disliked intensely. It's a shame Philip never really got on with Charlie. If he'd ever bothered to get to know these people with what he thought of as 'alternative lifestyles', he might have seen how interesting, kind – and laid-back – they all are.

An evening in their company is kind of relaxing.

I wonder how Guy would react to them. I suppose if his best mate lives in a camper van, then he'd feel right at home with them all. As I start to unwind, I begin to really enjoy myself, especially when a group in another corner of the pub pick up a random assortment of instruments, including a couple of banjos and a bodhran, and start jamming.

People's glasses are nearly empty. Despite being a skint single mum working in a very underfunded industry, I'm one of the least poor people in the group, so I guess it's my round.

"Who'd like another one?" I ask.

"Thanks… a Crusty Bath Ale for me, M'lover," says Tristain in his thick Bristolian accent.

"Ama," says Ama.

I'm momentarily puzzled, then laugh as I remember the one word of Cherokee I now know. "Tap or mineral?"

"Tap, obvs, Honey." She smiles. "No ice. Did you know the carbon footprint of a single ice cube is 0.2mg?"

I did not. But I do now.

Charlie also wants a Crusty, and Emily is after another G&T while she still can. I decide to join her in that and head towards the bar, although I'll probably end up having it warm now that Ama's guilt-tripped me.

I freeze. It's impossible to miss Debbie, even though she's in a dark corner of the pub. She's no longer wearing her Regency bonnet, and her mass of curls is loose around her shoulders, revealing streaks of pink and blue. She's wearing a low-cut T-shirt in shocking pink that strains over her capacious bosom. But what's really arrested my attention is the man talking to her in a very tense, confidential manner. I can't see his face clearly in the dim light, but it looks like Sebastian Seaton-Smyth.

Do I stop and wait for him to turn so I can be sure, or hide so he can't see me? Something tells me it would be better if he didn't spot me. Just before I turn away, I see Seb hand Debbie a Jiffy bag and Debbie give him one in return. I keep my head down as I duck back to the table.

"Have they run out of beer?" jokes Tristain.

"Her aura's changed," says Ama. "Something's stressing you out, Alice."

"I've just spotted someone, and I don't want him to see me," I stage-whisper.

"Who?" asks Charlie.

"That man talking to Debbie," I reply.

"Seb?" asks Tristain.

"You know him?" I ask.

Ama and Tristain look at each other and then at Charlie. "Charlie's aura wraps right round his the moment he walks through the door," Ama says with a teasing smile.

I raise an eyebrow, and Charlie blushes. "He is very good-looking," I admit.

I'm not sure whether to say anything about Maxine.

"Threesome?" says Charlie.

"Eeew! No, I mean, *ew*, Charlie!" Right, so this *really isn't* the moment to tell her about Maxine. "I can't explain now, Charlie, but I can't let him see me."

"Do you owe him money?" Tristain drawls.

"Something like that.... I need to know what he's doing, but I can't let him see me – watch his every move and let me know."

"Lamest excuse for not getting a round I've ever heard," grumbles Tristain. I toss a £20 note at him and dive for the toilets. Charlie runs after me.

"Alice! What's going on? How do you know Seb?" she asks.

"He's Guy's best mate from school, and he *works* at Tillingford Hall. How do *you* know him?" I ask, leaning against the sinks.

"What? No. Are you sure you've got the right guy? This is

Seb's local and I'm a regular here and we just kind of connected," says Charlie, twisting her hair with a frown.

"His *local*? It's a long way from Hampshire to Bath," I say, drumming my fingers on the edge of the sink.

"He's from Twerton. He's a skilled chippy so he's in demand all over the place. That's why he lives in a camper van and he's not around during the week – he's only here at the weekends," she explains.

"Charlie – he's not a carpenter; he's a loser! He did some kind of college woodworking course when he dropped out of Winchester and he does a bit of gardening at Tillingford Hall, but he's basically staying there because he's a druggy failed public school-boy who's too useless to get a proper job and Guy feels sorry for him. Did Seb say you were exclusive?" I ask.

"I never asked," says Charlotte. I just assumed we were, but now you mention it, we never actually said anything," she looks up at me and I can see tears in her eyes. "Is there someone else?"

I don't want to see her heart broken, but I think we're too far down the road for that. "Charlie, look… I'm not sure how serious he is about her but… "

"Go on," she says, biting her lip.

"I don't think you want to know," I say, leaning back against the sink again.

"You?" fire flashes in her eyes.

"No, of course not! It's Maxine – Lady Tillingford."

"Shit the bed! She must be old enough to be his mother!" Charlie says, her eyes flaming and a look of disgust playing across her face. "Wow! I didn't need to be exclusive, but I did at least need him to be honest!"

"Do you want to get back at him?" I ask, realising I've never seen her looking so angry. I'm thinking fast – there might be a way to figure this all out.

Charlie nods with gritted teeth. She's not one to hold back when she's crossed.

"Charlie, you don't have to do this, but do you think you can try, very subtly – obviously don't put yourself in danger or give too much way – find out what he's doing here? I saw Debbie pass him a Jiffy bag, and I need to know what's in it. I think it could be one of my missing miniatures or a reproduction of it."

Charlie's eyes widen in shock. "No!"

"Look, do you think you can… I don't know… maybe get him a bit pissed or stoned and try and have a look?"

"It will be my pleasure," she says, her eyes narrowing. I had no idea she had such a steely streak. Maybe life in the alternative lane has made her more hard-nosed than she used to be. "I wasn't planning to see him tonight cos you're here, but… we do usually spend Saturday night together, so he should be up for it." Her eyes are twinkling, like she's actually enjoying the intrigue.

But I'm absolutely terrified, and my hands are shaking. I've literally never once in my life been involved in anything remotely dangerous or criminal, and right now I can hardly breathe – but I can't let Sebastian get away with this!

"Thanks, Charlie. You're a good friend. Please don't do anything risky!" I beg as I give her a shaky hug.

"I might have to, if I'm going to stop him selling it – I think he's already gone outside and I'll have to explain it to the others somehow, 'cause I'm going to need their help. Wait here and I'll send Emily to you with an update when we've got a plan."

I close myself in a cubicle and breathe, though not too deeply because it's none too fresh. I hope I'm not being selfish and that Charlie's not really going to put herself in danger. But now that she's got fire in her belly because Seb lied to her, I don't think I could stop her if I tried. If she could just find out what's in that envelope, I could have all the evidence I need.

I'm fiddling with my oak-leaf bracelet and wondering how long I'm going to be sitting here when I hear footsteps outside the toilet window. I guess there's an alley running behind the pub.

"Here it is..." Seb's unmistakable drawl oozes through the window just above my head.

"It's not as good as the last one," a much harsher voice with a strong Bristolian accent replies. "Your missus holding them back now, is she?"

I stand on the loo seat and peer out through the opening in the tiny, frosted window. I can just see the top of Seb's fair curls and another head, shaven and tattooed with a scorpion, above leather-clad shoulders. I ease back down, hoping they don't notice the movement, and listen carefully. I'm scared, but I still have the presence of mind to draw out my phone and start recording. I have no idea if it'll come through or whether evidence like that would even be admissible, but I can at least play it to Guy or Giles.

"It's a Thomas Lawrence, you asshole," says Seb. "One of the best in the collection. Your Russian doesn't want poxy Banksies – he's an educated man of taste and culture. We had the head of the London Portrait Gallery over last weekend, and he valued this little beauty at £20k at least. So keep your end of the bargain. It's risky taking the best ones."

"What the f*** are you doing, drawing attention to it like that by putting it under some wanky neek's nose?" growls the man with the scorpion tattoo.

"We can't help who Grandad chooses to have over as guests, can we? We're trying to clear them out as fast as we can before he twigs."

"Will he call the cops?" asks the Scorpion man.

"No. He won't want the scandal," Seb reassures him.

"I'll give you 500g for it," wheedles the man.

"No, I don't have time to sell that much on. This time, I want cash, Scorpio."

"D'you think I carry that much in readies, you prick!"

"I know you'll have them somewhere. I've been in this business longer than you've been alive – and longer than you will be alive if you don't cooperate. Don't forget who I know," drawls Seb.

"And don't forget *what* I know, you pathetic…"

"Hey," says another voice, very mellow. I think it could be Tristain.

"What do you want, Hippy?" says Scorpio with a curse.

"For us all to be at peace. My friend Charlie here would like to go to bed, and you're keeping her up, so maybe you could just do what the Posh One says, and we can forget all about it?"

"It's not how I like to do business…" Scorpio spits.

"Nor me," says Seb. "You keep Charlie out of this, Tristain."

"Just thought you'd like to know the pigs are coming," says Charlie mildly. "They just parked outside the Swan, so they'll be at the Chase any minute."

I can't understand how she can play it so cool!

Four sets of footsteps recede along the alley, and I sit, trembling, on the loo, shutting my eyes so I'm not staring at a piece of graffiti that looks like it came straight from the mind, if not the pen, of Dame Tracey.

After a few minutes, I hear someone come in. I'm terrified, not sure whether to run or hide, or if I'll have to use the vegan food as an excuse if the police do arrive and find me in the ladies. Or maybe I'll tell them I was scared – and what I heard.

But then I think of Guy and Giles and how this is their story and what could happen to all of us if it gets out. I'm in much deeper than I feared, and I can't just go to the police without telling Guy first.

For once, I'm glad Hatty's safe in Basingstoke.

"Alice?"

It's Emily!

"I'm here," I reply from my cubicle, limp with relief. I open the door so we can talk.

"Charlie's with Seb now so Tristain, Ama, and me are going back to my AirBnB. It's a one-bed flat, so you can stay on the sofa if you'd rather not go back to Charlie's."

"OK, thank you," I say, creeping out of my hiding place and wondering what I'm going to sleep in and how I'm going to brush my teeth. I wish I could go home to Tillingford Hall, but my stuff's at Charlie's, my car's on the other side of town and I've had a couple of drinks. And, more importantly, I need to make sure Charlie's OK and find out what's inside that envelope.

As we hurry to Emily's AirBNB, it's fully dark and there's definitely an autumnal nip in the air. When we get to the flat, Tristain explains that while Scorpio is a notorious drug dealer, he's a mere stooge for the guy with the County Line who mostly operates in Bristol. Apparently, Scorpio's Bath chapter is notorious for dealing in stolen art and cars as well as drugs. The rumour is that their ultimate overlord is a Russian Mafia Boss who's an obsessive art collector. Ama is pretty sure Scorpio's gang was behind the recent theft of the two Gainsboroughs from the Holburne Museum, but the police haven't been able to pin anyone down.

Of course, I tell Tristain and Ama they should tell the police what they know, but they look at me incredulously. "We like to avoid the pigs if we possibly can," Tristain says, and I can imagine why both he and Ama feel that way. But it saddens me that big criminals are getting away with so much because people who have chalked up a few minor misdemeanours feel they can't put their heads above the parapet.

Once we've settled down a bit, Tristain and Ama make a massive spliff and offer it round. Even though I'm wide awake and totally wired, I say I'm exhausted, and Emily kindly lets me sleep in her bedroom so they can keep chatting – and smoking. When I shut the door, I don't know if it's the fumes from the weed, or the gentle drone of voices percolating through from the next room or sheer exhaustion, but I drop fast asleep in minutes. I wake up in the morning with the headache from hell and a strange buzzing in my ears.

When I hear voices and the door opening, I realise the buzzing must have been the doorbell. I pull myself together and poke my head into the living room. Charlie's just arrived.

Chapter Thirty

Charlie's face is pale and blotchy, and she has bags under her red eyes.

"I didn't dare go back to my flat," says Charlie, "in case the police come looking for me."

"Shit…" says Emily.

How am I going to get my stuff back? I think, selfishly, but I guess if I lose it, I lose it. At least we're all still alive.

"What happened?" everyone asks at once.

"I'll tell you in a minute," yawns Charlie. "I'm starving…"

"I'll get some breakfast together," says Emily.

I duck into the bathroom to freshen up while Tristain and Ama help Emily with breakfast. When I come out, the flat is filled with delicious smells. Emily's made vegan banana and coconut pancakes and proper coffee. I'm not complaining.

"So," says Emily, when we're all sitting on the floor, balancing mugs and plates on our knees because the bijoux pull-out kitchen table barely has room for two. "Tell us what happened."

"OK, so Seb seemed happy to go back to Neville, like we usually do on a Saturday," Charlie says, spearing a pancake. "When I saw him last time, I hadn't told him Alice was coming this week," she says, "so he was still expecting me."

"That's good – if you'd said anything about me, he might have put two and two together and realised who I was," I point out, reaching for the maple syrup.

"Yeah. It's such a weird coincidence," says Charlie, piling blueberries on her pancakes.

"There are no coincidences," says Ama, dreamily. I'm wondering if this is her personal philosophy or whether she knows she's quoting a noughties sci-fi action film, but I shake myself back to the point as Charlie carries on:

"The point is, he had no idea I knew anything about anything. So we, you know…"

"Got close?" says Ama at the same moment that Tristain says, "Got stoned?" and we all laugh.

"I wanted him to *think* I was stoned, but I needed to keep my wits about me," says Charlie.

"So…?" says Emily, passing the plate of pancakes to Charlie.

"I'm famished," Charlie admits, taking second helpings and passing them on. "And these are so good."

"So, tell us what happened!" I say.

"I will! Be patient! I've got to eat!" says Charlie. After a few more mouthfuls, while the rest of us are pouring more coffee and squirting syrup on our second helpings, she starts again. "When we were pretty cosy, I asked him if we were exclusive and he turns to me and says, 'Did you think that?' So I said, 'Well, I know I never asked, but I kind of supposed…' and he laughs a bit and goes, 'Hey, Babe' – I hate being called Babe," she says, angrily spearing her pancake, "it makes me sound like a talking pig – 'You never said.' So, I say, 'OK. Fair enough. We didn't talk about it, did we?' and he agreed we hadn't. So, then I ask, 'Who else is there?' and he goes all quiet. So, I say, 'Go on, tell me…' and I do some stuff that will make him talk..."

I see a look pass between Tristain and Charlie that makes me think *he* knows exactly what she's talking about. It makes me suddenly think of Guy, and my heart flicks with a beat of pain as I remember how much I miss him and how I've got embroiled in all this for his sake and he doesn't even know that all these strangers have put themselves in danger for him.

"So, did he talk?" asks Tristain.

"Yup," says Charlie, keeping us all in suspense as she munches another mouthful. "He told me – for about half an hour – about how amazing *Maxine* is."

"Who's Maxine?" asks Ama.

"Lady Tillingford," I explain.

"Oh my God!" say Ama and Emily together.

"Did *you* know this?" Tristain asks, pointing his fork at me accusingly.

"Yeah – I told Charlie when we were in the loos."

"It was you telling me that, more than the fact that he's been stealing pictures that made me agree to help you, Alice. He says he's fancied her since he first set eyes on her... when he was... get this..." gasps Charlie, biting her lip, "...fourteen. When they finally got together when he was nineteen, he said he felt like he'd 'become a god'." she makes quotation marks with her fingers and pulls a sickened face. By this point, everyone's jaws have dropped. "He's been seeing her on and off since then."

"Well how long's that?" asks Emily.

"Fourteen or fifteen years," I say.

"How old is she?" asks Ama.

"Early fifties I think – she had Guy very young," I explain

as though that somehow makes it any better.

There's a stunned silence.

"She is very well preserved," I say, and Charlie scowls at me.

"She's still twenty years older than him," she replies.

"Not as big a gap as President Macron and his wife," I point out.

And then everyone's talking at once. How old is President Macron? He's quite hot, isn't he? Lucky wife. Wasn't she his teacher? Bit creepy that she left her husband for him. Eeew. What will Guy think when he realises his best friend and his mum have been carrying for years? What about Guy's dad?

"Do you remember that lecturer at uni, Kevin Richards?" says Charlie with a cheeky look in my direction.

"But that's not the point, is it Charlie?" I say, over the babble to restore order and get her off that particular subject.

She looks wounded. "It is for me."

"I'm sorry," I say, leaning closer and rubbing her arm, "I really am. I wasn't sure whether to tell you, but…"

"No, of course you should have done," says Charlie, downcast, "And perhaps you should know that he says they're saving up to run away together and set up a surf school in Polzeath."

"What?" I say, absolutely incredulous, before I burst out laughing. "Lady Tillingford wouldn't dream of doing something like that for a second! She wears Louboutins to walk her dog, for God's sake. I can't see her in Polzeath at all, let alone messing up her hair in salt water and teaching snotty kids to surf."

Tristain throws his head back and laughs, but something here just doesn't add up.

"Anyway… I know you want to know about your miniature," says Charlie. "Pass me my bag, Tristain," she orders, and he grabs her velvet patchwork backpack and passes it to her. "Tada!!" she says after rummaging inside for a few moments.

"Charlie! You are amazing!" I say, taking the Jiffy bag from her and giving her a massive hug.

"What is it?" the others ask.

I open it. Inside is an original Thomas Lawrence miniature of a young man, clearly a Tillingford, along with a poor reproduction of the same picture. And even better – the envelope is a reused one, with Debbie's name and address on one side and inside an invoice for vapes she's bought on Amazon.

We all laugh.

"Oh my God!" I'm almost crying now. "I knew she was an amateurish artist but an amateurish criminal as well? It's brilliant!! I've got all the evidence I need!"

I hug Charlie again. "I'm sorry about Seb," I say.

She looks upset, though. "Nah… don't worry. He wasn't a long-term prospect…"

You can say that again, I think.

"…but he *was* amazing in bed…" she says quietly, biting her lip and looking away. Then she looks back at me sheepishly.

"What?" I ask, knowing she's itching to tell me something.

"Um… I did something a bit silly," she says, suddenly taking an interest in her nails.

Everyone's looking at her.

"What?!" we all ask when she doesn't come out with it.

"I… set fire to Neville and legged it!"

"With Seb inside?" asks Tristain.

We're all staring open-mouthed at Charlie, like a shoal of groupers.

She hesitates, avoiding everyone's eyes. "Yeah…"

We all gasp.

"Oh my God, Charlie! I hope he's OK!" I say.

"Look, I'm sure he'd've woken up pretty quickly. And after what he *did*…" she starts.

"Even so, Charlie," squeaks Emily.

Then we're all talking at once, and everyone's panicking that something awful might have happened to him. We know he's not a great guy, but we don't want him to have been fried alive in his own camper van like a sardine in a tin. What if someone comes after Charlie? What if she was followed? What if the police charge her for arson? We're all slightly panicking and agree we need a plan to find out if he's OK.

Emily, the least likely of us to be recognised locally, agrees to walk nonchalantly past Neville wearing jeans, a jumper, a hat and dark glasses to see what's happened, while Ama sets up a shamanic ritual to manifest Seb's safety and the rest of us clear up the breakfast things.

Half an hour later I'm leaning out of the window trying to get some oxygen through the fug of burning herbs and see Emily returning.

"What happened?" asks Charlie, tugging at Emily's sleeves the second she gets through the door, worry etched on her forehead.

"It's OK…" says Emily.

Charlie and I flop onto the sofa and Charlie bursts into tears and swears she never meant to do it – she was just so angry –

while Tristain heaves a sigh of relief and Ama chants some more incantations that sound thankful.

"There was a fire engine and a police car there," says Emily. "Seb was talking to the police wearing nothing but his boxers. I can see what you're on about, though, Charlie – he's pretty hot."

"Especially after Charlie set fire to his camper van," says Tristain, and we all laugh hysterically, as much out of relief as amusement.

"But anyway," says Emily, "Neville looked a bit…. well, not very drivable. But Seb was definitely fine – just a bit stressed."

"But he'll name me to the police. They might be round my flat right now," whimpers Charlie.

My heart is in my mouth. All my stuff – except my handbag thankfully – is there. If I go to get it, I might meet them, and they'll question me. I've got a very valuable picture on my person which they'll find if they search me. My pulse is thudding in my neck.

"My stuff's there," I say weakly, "and I need to get Hatty soon."

"Who's Hatty?" asks Tristain.

"Her daughter," says Ama. I don't know how she knew that – I'm sure I hadn't mentioned her. Ama closes her eyes. "Hatty is safe," she says in a weird voice. "I can see her laughing, with an old woman. But you must go to the flat now and retrieve your burdens." She blinks. "Seb's never been to Charlie's flat," says, her voice back to normal. "By the time the police work out who she is and where she lives, you – and your Thomas Lawrence – will be safe at Tillingford Hall."

Everyone seems to agree this is the best idea. So, I scurry over to Charlie's, grab my case, and lock up, leaving the key under the wheely bin and practically run to my car. Torn between a desire to get away as quickly as possible and a fear of drawing the eye of the police, I spurt between speed cameras in a state of panic. It's not until I get to the Popham Services that I stop for a comfort break and breathe a sigh of relief.

Chapter Thirty-one

When I finally get back to Tillingford Hall with Hatty, Giles and Desmond are out on the front drive, attempting to put Desmond's enormous suitcase in the diminutive boot of his MG. Algie and the beagles bound up to us as we get out of my car and shower us in drool. We put them off by totally ignoring them as Guy showed us, telling them in dog language that they're beneath contempt.

"Are you alright?" asks Giles, grabbing Algie's collar.

"Rough weekend?" asks Desmond.

I must look pretty bad, then. "The roughest…" I glance down at Hatty, who is giggling as Mr Biggles humps her leg. I raise my eyebrows at Desmond, and I can see he understands that now is not the time or place for an explanation.

"Perhaps we can have a little catch-up after supper?" he suggests. "I need to go back down to London tonight, but I don't mind making it a late one," adds Desmond, kindly.

"Thank you. Hatty and I will go and freshen up, and we'll be down in a minute," I reply.

"No rush," says Giles. "It's just us four for a cold supper – we can wait for you."

So, Guy's still away.

Since Ama's vegan pancakes this morning, I haven't eaten anything except the stale emergency Frusli bar I keep in the glove compartment. So I don't really care what we have as long as it's not got beans in it.

After a supper of beautiful homemade gala pie which wouldn't look out of place in *Good Housekeeping* circa 1981, I get Hatty settled upstairs reading a new book called *The Mysterious Castle,* which Granny found in her local charity shop and seems highly apt.

Luckily, Giles says he has some paperwork to do, so I can sit down alone with Desmond at the Kitchen table with tea and biscuits and tell him what happened in Bath. He listens silently, his eyes wide as saucers as I give him a blow-by-blow account of the entire weekend.

"And did this shaman girl actually do a ritual?" he asks at the end, pouring himself another cup of tea.

"Desmond… I think you've missed the point of the story!" I chide.

"Of course, I haven't… I just mean, I've never met anyone like that. I'm intrigued." He takes a biscuit and dips it delicately in his cup.

"The only snag is," I point out to him, cradling my mug, "all I've got is this envelope and what I managed to record on my phone, if that's even admissible evidence, which I'm not sure it is. I still can't *prove* who's doing this – though I've got a pretty good idea – and I still don't understand *why*."

Desmond dunks his biscuit for slightly too long and tuts as it disintegrates into the cup.

"Who do you think it is, then?" he says, digging around in the cup with a teaspoon to retrieve the sludge.

"The Scorpio guy said something about Seb's *missus*…"

Desmond looks up, biscuit forgotten.

"Do you think he meant Maxine?"

"They must be in this together," I say, "but surely Maxine can't really be planning to set up a surf school with Seb?"

Desmond's jaw drops as though he's suddenly realised something. "We've *got* to tell Giles," he says.

"I don't have any solid evidence! It's just a hunch – and I'm worried about giving him a shock," I admit. "Or what if he's in it too?"

"Oh no, I'm sure he's not," says Desmond, "and I don't think he'll be as surprised as you expect," he says, spooning up some mush from the bottom of the cup.

"Oh really?" I reply, looking at the remaining biscuits on the plate but not really fancying them now.

"Maxine hasn't been home for two weeks, her phone's on an international ringtone and she isn't picking up," he says, giving up on the biscuit fishing.

Sounds a bit like Guy, I think.

"We have to talk to Giles," insists Desmond again.

"And ask him about Sir Nicholas at the same time – it might all make sense if we put it together," I agree.

Desmond scoops up the sleeping Mr Biggles, who lets out something between a growl and a yawn, and we traipse up to Giles's Study, stopping by the Salon to pick up the photo of Brad and Chelsea from the piano.

Desmond knocks lightly on Giles's Study door then pushes in. "Giles, m'dear," he says.

Lord T looks startled at this endearment as he spots me coming in too.

"Don't worry, she knows," Desmond reassures him.

"You... *told her*?" Giles says, nervously shuffling the papers on his desk.

"Don't be silly – she saw us in the Lake," Desmond explains.

Giles goes white. "Was Guy with you?" he asks, turning to me.

"Yes," I reply, fending off a rather damp investigation from the beagles.

Giles slumps back in his chair and looks heavenwards, raking his hands through his hair, just like Guy does.

"Giles," I say gently, "I guess Guy's trying to work out a lot of stuff right now. Seeing you and Desmond together wasn't the first thing that's thrown him this summer. In fact, it's maybe helping him make sense of it all."

I put the miniature of *Sir Nicholas* on his desk. "Have you seen this before?"

"I think so," says Giles. "It's normally in the Billiards Room, isn't it? I think he's Sir Thomas, who was a captain at Trafalgar or something – or was that Sir William? I think they were brothers. But I've never paid them much attention. It's not very good, is it?" he says, peering closer.

"No – dreadful!" agrees Desmond, depositing Mr Biggles on the floor.

"Who is it of?" I ask.

Giles picks up the miniature and turns it over. "Sir Nicholas Tillingford – says so on the back."

"Who was he?" I ask.

"Not really sure – I've got so many bally ancestors, I lose track of them," says Giles, waving his arms towards a selection of portraits on the walls.

"Look closely," I urge him. "Does he remind you of anyone?"

Giles is squinting at the picture, holding it up to his face to look more carefully. I can see cogs whirring. He scratches his head, then looks out of the window. Then I see a light come on in his head. "Good God," he says. "It's that bloody Yank."

"Do you agree it's a portrait of Brad Masters?" I say, handing him the picture from the piano.

"Indubitably so. I don't need that photo." He pauses, thinking. "But why? I mean, why not just have this ghastly daub done and write *Brad* on the back?"

"That's what we're wondering," I say, as Mr Biggles wanders over to investigate a sleeping Algie, eliciting a barely audible growl from the enormous hound that sends him skittering back to Desmond.

"Do you think someone was trying to hoodwink you?" asks Desmond gently.

"Maxine, you mean?" says Giles.

Desmond and I say nothing, willing Giles to tell us what we need to hear.

Giles gets up from his desk and crosses to the window. He stares across the parkland for a few moments, and Algie grunts as the ornamental clock on the mantlepiece chimes the quarter hour.

"I've always known Guy wasn't mine," Giles admits without turning his head, "I just hadn't ever thought to question whose he *was* – I love him so much," he says, pursing his lips and gulping. "I've always accepted him as my own, and God knows, I've been a decent father to him. I never wanted him to be left to the mercy of a string of nannies and then boarding school from the age of eight like I was. I still wake up with nightmares about the stuff that happened there.

"Maxine and I did all the real mummy and daddy stuff ourselves: the nappies, the feeding, the first pony ride, first shooting lesson – you know, the things that normal parents do…" I try my utmost not to catch Desmond's eye at this moment. "We did all of those things. I didn't want to send Guy to Winchester, but Maxine insisted it would be best for him, so I agreed to it only if he could be a weekly boarder and always come home at the weekends. He used to bring his friends over to give them a break, and the house was always full of lively boys having fun.

"I miss those days. This house should be full of children again. And then there was Sahara. I can't help feeling bitter that she broke his heart and wasted his time. I know that's not a nice thing to say, but I feel like she's the one who's stood in the way of us carrying on the family line – although it's not like I made much effort in that department. I just couldn't… *face it.* I'm just not made that way."

Desmond picks up Mr Biggles and ruffles his ears.

"I suppose the title will go to my cousin's son and his children eventually," Giles goes on. "Pity… unless…" he looks at me significantly. "I thought maybe you were the one to make Guy smile again – he seems to have been happy for a moment this summer, but…" He pauses and sighs as he fiddles with the curtains. "God, aren't families complicated?"

He paces back to his desk and flops into his chair, gazing at the ceiling.

"God knows, I tried to make Maxine happy," he carries on. "It was a whirlwind marriage. We met at a ski lodge in Zermatt when she was a chalet girl. I was already in my thirties, and my friends were joshing me for not having found a mate yet. I guess I just got swept away with the serendipity of it all. It was the height of the AIDS pandemic, and I didn't dare tell them the truth… about me, about the way I felt. They were farmers and hearty rugby types who thought that 'gay' was how you'd describe the colour of your tractor. Maxine and I got talking late one night in the bar. She cried on my shoulder and told me she was in trouble. She didn't want to have an abortion, but she was scared of what would happen to her if she didn't. She would never tell me who the father was, just that he wasn't going to leave his wife for her. She thought the only way to save the baby was not to tell the dad.

He picks up a photo of Guy from his desk and hands it to me. "Worth saving, huh?"

And I nod, a tear pricking my eye at the thought of what could have happened to him.

"And so, we married there and then in Switzerland and told everyone Guy was a honeymoon baby. Don't get me wrong, it wasn't purely cynical. I was – I am – very fond of her; she's beautiful, vivacious and plucky, the life and soul of the party. I knew she'd be a brilliant hostess, the perfect Society wife. It seemed like an ideal solution. She obviously never told Brad about the baby.

"Of course, I knew Guy wasn't mine, but I wanted him, and I needed her, and Tillingford Hall needed all of us, and so we never talked about it again. And I let her live her own life, so long as she was discreet and kept our secret and turned up to hunt balls looking pretty. And to be fair to her, she did – I've never once heard a hint of her affairs, though Lord knows I encouraged her enough to have them, but I never really wanted to go down that road myself. Maybe I just never found the right person, but I understood she had her needs, and I didn't want to risk what we had.

"Do you think she had the portrait of Sir Nicholas done?" asks Desmond.

"I suppose it was her attempt to hoodwink Guy – or anyone else who came snooping – into thinking that somewhere in the Tillingford line were some handsome blond genes, to show where Guy got his good looks from. I never thought to question it; there are so many bally pictures in the house."

Desmond and I catch each other's eye.

"You know these aren't the only fakes and forgeries?" Desmond asks.

"Guy had his suspicions," Giles admits. "That's why we called you in. He didn't have the time or the knowledge to check everything; he works so hard in Town and he helps me look after the accounts and the house as well. He must get his business head from Masters as well."

Giles turns and looks sadly at both of us.

"I'm sorry to do this to you, M'dear," says Desmond.

"No, you mustn't apologise! It's not your fault!" he gets up and crosses to the window again. He turns back to us and says, "I'm sorry to wash our dirty linen in front of you both, although it's honestly a bit of a relief to have it in the open. But not *that* much in the open; I do hope you'll be discreet," he says.

"Of course!" we both say.

"We're here to help with the miniatures," I add gently. "We're trying to get to the bottom of what's going on with the collection."

"We've told you that some are fakes," explains Desmond. "Just completely made up, maybe just for fun, like the Sir Nicholas one. But some are forgeries; the originals have been replaced with copies while the originals themselves have then presumably been sold. There are quite a lot, about thirty, like that."

"And we think we've worked out who's doing it," I say.

I explain to him what happened in Bath. "We know Seb's bringing Debbie the pictures, and she's copying them. Then he sells the originals to Scorpio for drugs – or cash, though generally drugs, I think – and Scorpio passes the art on to a Russian collector."

"That good-for-nothing layabout!" growls Giles, walking back towards the desk. "I told Guy we shouldn't take him back in. He's a cuckoo in the nest… worse than his sister!" he says, slapping his hands on the desk and leaning towards us both.

Desmond and I look at each other.

"I don't think he's doing it for himself," I explain.

Giles looks startled.

"Giles… he's in love with Maxine," says Desmond.

"He has been since he was a teenager," I add. "They've been lovers for the past fifteen years."

Giles drops heavily back into his chair, and we sit in silence for a moment as this all sinks in, lost in our own thoughts. "My poor miniatures...," he says after a minute, "stuck in a vault in Switzerland or some zillion rouble dacha in Siberia."

Algie stretches loudly, and a faint, foul odour fills the air as he opens his maw in an enormous yawn and walks over to the desk.

"But… why?" asks Giles, scratching the Great Dane's head. "The affair, I understand. It's a bit..." he pulls a face, "...odd, but they're adults and he's a very handsome young man. I'm sure he's been giving her what she needs," he smiles bitterly. "But… why sell the family silver?"

Both Desmond and I stay silent. We want Giles to reach his own conclusions.

"I can only suppose she's been pocketing the cash," he goes on. "Maybe trying to make her getaway. She was always moaning in the early days about not having enough money to do the place up. She wanted to strip it and modernise it. The pool was my one concession to her need to turn this place into some kind of Dallas-style ranch. But pin money, money for clothes and so on? I don't know why she didn't just ask. I'm sure we could have come to some arrangement. I'd do anything to have the collection back, but if *Maxine's* gone… well…" he looks significantly at Desmond. "I expect I'll manage…"

We all laugh hollowly.

"We need something to link Maxine to all of this," I say. "Seb probably won't testify against her, not least because it'll bring up a whole heap of trouble for him. I wouldn't be surprised if he's scarpered already."

"I don't want to involve the police," says Giles firmly. "Certainly not until we're absolutely sure what's happened. Can you imagine the field day the media would have? We'd all be involved – you two included."

A look of horror crosses Desmond's face, and I imagine not being able to leave the Hall for paparazzi. I take a deep breath and agree that Giles is right.

"Why don't we check her room?" says Desmond. "It's somewhere to start."

So, we traipse up the Grand Staircase under the disapproving eyes of Giles's ancestors. Maxine's door is locked, and the duplicate key has been taken from Giles's stash, but with my newfound locksmithing skills, it doesn't take much to unpick it. As we push open the door, the room looks abandoned: bed made, photos on the bedside tables and mantlepiece, a couple of dusty Jilly Cooper novels on the fitted alcove shelves next to the fireplace.

I open the drawers of her dressing table, but apart from an old pair of tights in one and some dried-up lipstick in another, they're empty.

"There's practically nothing here," says Giles in astonishment. He opens the mirrored wardrobe, which aside from a couple of puffy-sleeved eighties taffeta ballgowns, is totally bare. He bangs about in the back of the cupboard. "Even the safe is empty…"

I lift up the pink flouncy valance and pull out a Salvatore Ferragamo shoe box from under the bed. I open it, revealing a load of receipts.

"What about this?"

We sit on the bed and spread them out – Prada, Christian Louboutin, Oscar de la Renta, Cartier, Tiffany, Rolex, Harrods, Selfridges – hundreds of receipts for luxury goods from shops in London, Milan, Paris, and New York.

"I didn't buy her any of this," admits Giles. "I mean, I got her lots of jewellery when we were first married and a few bits for anniversaries but nothing like this much stuff."

Desmond is rifling through Maxine's bedside drawers. He tosses an empty condom packet towards the bin, tuts as he misses, and goes over to put it in properly. "Hang on…" he says, peering into the bin.

At the bottom is a scrunched-up Jiffy bag.

"Let me look at that!" I say, taking it. "It's a perfect match!" I crow. There, on the envelope, is the name *Seb,* written in the same weird, loopy handwriting that's on the envelope Charlie gave me in Bath. And, inside – joy of joys! – another receipt for vapes addressed to Debbie Crowder. I snap a photo of the envelope, the contents, the bin, the room.

"She's gone," says Giles, sitting heavily on the bed.

Desmond sits down next to him and puts his arm around his shoulders.

"Silly me," sniffs Giles. "I thought we had an understanding, but it obviously wasn't enough. I'm going to miss her, you know… I was very fond of her." A solitary tear rolls down his long nose.

Desmond nods at me, as if to say: *I think we need some time alone*.

"I'll go and put this envelope with the other one," I offer, walking out of the room and leaving them to it. But as I walk down the corridor, my head is pounding. Where does Guy fit into all of this, how much does he already know, what should we say to him when we see him?

And, more importantly, where *is* he?

Chapter Thirty-two

Our time at Tillingford Hall has come to a close. New school shoes and pristine exercise books beckon. The nights are darker, the last few blackberries on the briars are small and sour, and a faint wash of autumn colour is starting to creep across the Tillingford estate.

As always happens when one goes away, we seem to have more stuff now than when we arrived, and Hatty and I end up packing a couple of those super strong Lidl shopping bags with our extras, including the Jane Austen mug Guy got me in Chawton, Aurora's Castle, and some dresses and shoes that Lily and Poppy have grown out of and passed on to Hatty.

Luckily, she doesn't start back at school until Tuesday, and I've got Monday off, so we'll have a day to get settled in at home once she's back from her Dad's. Of course, I was meant to travel down on Saturday and use the whole weekend to prep, but I wanted time to wind things up here and say goodbye to Guy properly. I must be a sucker for punishment – it would have been much easier just to creep away, knowing I've done what I came for. That way, I could forget that I was ever such an idiot as to let a man I barely knew into my life.

But he did ask for two weeks. So I shall give him the chance to explain himself before I close and archive my file marked *Tillingford Hall Escapade*.

Hatty's trying to stuff all kinds of things into her little pink wheely case when I hear the crunch of tyres on the gravel below. I'm determined to ignore it, but Hatty runs to the window.

"It's Guy!" she says excitedly. In the James Bond Car! *Please* can *he* take me to Granny's, Mummy? I really want to ride in his car."

"I'm sure he'll be too tired," I say with a sigh. I really don't want to get into this now. "Why don't you run down and say 'hello' while I finish packing your bag?"

A few weeks ago, my little girl would have baulked at straying that far from me, but she's gained so much confidence and is clearly so fond of Guy that she's off like a rocket. I pull together a few more things, putting what she needs for Granny Janet's into her wheely case and shoving anything that can come to Morden with me wherever I can find space.

I hear a car door bang and small, excited steps hurrying across the gravel. I'm too curious; I look out of the window to see Guy scooping my little girl up in his arms and giving her a big hug. She wraps her arms around his neck as he holds her.

His body language speaks of genuine affection, but I don't want her to be sad that we can't take him home with us. Guy would have been such a brilliant stepdad: hardworking, practical, and strong, but also playful and fun – not to mention solvent(ish) with a GSOH. He's given her something with one hand and taken it away with the other, and my heart clenches at the thought of Hatty going back to putting up with just *Silly Mummy* and *Boring Old Daddy*.

I sigh. The little pilot light of hope that I've tried to keep burning is so dim that it's almost gone out. I don't want to have to explain why we won't be seeing Guy again. I'm hoping that once Hatty gets back to the busyness of the new school year, she'll forget about Tillingford Hall and everything it meant to us.

But I know *I* never will.

Hatty bursts into the room as I'm reaching into the land of dust bunnies under her bed, looking for any stray toys or gel pens or hair grips. My bottom's in the air, like a mother rabbit digging a warren; I'm just missing the little white tail.

I clasp the leg of poor, forgotten Beebee, who's lying, dusty and no doubt uncomfortable, on top of my long-lost vial of Rescue Remedy.

"Guy says I can ride in his car if you say it's OK," says Hatty to my bottom.

I really don't want Philip to see Guy and get the wrong impression. And I'm annoyed with Guy for being so affectionate towards Hatty when we're probably never going to see him again. I suck in a breath – and cough on a mouthful of dust, banging my back against the underside of the bed frame.

"Ow!" I wiggle backward, extracting myself from under the bed. "I'll have a word with him. Why don't you go and say goodbye to Mrs Powell and Gile... Oh! Guy!" I exclaim as I realise he's been standing in the doorway and just got a full-on view of my none-too-pert hindquarters sticking out from under the bed. I shoot to my feet, get a headrush, and have to flop down on the bed, my cheeks red as a radish. My heart stops. He's even more handsome than I remember. He looks tired – his hair a little unkempt, his beard untrimmed – but his face is all smiles.

"I don't *want* to say goodbye to them!" says Hatty, pouting.

"Whyever not?"

"I don't *want* to leave! I like it here, and I like Guy and Giles and Mrs Powell."

"Oh Hatty," I say, drawing her into a hug. "You know I came here to do a job and that job is done now. And, more importantly, school starts next week."

"Can't you homeschool me *here*?" she asks.

"No, Sweetheart. I need to work at the Gallery to keep you in pretty dresses, so where would I find the time to teach you?"

"Giles can – he doesn't have much to do, and he's very clever."

Guy snorts as he stifles a laugh.

"Oh Hatty," I say, looking up at Guy. The glint of amusement in his eye making me smile, even though my heart is breaking. "Giles is actually very busy…" But I can see this isn't going to go anywhere. "Aren't you looking forward to seeing all your friends?"

"Like who?" she asks, crossing her arms defiantly.

"Sapha? Or what about Milly? And Freya?"

"Sapha's silly and Milly's mean. And Freya doesn't like me," she claims, scuffing the floor with her little pink shoes. "And Lily and Poppy are my friends now."

"Come on, Hatty," says Guy, kindly, holding out his hand, "let's go downstairs and give Mummy a minute to finish your packing. I'll let you sit in the driver's seat and you can press that rocket launcher button I told you about!"

Hatty clings to his legs, and I look at Guy with an apologetic eye roll, but he smiles reassuringly while he strokes Hatty's hair. Then he shuffles towards the door, dragging Hatty out of the room while she's still clinging to his leg. After three paces, she's giggling hysterically. They go all the way down the corridor like that, until he picks her up like a sack, hefting her under his arm to carry her down the stairs, with her screeching and wriggling her legs all the way.

A big lump makes its way up my throat, but I swallow it back down. I shake Beebee to try to get the dust off. His sweet bunny face looks up at me, and I sit on the bed, hugging him, unable to stop the tears from flowing.

There's a soft knock on the door, and I don't have time to sort myself out before Guy's head appears. "Alice?" he says. "Hatty's with Mrs P. I just came to..."

One look at my face, and he sits on the bed next to me. He takes a deep breath.

"Alice, I'm sorry I've been such an arse," he says, turning to me. "I've had a lot to think about, and I didn't have the headspace for 'us', but I never wanted to hurt you."

"I understand," I say, itching to ask where that puts us now. I stand up and reach for Hatty's case.

"Here, let me put that in the car," he says, picking it up and striding to the door.

"I'm not sure we should go in *your* car," I say.

"Philip's going to have to know about us sooner or later, Darling," he insists, standing in the doorway and looking at me with such intensity that my little pilot light bursts into sudden flame.

The fire in his eyes brooks no contradiction, but it's not enough. I need to know.

"*Us*, Guy?" I say. "Is there an *us*?"

"Don't you… don't you *want* there to be?" he asks softly, his shoulders falling.

I sigh. "Honestly? I don't know, Guy. I have no idea what's going on in your head," I say. "I don't want to go any further if you're not totally sure about this – about *us*. I'm too old and tired to have my heart broken again."

Guy sinks down onto the bed next to me, his elbows on his knees and his head in his hands. "Alice... I..."

There's a knock on the door.

It's Giles – and some dogs. "Sorry to interrupt!" Lord T says brightly, but his face is dead serious. "Guy, my boy, I'm so glad to see you're home. We need to talk – all three of us."

"Yes, Dad, I know," says Guy. He reaches for my hand and gives it a squeeze. "That's why I came back early."

"Come into my Study and we'll have a pow-wow," says Giles, herding Bailey and Bertie back into the corridor before they can start exploring my room in earnest.

"I need to take Hatty to her dad's first," Guy replies, looking at his watch. "Why don't we talk over dinner instead? I guess we'll just eat in the Kitchen?"

"Yes, I asked Mrs P to make her famous fish pie and leave us to it. I couldn't be bothered with drinkies and all that business," he says, grabbing the beagles' collars.

"Fine by me, Dad. We'll be there," says Guy.

He picks up Hatty's case again and pushes through the seething sea of fur with it. We hurry towards the Kitchen, where Mrs P is writing down a cookie recipe for Hatty, a half-made fish pie in front of her.

"It's time to say goodbye, Hatty," I say firmly.

"I don't want to!" exclaims Hatty, banging the table with her hands as her face turns red. "I. Don't. Want. To. Go!"

"Now, now, Hatty," says Mrs P holding the piece of paper with the recipe on it high up where Hatty can't reach it. "Your dad's been looking forward to seeing you all fortnight – you don't want to let him down, now, do you?"

Hatty pulls a face.

"Besides," adds Mrs P, "if you behave, you can come and visit us anytime. Isn't that right, Guy?"

"I insist on it!" he says enthusiastically.

Hatty's face lights up. I have no idea how I'm going to explain my way out of this one. We haven't even begun to talk about *us* and what that means or how it would work – or even if we're ready for it.

"And remember," says Guy, grabbing a bit of grated cheese off the chopping board, "during the week, I live in London, just like you. So maybe, if I'm not too busy at work, I could come over for supper at yours," he says, looking hopefully at me. "How would that be?"

Hatty jumps up and down yelling, "Guy's coming to our house! Guy's coming to our house!"

Now he really is putting me in a double bind. But my heart is doing a happy dance at the idea of Guy sitting at our tiny Ikea table in Morden.

"Shall we go and say goodbye to my dad?" asks Guy as he goes in for another helping of cheese. Mrs P smacks his hand.

We traipse upstairs to the Study.

"You're a very clever, and helpful little girl, young Miss Hatty. It's been such a pleasure having you here," says Giles, shaking her hand. "I do hope we'll be seeing you again."

Hatty nods vigorously, then puts her arms around Algie's neck and gives him a big kiss, and giggles as Bertie and Bailey snuffle her, trying to lick her face. As we get in the car, we can't find Beebee, so we rush back to the Kitchen and discover him propped up against the salt cellar.

I'm worried we'll be late, but the Aston Martin eats up the miles and we arrive at Granny's earlier than expected.

"Hello Alice, dear," says Granny Janet.

I always was fond of my mother-in-law, but our relationship is obviously a bit awkward these days. And once Guy jumps out of the car, there's no hiding him. So I introduce him formally – as my employer – even though it makes him wince.

"Pip won't be here for another twenty minutes, so why don't you pop in for a cuppa?" says Janet. "It would be nice to have a quick catch-up."

If I were alone, I'd quite enjoy that, but with Guy here... I don't want Janet to find out everything about him and get the wrong idea and tell Philip how I'm going to be rich and how I won't need his maintenance payments anymore, and besides, I want to get back to Tillingford Hall for supper so we can get our meeting with Giles over and done with.

But Guy looks at his watch. "We're not due back for a bit, Alice, so we could stay for a quick one, if you'd like," he says, squeezing my shoulder reassuringly.

While Guy gets Hatty's case from the car, Janet ushers us inside and tells Hatty that Rocky the cat is on her bed – a rare thing, as he normally hides – so Hatty runs upstairs to see him, while Guy excuses himself to take a call. As soon as we're alone, Janet turns to me, kettle in hand.

"I know it wasn't your fault, Alice, how things worked out

between you and Pip. It's just one of those things..." It makes me wonder if she knows about the affairs, which definitely weren't 'just one of those things', but I suppose a mother will never see her little boy's faults. "I'm glad you've met someone else," she goes on. "You're a lovely girl and you deserve to be with someone nice. Anyway it's about time you moved on. I don't want you to be miserable."

"But I'm not *with* Guy, Janet. He's just giving me a lift!" I protest.

She turns on the tap. "Don't try to pull the wool over my eyes," she says with a smile as water pours into the kettle. "I've known you long enough. You're still a daughter to me, even if my son isn't your husband anymore. I've never seen you light up like this. This man's good for you. And it looks like Hatty's keen on him too – she never stops talking about him when she's here. She deserves a happy family life." She turns off the tap and snaps the lid on the kettle. "I've said my piece. I won't say any more."

"Thank you, Janet," I say, but I avoid looking her in the eye in case she sees the moisture gathering there. Weirdly, I feel like a weight has been lifted, like somehow Janet's blessing has given me the permission to move on that I didn't quite feel able to give myself.

But I'm still not sure Guy's the person I should be moving on with.

"How do you take yours?" Janet asks Guy as he walks back in.

It turns out that a good cup of builder's tea with some homemade ginger cookies is just what I needed. We catch up on Janet's job at English Heritage, where she works part-time as a fundraiser. She's not keen fully to retire quite yet and is saving up for a cruise. When we tell her all about Tillingford Hall, she says she would love to come visit one day. Guy promises that he'll show her round soon and that he'll be very happy to pick her brains about fundraising.

All too soon, Philip arrives.

Thankfully, both men are civilised and gracious, shaking hands as I introduce them.

"Your daughter's utterly charming," says Guy. "A real credit to you both. We'll miss her."

Philip looks proud and ruffles Hatty's hair. "I miss her all the time," he says, "but she couldn't have a better mum than Alice," he adds.

I feel a bit overwhelmed with the weirdness of my ex praising me at all, never mind to a man I hope might be my next partner, and I'm not sorry to get back in the car as quickly as possible. As soon as we're on the country roads, Guy puts the Aston in sport mode, and it hugs the curves like a Pendolino train, eating up the miles.

"Alice, I've missed you so much," says Guy, flicking his eyes from the road to me, to the mirrors and back.

My heart swells with desire mixed with excitement – and dread. "Guy, I'm going back to London on Sunday."

"That gives us two days," he insists, "and besides, what I said to Hatty is true. I'll see you during the week as much as I can. And at the weekends, we can all come home together – Hatty too, every other weekend. Alice, I don't want to be apart from you anymore."

My hand clasps the silver acorn he gave me, which I still wear every day. "Guy, you can't just swan off for two weeks, totally ignore me, give me no idea of what you're up to, then expect to pick up where we left off."

He frowns and his grip tightens on the steering wheel, the speedometer flicking up.

"Guy! Slow down."

He eases back on the accelerator with a glance at me. "Sorry," he says. And then he grins. "Or did you mean that metaphorically?"

I laugh – just a bit. "Literally *and* metaphorically."

"I get it," he says. A massive green and yellow tractor pulls out from a farm gate ahead of us, and he's forced to slow the car right down. "You're right."

I look at him as he concentrates on overtaking the tractor before we hit another blind corner. He's even more handsome in profile – and I like it that he can admit when he's in the wrong.

"No one's made me feel like you do, Guy. Ever," I confess. "But you shut me out just when I'd opened up to you. I need to know what's going on, and I'm stressed about this talk we have to have with your father this evening."

"Me too, Alice," he admits. "I'm more than stressed, I'm bloody terrified."

My breath catches. "OK." Somehow knowing that he's freaked out too makes it worse. I don't know how much he already knows, or whether the news we have for him is going to destroy everything.

He pulls into a lay-by and turns to me.

"Alice, I was hoping for a different setting for what I have to say, but I need to talk to you before we meet Dad." And looking at me with smouldering eyes, he leans forward and kisses me on the lips and I can't help but respond.

"I love you," he says as we pull apart. "Alice, I've been thinking about you every single day these past two weeks. I know I should have involved you in what was happening, but I was too ashamed, too confused about it all. I thought if I just kept everything to myself, it would all go away, and I'd be able to turn up like a knight in shining armour to sweep you off your feet and rescue you but now I realise it was me who needed rescuing."

He runs his hands through his hair. "My family and my heritage was everything to me. Then suddenly I discovered I'm not who I thought I was, and it's been hard – really hard – for me to deal with. I've questioned *everything*. Who I am, why I'm here, what's going to happen now, what I should do," he sighs. "And I realised I'm not the knight in shining armour after all. Turns out I'm just this guy: a boring hedge fund manager trying to keep a roof over his family's head, except I don't know who or what my family is anymore."

I reach over to take his hand, and he lets me.

"I totally understand if you never want to see me again," he says finally. "I don't blame you if you want to have nothing to do with these crazy, dysfunctional people. You've already done so much for us – for *me*. I don't deserve to ask for anything more, but I hope, I really, truly *hope*, that you'll forgive me for shutting you out when I should have turned to you for support." He squeezes my hand. "So here I am, asking for another chance. I want to move on from all this and figure out who I am, really. I want to start something new at Tillingford Hall, if Giles will let me."

He looks up at me, his eyes pleading. "And I want to do it with you by my side, Alice, if you'll have me."

So, here *I* am, sitting in a £150k car with the most handsome, eligible man I've ever met, a man who shares my passions and my values and who can be vulnerable and humble, a man who has apologised fulsomely for the one thing he's done to hurt me and who is now begging me to take him back on. What's a girl to do?

What would Brave New Alice do?

I twist round, reach my hands towards his face and pull it close to mine so our lips can meet, gently at first, then more passionately – and awkwardly, entwined across the console – until my cardy gets tangled in the gear stick.

I giggle as he untangles me. "I love you too, Guy," I say, "and if you can promise you'll never shut me out again, I promise I'll be there for you, whatever happens."

He smiles and strokes my cheek. We stare at each other goofily for a few seconds, before the car starts to shudder as the tractor comes back into view behind us.

"Then onwards and upwards!" says Guy, putting the gear into drive and leaving my stomach in the lay-by as he tests the theory that his Aston Martin can go from 0 to 60 in 3.6 seconds.

Chapter Thirty-three

Giles is all but hopping from foot to foot as he waits for us on the doorstep like some latter-day Noah with dogs of all sizes milling impatiently round him. "Come, come, supper's ready," he says, urging us into the Hall. "Mrs P's going to serve up and then go out, so we four should be alone in the house," he says.

In the kitchen, Desmond is helping Mrs Powell to put the fish pie on the sideboard, along with bowls of braised chard and steamed green beans, and Giles hands out plates so we can help ourselves. The food looks amazing, but my mouth is dry and my stomach churning. I gingerly put a small portion of the cheesy potato-topped pie on my shaking plate and add a few vegetables. Mr Biggles looks up at me wistfully, licking his lips, willing me to drop something.

The only thing that goes down well for me is a long swig of the golden, smoky Pouilly-Fumé.

"Well, Guy, seems we've got ourselves in a pickle, doesn't it?" says Giles once we're all seated.

"Looks like it, Dad. Where do we start?"

"Perhaps Alice should explain," replies his father.

"OK… well, here's how it is… I mean, I'm going to talk about pictures, obviously. Your family goings-on are yours to discuss."

Giles, Guy and Desmond glance at each other sheepishly.

"Go on," urges Giles.

"So, you knew that there was something wrong with your miniature collection. That's why you called Desmond in the first place. He and I have been working on it together, and we figure you should have approximately one thousand original miniatures dating from 1500-1900. However, thirty or so of the pictures are missing. I believe someone has deliberately taken them, had them copied – quite badly, I might add – and inserted the copies into the collection in their place," I say, taking another sip of wine.

"My theory," I go on, "is that they have been selling the originals on the black market to raise funds for an extravagant lifestyle. I've found a few of the missing miniatures in sale catalogues of obscure foreign auction houses from the past ten years or so, but most of them seem to have disappeared, possibly into a private Russian collection.

"There is also one entirely new portrait, which is obviously of Brad Masters but has been entitled *Sir Nicholas Tillingford* and inserted in the family tree in the Billiards Room. Make of that what you will. I'm not sure if it was created deliberately to mislead or as a joke."

I take a forkful of the fish pie, but it's now cold and even more unappealing. At this moment, Desmond puts down his knife and fork, having cleared his plate with gusto.

"The whole collection," says Desmond, "were it all originals, would be worth £3-5 million." Guy lets out a low whistle. Desmond goes on, looking right at him, "With so many gaps – and it's mostly the most valuable ones that are missing – it'll be more like half that. However, it's the extent and integrity of the collection that makes it so special. It would be a real shame to break it up by selling it. I would love to see it as a special exhibit at the

London Portrait Gallery – if it couldn't be opened as a museum collection in its own right."

"Tell us about what happened in Bath, Alice," says Giles, after a thoughtful sip of wine. "I take it you haven't told Guy yet?"

"No – I haven't had a chance," I admit. "Thanks to my friend Charlotte, I discovered an artist in Bath called Debbie Crowder. Desmond, I think you'll agree her technique directly matches that of most of the copies – and of the new pictures."

"Definitely," agrees Desmond, walking over to the sideboard to help himself to seconds. "There's a clear similarity between them all, and we've got other evidence to link her to the forgeries, which Alice will explain in due course."

"You have something to say about Sebastian too," I believe, says Giles.

"Yes, I saw him in the George and Dragon pub in Bath, receiving an envelope from Debbie. Moments later, I overheard him trying to sell a Thomas Lawrence to a drug dealer rumoured to work for a Russian mafia boss who happens to be an avid art collector. In this deal, Seb was asking for cash, but it sounded like he would normally take payment in drugs. The sale was interrupted when my friend tipped them off that the police were on their way."

Guy's glass is halfway to his mouth. He puts it back down, clearly angry. "You're telling me Seb's been selling *our pictures* to keep himself in drugs?"

Giles, Desmond and I all look at each other, and Giles nods at me to explain the truth to Guy.

"No, Guy," I say, hesitantly. "It was your mother – Seb's just her stooge."

"What?" The colour drains from Guy's face.

"Guy…" I say softly. "I don't know quite how to put this. Seb thinks he and your mum are going to run away and set up a surf school in Polzeath."

And then, Guy does something I don't expect: he bursts out laughing. "Oh my God. What is he like? *Mum in Polzeath…?*" He looks at me bewildered. "Obviously I'd realised they were… seeing each other," he says euphemistically. "But… how long…?"

"Apparently he thought she was a MILF since the first time he came here," I say.

Guy swears under his breath. "But he must've been, like, fourteen!"

"Exactly," I agree.

"So, she's a paedo?!"

"Well, not quite," I say. "More of a cougar – apparently he was nineteen when they…"

"I'll kill him…" says Guy rising from the table.

Giles and I put our hands on his shoulders and make him sit down.

"She *used* him, Guy," I say. "You told me what he and Sahara went through as children, how vulnerable and needy they were. It wouldn't take much to get confused when a mother figure came along. It may even be her who got him into drugs in the first place, he who passed that habit on to Sahara. And he was the one who did the dealing, the trading, all the dangerous and dirty work. He must have risked arrest for her dozens of times."

"Shit," he says, elbows on the table, running his hands through his hair. "And I thought I was *helping* them by bringing them here…"

"Tell Guy what else happened in Bath, Alice," says Giles.

"Charlie has been seeing Seb for a year or so. He told her he was from Twerton and that he was a jobbing carpenter who worked on contracts out of town during the week and she had no reason to disbelieve him."

"His dad's house is actually around there somewhere," says Guy.

"Well, that explains the Bath connection, then," I say. "Charlie obviously didn't know about Maxine, so she was pretty annoyed when I told her. More than annoyed, actually. So, she was happy to help me out by using her feminine wiles to recover *this*." I put the Jiffy bag on the table and gently shake out the contents onto a clean napkin. "As you can see, it contains an original Thomas Lawrence, a poor reproduction of the same picture, and most importantly – " I triumphantly hold up the paper I found inside, "an invoice for vapes that proves this envelope was in Debbie Crowder's possession.

"I've also got this." I show them all a WhatsApp photo my mum sent this morning of the miniature of Hatty. I'm gratified that they all coo over it, saying how sweet Hatty is – until Desmond breaks the spell by scoffing at the picture's poor quality and how it really doesn't do Hatty justice (which I agree with). Then he points out how the technique, particularly the fake patina (which is probably done with Windsor and Newton's Nut Brown acrylic ink), exactly matches all the other dodgy pictures in the collection.

"So, where's Seb now?" asks Guy.

"Here," says Giles. "He came back from Bath on the coach, feeling sorry for himself. Apparently, Alice's friend set fire to his camper van."

Guy looks at me for corroboration, and I nod. After a moment, he lets out a chuckle, and then we all burst out laughing, and Guy is still mouthing *Polzeath* to himself a few minutes later as we clear the plates and Giles pulls another bottle of Pouilly-Fumé from the wine fridge.

"Seb tried to touch me for repairs to Neville," says Giles as we help ourselves to Mrs P's Tipsy Eton Mess laced with Chambord. "Of course, I said no, but I told him he could stay here a bit longer. I'm not sure Herbert's pleased to have him in the Cottage, but I thought it would be useful to keep him under observation. He asked if I knew where your mother was, so I told him she was shopping in London and would be back soon to keep him off the scent. But actually, when Desmond, Alice, and I looked in her room, *everything* was gone, save a box full of receipts for jewellery and designer clothes. When I tried to call her, the ringtone was international, and she didn't pick up."

"I can explain that," says Guy. "She's in Boston."

"What?!" says Giles.

Guy takes a very large swig of wine, then a deep breath. "She and I have been there the last two weeks with my biological father and my half-sister."

Giles drops his spoon with a clatter and goes white.

"I think Mum's going to stay there…" says Guy, "permanently."

Giles chokes on a piece of meringue, and Desmond jumps up to thump him on the back. A few coughs and a glass of water restore him to normality.

"Are you alright, Dad?" says Guy. "I can still call you *Dad*, can't I?"

Giles looks dismayed. "I hope you always will, Guy," he says. "I've always known you weren't mine, biologically speaking – your mother was pregnant when I met her. But I loved you as my own right from the start. You are *my* son, and I am your father!"

"Thank you, Dad – and I love you too. You've been the best dad anyone could hope for."

Giles breaks down, and Desmond goes to put his arm round his shoulder, but Guy and Giles have risen from their seats and are hugging each other tightly, tears rolling down their cheeks.

Desmond and I look at each other awkwardly. I wonder if we should tiptoe out of the room and leave them to it, but Giles and Guy quickly settle back into their seats, and Giles, after blowing his nose on an outsize hanky, tops up everyone's glass again. Guy takes a deep swig and exhales deeply, looking down at the table.

"Your mother never told me who your father was," says Giles. "And when I decided to raise you as my own, I didn't want to know. We never talked about it. I feel a bit stupid now that I never worked it out – you do look awfully like him. They were old family friends of hers, but I can't understand why your mother kept in touch with them and let you get fond of Chelsea. She must have known it might go too far one day. How is the poor girl?"

"Nursing her wounds," says Guy. "I think she'll get used to the idea eventually. I swear I never saw her as anything other than a friend, but she wanted more." He looks significantly at me. "She misinterpreted an email I sent a few weeks ago when it was all starting to dawn on me. I was trying to drop a hint that she might be my sister without dropping a bombshell, but she misunderstood. I said something like *I think we have a closer bond,* and she thought I was interested romantically, poor thing. I feel like such an idiot. My God… imagine what could have happened? There was a moment when I was with them during my internship in Boston…" he trails off with a shudder.

"A narrow escape?" asks Desmond.

Guy nods. "Luckily, I was still bewitched by Sahara back then – and I told Chelsea so. But you should have *told* me, Dad!" He sounds quite angry.

"Believe you me, son, I wanted to have it all out in the open," admits Giles, "but your mother would never confirm it was Brad. I realise it seems obvious now, but your mother isn't exactly a one-man woman. She was happy to go along with the pretence that it was me. I think she was afraid that if anyone knew, it could cause a scandal, might cause problems with the estate and the succession, although I did consult a genealogist and a lawyer just in case. I don't think it would have been a problem legally or constitutionally, but, you know, still, it could've been awkward…" mutters Giles.

"She told me she kept visiting them, hoping that the right moment would come up to tell Brad," explains Guy, "but over the years she became fond of Chelsea, and she really respected Brad's wife Barbara. She felt bad about what had happened and didn't want it to destroy their happy family." He sighs. "She should at least have told Brad, though. Do you know he genuinely didn't realise? Chelsea and I had to show him the results of the DNA test we had done in Harley Street, and he still insisted we have another one done in Boston – that's why I was away for such a long time."

"You'd have to be blind not to see the family resemblance," comments Desmond.

"Hey that's my dads you're talking about!" says Guy with a smile. "But yeah, I mean, surely, one of them would have put two and two together?"

"I guess anyone can be blind to an inconvenient truth," Desmond shrugs.

We all nod thoughtfully at that while Mr Biggles, who's been asleep through all of this, yawns loudly, which makes us all titter, probably as much from nerves as anything else.

Guy takes the pudding plates away, while I bring over the cheeseboard.

"What does it mean, though, Dad," says Guy, giving everyone a cheese plate, "for the Hall, I mean, for the succession?"

"Nothing. I'm your father on your birth certificate," Giles says, spearing a wedge of Caerphilly. "As far as the law is concerned, you are my natural son. And you are the heir of Tillingford, natural or not. Nobody cares about this place, this *family*, more than you. You just need to produce an heir yourself now. Find yourself some young filly," he says, looking significantly in my direction as I almost drop the cheese biscuits.

"That's not very PC, Dad," says Guy, smiling at me.

"Oh, stuff PC, you daft boy," he says, getting to work on the Stilton. "You two are besotted with each other. You even adore her daughter! Get married, you silly people, come and live here, and manage the place. It's about time someone gave me a break. I'll go and live with Desmond and enjoy all the delights that London has to offer."

Giles pushes the cheeseboard towards me, but his eyes are locked with Desmond's, and a broad grin breaks across Desmond's face and his eyes glisten.

Utterly disconcerted, I cut the tiniest piece of Lincolnshire Poacher and pass the knife to Guy.

"I'm a bit old to be a mother again," I mutter into my plate.

"Nonsense!" says Giles. "Not by today's standards. Plenty of women five or even ten years older than you are having babies these days – look at Cheri Blair or the clever girl on that quiz show, you know, the fruity blonde one with the comedian husband. You're pretty fit and healthy – I've seen you powering up and down the pool in the evenings." It's certainly true that I've got fitter in the last six weeks since I started swimming daily. "And you're an experienced mother to boot, so why not?"

I glance at Guy, and the look he gives me makes me burn.

"We'll give it some thought, Dad!" says Guy with a stiff grin, rolling his eyes and placing his hand on mine. "Let's not rush into anything."

"Well, don't leave it too long, is all I can say!" his father declares as I cross my legs, a mass of confused emotions.

"But what are you going to do about Seb, Maxine, the drugs, the missing pictures?" I ask, swiftly changing the topic. "Are you going to involve the police?"

Giles and Guy look at each other. "Hopefully not," says Guy.

"If any of this gets out, it'll blow us out of the water," agrees Giles.

"I think we need to find out everything we can – there are still a lot of unknowns – before we decide what to do," Guy points out.

"I've thought and I've thought," says Giles and I really don't know what the best thing to do is. For starters, Maxine hasn't made her intentions clear, but obviously we can't stay married." Giles puts his hand over Desmond's and squeezes it.

"I don't know if this helps, Dad, but I've never seen Mum looking happier. I genuinely think she's found her match in Brad."

"Well, that's something, I suppose, but I don't know where to begin discussing a divorce," admits Giles. "I mean, it could ruin me… ruin *us*. If she demands half of everything, the Hall will end up sold to some Chinese developer or some ghastly footballer with a pneumatic wife, and the collections will have to be auctioned and broken up."

Desmond and I look at each other in dread.

"Better get some very good legal advice then, Dad, and not be caught on the back foot," says Guy.

"Well, that's that, then," says Giles. "I shall call Hugo in the morning."

"No, Dad," says Guy firmly, "I mean *good* legal advice. Mum and Brad will find some hot shot Bostonian attorney, and you and Hugo will be mincemeat." He slices the corner off a block of Manchego. "One of our senior partners got divorced last year and swears by this guy in Blackfriars. The best in the business, he says. I'll get his details."

"But what about Seb?" I ask, reaching for a biscuit.

"The fact he's dared to come back here," says Guy, "makes me think he genuinely didn't know what Mum was up to. I reckon she's double-crossed him."

"I think we'd better get him in, don't you?" says Giles.

Chapter Thirty-four

While Guy goes looking for Sebastian, Desmond makes coffees and Giles pours everyone a scotch. When eventually Guy and Seb appear, Seb looks dishevelled and contrite. He flops down into a chair.

"I always mess everything up," he says in tears, wiping his nose with the back of his hand. We have no idea what Guy has said to him so far.

I hand him a piece of kitchen towel, and he mops himself up a bit. He refuses scotch or a coffee but agrees to have some of the tisane I've made with lemon verbena from the garden.

When everyone's settled, Guy turns to him. "I gather you've been helping my mum liquidate our assets."

Seb looks like a deer in the headlights. He pulls at his beard, but when he sees us all looking at him expectantly, he sighs and says, "Yeah… I'd do anything for her."

"Even steal a load of priceless art from your dearest friends, sell it for drugs, and infest my laptop with spyware?" I snap at him.

Seb looks imploringly at his friend's stony face.

"Come on, Mate. You know how persuasive she is. And she's a total MILF. All the boys at school fancied her. Why do you think everyone was over here every weekend?"

Guy looks like he's been shot.

"I thought I was the cat that got the cream," admits Seb, looking at the floor. "To be honest, I thought Josh Alderton was going to have her fir–"

"That's… pretty hard for me to hear, Seb," Guy interrupts, the muscles in his jaw tightening. "I know my mother's… well-preserved, but some people are out of bounds! You just don't sleep with your best mate's mum – no matter how much of a MI… no matter how attractive she is."

"She's quite hard to turn down," mutters Seb.

There's a strange gurgling sound from Giles, who starts to cough. Desmond puts his hand on his shoulder. Giles and Guy look at each other. I can see they don't disagree with Seb, but it's not exactly what they want to hear.

"I'm not sure I really want to know this, Seb," says Guy after a pause, "but I'm going to ask anyway. How old were you when…."

"Nineteen," Seb mutters, fiddling with the leather thong on his wrist. "It was the Calvin Klein campaign that did it. I guess she stopped seeing me as a kid after that – her and half the housewives of Britain, apparently."

"Christ!" says Guy. "You mean you've been having an affair with my mother for *fifteen years* and none of us realised?" He drains his scotch in one swig.

"No! More like… there were a few times that summer and maybe a few other times after that when you were still at Uni and I used to visit," he says. He twists his hands together nervously before sitting on them. "After that, I didn't see much of her for years, not until I had my bad patch last year and you invited me to stay – so, like, it was just this year, really."

"And I'm just curious, Seb," says Guy with extraordinary equanimity, "but when did you and Sahara first take drugs?"

"What's that got to do with it?" he asks.

"Just tell me, Seb."

Seb looks at the floor and says, "Our dad and stepmother just had them lying around, you know. Sometimes they used to send us out to get stuff for them from these kids who used to hang around on the estate near our house. The gang offered me a job – I suppose they thought I'd blend in better with their richer clientele than their usual runners – until they twigged I wasn't around in term time. And my dad's friends kept giving us stuff at parties. We were probably like eleven or twelve when we first tried dope, maybe fifteen when we had coke." He looks up to meet Guy's glare. "Like you."

"No, actually, Seb. Not *like me*. There were maybe a couple of times in sixth form..." Giles looks dismayed but Guy ploughs on, "but after what happened at Sahara's seventeenth, I never touched the hard stuff, and *anyway,* this isn't about me! The point is, I can't lay your drug problems at Mum's door," he says grimly.

"God, no! She tried to tell me off for it, but she wasn't much of an example herself, so that didn't really work." He laughs hollowly. "I've been really careful since Sahara went into rehab, but it didn't stop Max.

"But look, Bro, I know this seems like really awkward, but hear me out – I've got it all figured. You know your Dad and Desmond are like, well…"

"…together now," supplies Desmond, and Giles smiles dopily at him.

"Yeah! So Max and me are like solid, OK? And maybe it's

time…. time for her to leave now, cos Giles isn't so much in the wife line anymore, right? So me and Max being together isn't so bad, is it? I think we've saved enough for our surf school now. Although, with Neville gone, I don't know how we're going to get down to Polzeath. I guess we'll have to get a loan if we can, or maybe she can sell like a necklace or something to buy a new camper van, and then we can be out of your hair, and you can just forget about us…"

"Sebastian," says Giles firmly. "There is not going to be a surf school. Nor a camper van."

"How are you going to stop us?" exclaims Seb. "And what's it to you anyway? You don't love Maxine."

"Actually, I *do*, I'll have you know – just not in *that* way. She was the light of my life, and we had an understanding. Her betrayal has hurt me more than anyone. But this isn't about *me*, Sebastian – you can set up a flying pig farm in Portishead or a swan sanctuary in Swansea for all I care. But my wife – my soon to be *ex*-wife –" Giles corrects himself, "is now living in Boston with a ludicrously rich property developer who will be able to supply her with every sports car, fancy watch, and designer shoe her little heart has ever desired. I don't think she's going to be setting up a surf school in Polzeath any time soon."

Seb looks up at us all, and the colour drains from his face.

"She's duped you just like the rest of us, Mate," says Guy.

My heart goes out to Seb. I know he's not the good guy here, but he's right when he says he always messes things up, and there's no doubt Maxine's used him. I can't help but pity him.

"But she promised me Polzeath!" moans Seb, twisting his fingers through his beard.

"I'm sorry that someone close to you has let you down again, Seb, and I want you to set up your surf school, I really do," says Guy. "But I'm not sure you're ready for it yet. Why don't you just take off for a while… you know… go and find yourself in Waikiki or something? Before the police find out about that conversation in the alley behind the George and Dragon…"

"How… how do you know about that?" Seb asks, his shoulders hunching.

"I've got my methods, Seb," says Guy. "So please just go. I'll tell Sahara and James you're leaving, and they can help you move your stuff. And, Seb… I'll need a while before I'm ready to see you again, OK?"

"Yuh, huh, I totally get it, Dude…" says Seb, gripping the edge of the table as he leans forward, "but I'll need my share of the cash."

Giles explodes. "You good-for-nothing layabout! That money was never yours! Besides which, she's already spent it, you fool!"

Suddenly, the dogs outside start barking, and Mr Biggles attempts to raise his fat head and whine a bit in response.

"There's someone outside," says Guy. "I'll go and look."

He bounds out of the Kitchen, and moments later, there are voices in the Hall – evidently, we have a visitor.

"Hope he'll send them away, whoever it is," growls Giles.

But footsteps sound on the stairs, and then Guy comes back in, accompanied by a tall, blond man who is the spitting image of Sir Nicholas Tillingford.

"Brad! My, my, this is a surprise," says Giles haughtily. "You should have rung ahead. We could have saved some supper for you."

"Hey, don't worry about it! I had my chef whip up a little something for me over the Atlantic," says Brad in a gentle American drawl, pumping Giles's hand.

We all stand awkwardly for a moment, not knowing quite what to say.

"Please, sit down," says Guy after what feels like about ten seconds too long. "Let me get you some wine…"

"Thanks, Son," says Brad as Guy hands him a glass. He takes an appreciative swig while Giles has another coughing fit.

"So, Brad," says Lord T once he's recovered, "you are of course, welcome, but to what in particular do we owe the pleasure of this surprise visit?"

"I have a proposition for you," says Brad, looking him directly in the eye, "which I wanna discuss privately."

"Let's go up to my Study then," Giles says, pushing himself up from the table.

The two disappear upstairs, and there's a moment of awkward silence as those of us left round the table look at each other, except for Seb, who's quietly weeping while rocking himself backwards and forwards. "I'm sorry, Guy. I can't believe I've messed up again. I'm such a tosser!"

"I'll call Sahara," says Guy with a sigh, getting up and moving to the far end of the room for better signal.

"I guess we'd better clear up," I mutter to Desmond.

We begin stacking the dishwasher and wiping down the worktops while Mr Biggles flops down by the Aga, snuffling slightly. We distance ourselves from the Tillingford family drama unfolding under our noses by chatting about Desmond's summer holiday plans. He's going to Trinidad to see his mother, who returned there when she retired. He tells me all about his aunties and their colonial-style house surrounded by crabwood, kapok, and hog plum trees, but I'm all too aware of Sebastian sitting there snivelling, his knees pulled up to his chest.

"Sahara's coming," says Guy after a few minutes on the phone. "Come on, Seb. Time to go."

"Shit, Bro," mutters Seb, unpeeling himself from his near-foetal position and putting his head in his hands. "Can't you see? I'm losing my home, my woman, and my best friend… all in one night."

But what about Charlie? I think. How does he think she felt? And Giles and Guy… what about them? My sympathy for Seb is wearing thin, to the point where I'm starting to feel glad Charlie set fire to his camper van. I have no idea how Guy is staying so calm.

"I need a break, Seb, but I'll never stop being your friend," he says, pulling him to his feet. Seb turns to weep on Guy's shoulder, while Guy pats him awkwardly on the back.

"I'll miss you…" Sebastian sobs.

"Let's go, Sahara will be here in a sec," says Guy.

"Bye, Seb," I say to his receding back, but he just throws me a filthy look as though somehow this is all my fault.

And I wonder if maybe it is.

"It's not your fault, Alice," says Desmond once we're alone, as though he's read my mind. He sits down and pats the chair beside him. "They asked us for help and, man, did they need it."

"But we were supposed to catalogue a collection of pictures, not destroy a family," I say, chasing a crumb with my finger.

"Listen, Alice," says Desmond, smiling kindly, "that was

all going to happen anyway, and now we've made three new families."

"I suppose… but I just feel bad about it. And also... I'm not sure I want your job; I want to finish my PhD!"

"That's great," he says, putting his hand over mine. "And how will you live?"

"I want to live here with Guy. I want to help him open Tillingford Hall to the public, and…"

"You want to have his babies," he teases.

"Don't!" I squeal, smacking his hand as my face cracks into a huge smile. "That's not…"

Desmond leans back in his chair and laughs, but then I burst into tears.

"Oh God, I'm sorry," I say, as he hands me a beautifully laundered hanky – well-ironed and smelling slightly of lavender – and I drench it. "I *know* it's mad! I've only known him for six weeks!"

"Sometimes, Alice, you can't get to know someone in sixty years. But sometimes you just know, in a flash, that someone's perfect for you."

I look at the soaked hanky, not quite sure what to do with it. "It's been an emotional day, Desmond. I think I'll turn in," I say wearily, even though it's only nine pm.

But just as I'm getting up, Guy reappears in the doorway. "Alice," he says, closing the gap between us. I'm pressed against him, breathing him in, while his arms encircle me, and I've never felt more *right*.

I won't be sleeping alone tonight.

Chapter Thirty-five

When Guy and I wake, we're so tangled in each other we can hardly move. Gradually we untwine ourselves, and softly, we sigh and kiss and tell each other all the things that lovers say when they're looking out together across an ocean that no one has seen before.

When we come down for breakfast, Brad is in the Kitchen, tugging at drawers and pulling open cupboards, looking very much like a man in need of a cup of coffee.

"Hiya, Son," he says to Guy, poking his head around a cupboard door.

"Hello, *Dad*," says Guy. "I haven't introduced you properly to Alice."

"Hey, Alice. I've heard all about you, the amazing, clever lady who's stolen my son's heart," Brad says in his gentle American accent. "I'm looking forward to getting to know you, but I just do not function without coffee, so Guy, *pleas*e tell me where it is!"

We get Brad to sit down and relax while Guy fires up the Nespresso machine and I make toast for the three of us. When we've emptied our plates, Brad says, "Come on, kids, I want you to show me the whole place and everything you've got planned!"

"OK!" says Guy, lighting up. "But first I need to know what you agreed with Giles last night."

"Well, we had a full and frank discussion," says Brad, peering into his empty mug, as if hoping for more coffee.

Guy gets up to make him another cup. "And?"

"You know I love your Mom, Guy," says Brad, taking a grateful sip. "I've loved her forever. Our families had been friends since I was an itty-bitty boy. I knew Maxine when she was just a child, and she was so beautiful and vivacious… and too young for me." He coughs. "So, I married Barbara. But one winter I went to Zermatt for a conference and there she was, working as a chalet girl. I realised little Maxine had grown up and…"

He takes another swig of his coffee.

"I never meant it to go so far, but I'd always been crazy about her, and she doesn't hold back. I'll be straight with you, Guy, I felt pretty bad. I kept trying to tell her it couldn't be, but she's hard to turn down, your mother, and when she wants something, she gets it. And then Barbara was expecting Chelsea, and of course, Maxine never told me she was expecting you, and it was convenient to forget all about what had happened between us, especially once she married Giles. So, I settled back into my life with Barbara and Chelsea and never thought about it again."

"Didn't anyone notice how we look like each other?" asks Guy.

"Did you?"

Guy shakes his head.

"Although, when you came to live with us when you had that internship," Brad goes on. "Barbara did once say something about how much you looked like me, but I genuinely didn't see it, and Barbara didn't make it a thing."

"Chelsea and I were born just three months apart," Guy

explains to me, while Brad looks sheepish. "Maybe that's how it never occurred to anyone we might be siblings."

"I honestly had no idea Barbara was expecting Chelsea when I slept with Maxine that one time," Brad says, as though this somehow exonerates him, "but I'm glad it didn't come out until now and that Barbara and I had a normal, happy marriage without recriminations. I do wonder if she passed away wondering about it. But she never said a thing – no need to settle the question on her death bed or anything like that – and I certainly didn't want to bring it up and take her peace from her. But now? For Giles finally to be able to stop pretending and Maxine to get what she's really wanted all this time is good for all of us, ain't it?"

"So, what was the proposition?" Guy reminds him as Brad investigates his empty coffee cup.

"I want to take your mom on, Guy. I've never stopped adoring her and she keeps me on my toes and makes me feel so alive. I want to give her what she wants – I don't think she could spend everything I've got left if she tried," Brad says, spreading his hands generously.

"I wouldn't be sure of that," says Guy solemnly.

"Obviously I'm aware she's done some real bad shit, though," says Brad, "so I've made an agreement with Giles: a no-fault fast-track divorce. You forget about the pictures and don't hand her over to the cops, and she won't claim a penny from Giles. How 'bout that?" Brad pops a corner of cold toast into his mouth.

I can see Guy doing calculations in his head, relief gradually spreading across his face. "That's fair," he says at last. "Thank you. But what do you mean *everything I've got left*?"

"I'm retiring so I can make up for lost time with your Mom.

I'm going to sell my half of Masterbuild to my brother – he's raising the finance now to keep the whole business in the family. Then I'm splitting my assets. Half for me and Maxine, a quarter into a trust for Chelsea, and a quarter into a trust for you. That way, you can afford to leave work and look after this place. I've also consulted the right people and found that if you set up Tillingford Hall as a Registered Charity, I can make some tax efficient donations to get you started."

Guy collapses into his chair and throws his head back, running his hands through his hair. He rights himself and looks straight at Brad. "Thank you!" he says with an enormous exhalation. "Thank you, Brad… *Dad!* You have no idea how much that means to me!"

"And, I have something else for you," Brad says, winking at me. But when he takes out a square box of midnight-blue velvet – about the size of an extended hand and tied round with a satin ribbon – it's Guy he hands it to.

Guy gasps. "How did you persuade her?" He hugs the box close to his chest and kisses it. But then, instead of opening it, he passes it to me while Brad beams.

"Go on, open it," says Guy.

I undo the clasp and lift the lid.

Inside is an exquisite necklace, delicately set with a dozen diamonds, and a pair of earrings fashioned from glittering stones as big as sultanas.

"Oh my God!" I gasp. They are probably worth as much as my flat, and I'm hoping I'm not actually being offered these priceless jewels as a gift.

"These are the Tillingford Diamonds," says Guy. "Brad's persuaded Mum that she really should return them to the family for the next Lady Tillingford to wear. And I hope one day you might do me the honour of being that person."

I look at Guy, and I start crying, my hand flying up to the little silver acorn he gave me.

"Oh, Alice," says Guy, sitting up and taking my hands, while Brad looks on, bemused.

"What's eating her?" he asks.

I purse my lips to try to stop them wobbling. "I… I just can't believe this is happening. I think I must be dreaming!"

Brad laughs. "I've noticed that people get used to money very quickly, so enjoy this feeling while it lasts!"

"I think I'll just wear *this* for now," I say, touching my silver acorn again.

"And that's just fine," says Guy, kissing me tenderly.

And before I can burst into tears again, Brad's jumped up.

"Now, take me on a tour, kids! Show me everything! I wanna hear all your exciting plans for restoring this place!" He clamps his arm onto Guy's shoulder. "I'm so proud you're going to be a property developer like me, Son!"

And, as we open the kitchen door and Guy takes my hand in his, I look up at Tillingford Hall and out across the estate, and I think this might just be the best morning of my life so far.

EPILOGUE

Extract from *Hampshire Life*

At Home with the Tillingfords

The Honourable Guy Tillingford and his charming partner, Dr Alice Merrow, couldn't be more welcoming as they invite me into their beautiful home, Tillingford Hall, immediately putting me on first-name terms.

So often, we journalists are made to use the Tradesman's Entrance, but not here at Tillingford Hall.

"We want to give all our visitors the warmest of welcomes," Guy explains.

"I find the Tradesman's Entrance cosier," admits Alice modestly, as she bounces baby George on her hip. "But you get the full effect of the Grand Staircase when you come to it through the Front Entrance."

And what a staircase! At the time of my visit, it is garlanded with hop bines from the Tillingford Manor Farm, which is run by their nearest neighbours and longstanding family friends Allegra and James, son and daughter of the late Formula1™ driver Sir Jason Irving-McAuley.

"We love to work with the seasons and bring the outside in," explains Guy. "James and Allegra have been farming organically for years, and now they're looking to rewild a portion of the farm. Obviously, we're super supportive of that."

"It's nice to know our children aren't breathing in

pesticides and other rubbish when they're playing outside," agrees Alice, who is also mother to daughter Hatty, nine, from a previous relationship.

With baby George in a sling on Daddy's chest, we take a tour of the magnificent house.

"Thanks to a substantial donation from an anonymous donor, we're gradually opening more rooms to the public," explains Alice. "We want to show everyone the beautiful things the Tillingford family have been collecting over the centuries."

The Tillingfords are especially proud of their extensive collection of over a thousand miniature portraits, second in importance only to the Royal Collection. "We've applied for Heritage Lottery funding to open a dedicated museum in the former dairy," explains Alice, who originally came to Tillingford Hall on secondment from the London Portrait Gallery to catalogue the collection. "I fell in love with the Hall, the collection – and Guy, of course – and never left!" Thanks to the move, Dr Alice Merrow was recently able to complete her PhD on Richard Cosway, the regency miniaturist. "I put the binding on it just as I was going into labour with George, and honestly, childbirth wasn't half as painful as finishing a PhD part time!" she jokes.

But Dr Merrow has no plans to return to academia. "I'm excited about the future here," she says. "Tillingford Hall hasn't been open to the public since the 1920s, and there's a lot of updating to be done to the facilities to make it more visitor friendly. We've just opened a lovely tearoom and put toilets in the Old Stables, and we're working on a sensory garden and improving disabled access."

"We really want to share our heritage with the nation and manage the whole estate for future generations to enjoy," says Guy.

Guy jokes that since he's taken over the estate from his father, Giles, the seventh Lord Tillingford, he's gone from hedge fund manager to hedge*row* manager. He takes me for a tour of the extensive grounds and farmlands that surround the house while little George has his nap. Guy intends to turn twenty acres of rough grazing into woodland and wetland to encourage biodiversity and create work for ex-offenders. "We already have ten acres of good-quality woodland. I've got a forester and two apprentices managing it so that we can use the timber in our building work. They're good lads. I met them when I was a volunteer mentor on a scheme in Southwark for boys who were at risk of getting into gangs. I knew they had potential, so I brought them down here, and I think it's safe to say they're out of the woods, as it were."

The crowning glory of the estate is the formal gardens and parkland designed by Lancelot 'Capability' Brown, managed by Charlotte Patcham, a long-term friend of Alice's and expert on historical gardens and landscapes. Charlotte, previously curator of the Bath Phyzick Garden, has worked at some of the country's most famous estates, including Hampton Court and Chatsworth. "Bringing the grounds back to something Capability Brown would be proud of has been a huge undertaking, but the restoration of the walled Kitchen Garden as an organic potager to supply vegetables to the House and Tea Rooms is the project closest to my heart," she says.

As we wander through the gardens, we come across a group of children in cheerful green tabards. "They're the Tilling Forest School," explains Guy with a smile. "We love having them around – there are 24 kids at the moment, and they're planning to expand to 48 next year. We'll be over-run soon!"

As we sit down to a delicious slice of homemade coffee and walnut cake and a cup of Darjeeling in the Old Stable Tea Rooms, served up by the legendary Mrs Powell – who has been working at Tillingford since the 1970s – Guy tells me he wants Tillingford Hall to be a happy place for everyone to enjoy.

After my short visit, I can say it definitely is.

Tillingford Hall is open 10am-5pm every Wednesday to Sunday from 15 March to 15 November. Visit www.tillingfordhall.com for more details.

Tillingford Hall

Half-term Spooky Owls Experience

22-31 October

Kids go free with this voucher

Giles and Desmond

invite you to

Cocktails and Cabaret

at

24 Clarendon Mansions

Pont Street, Belgravia, London

RSVP

Dress: Resplendent

Acknowledgements

Thank you for reading this book. I hope you've enjoyed it. I couldn't have written it without the love and support of all these wonderful people:

- My husband, Martin, for building me a posh writing shed and always believing in me.
- My son, Alfred, for being president of my fan club and always encouraging, inspiring and critiquing my writing and for reading this book, even though he'd rather have been reading Proust.
- My hilarious stepsons, Alexander and Luke, for keeping me up to date with modern culture and giving me an excuse to bake.
- My mother and father for their eternal support and their example as learners and authors.
- The wonderful novelist Milly Johnson for giving me, a complete stranger, friendly encouragement.
- Writing coach Alison May for coaxing me towards a first draft, and my friends Susie and Brenda for commenting on it.
- My friends Katie, Rose and Jo for reading and commenting on the second draft.
- The authors Ruth Kramer, Jacqueline Malcolm and Hannah Langdon for making helpful comments on the text.
- Julia Boggio, author of the award-winning *Shooters*, who has encouraged me and put me in touch with editor Amy Borg, who helped me polish this final version.
- Lumina and Holly the cats, for being just that.

Flora Dunn: about me

I wrote my first book when I was five. It was about a cow and a bed because those were words I knew how to spell. Then I wrote a three-page graphic novel, *The Crazy Book,* about a gang of kids who went back in time, and seventy-two issues of a magazine about Bunnyland.

I fell in love with romance when I read MM Kaye's *The Ordinary Princess*, a touching children's book about a sassy runaway princess called Amy, which was one of the first books to turn traditional fairy stories on their head. Later I got into Jane Austen, the Brontës and all the classics, until I finally picked up a Mills and Boon and my fate was sealed.

When I'm not being a mother, wife and professional charity fundraiser, I'm writing feel-good, funny romances and now I want to share them with you.

Whether they are about romance, friendship or camaraderie, love stories – how we feel about other people, how we treat them, how we make mistakes and are forgiven and learn to forgive in our turn – are what makes the world go round. You can tell those stories in a light-hearted way but that doesn't change the depth of the message – that true love is what sustains our very existence. Even The Bible is a love story between God and his people (and that ending when you think it's all over, but it isn't, is just the best plot twist ever).

My stories are set in and around the modern-day fictional village of Tillingham in leafy mid-Hampshire (known to some as Jane Austen Country). The characters are dotty but, I hope, believable.

Summer at Tillingford Hall is the first book in the Tillingford Hall series. It will be followed by *Christmas at Tillingford Hall*, narrated by Charlie who comes to the Hall to help Guy and Alice restore the gardens. And there are more in the pipeline including Elizabeth's story. If you subscribe to my newsletter, you'll be the first to hear about them.

I write from a posh shed set in a beautiful garden in Wimbledon in South-West London. I live with ten beautiful koi carp, one boring fat cat, one mad skinny cat, three teenagers and my husband, a hunky gardener with a growing collection of tractors. When I'm not working or writing, I'm to be found baking cakes (which I try not to eat) and cooking my home-grown veg (which I do).

Keep in Touch!

If you would like to learn more about the history of
Tillingford Hall, the romance of the English countryside,
get some of Mrs Powell's recipes,
and hear about my forthcoming books,
exclusive offers, events and giveaways,
then please sign up for my newsletter at
www.floradunn.com
or follow me on Instagram @floradunnbooks.

Printed in Great Britain
by Amazon

51410440R00182